D0015442

MORTAL REMAINS
IN
MAGGODY

MORTAL REMAINS IN MAGGODY

Joan Hess

A DUTTON BOOK

DUTTON
Published by the Penguin Group
Penguin Books USA Inc., 375 Hudson Street,
New York, New York 10014, U.S.A.
Penguin Books Ltd, 27 Wrights Lane, London W8 5TZ, England
Penguin Books Australia Ltd, Ringwood, Victoria, Australia
Penguin Books Canada Ltd, 10 Alcorn Avenue,
Toronto, Ontario, Canada M4V 3B2
Penguin Books (N.Z.) Ltd, 182-190 Wairau Road,
Auckland 10, New Zealand

Penguin Books Ltd, Registered Offices:
Harmondsworth, Middlesex, England

First published by Dutton, an imprint of New American Library,
a division of Penguin Books USA Inc.
Distributed in Canada by McClelland & Stewart Inc.

First Printing, October, 1991
10 9 8 7 6 5 4 3 2 1

Copyright © Joan Hess, 1991
All rights reserved

 REGISTERED TRADEMARK—MARCA REGISTRADA

LIBRARY OF CONGRESS CATALOGING IN PUBLICATION DATA:

Hess, Joan.
 Mortal remains in Maggody / Joan Hess.
  p. cm.
 ISBN 0-525-93368-9
 I. Title.
PS3558.E79785M67   1991
813'.54—dc20   91-10525
                                                        CIP

Printed in the United States of America
Designed by Eve L. Kirch

PUBLISHER'S NOTE
This is a work of fiction. Names, characters, places, and incidents either are the products of the author's imagination or are used ficti-
tiously, and any resemblance to actual persons, living or dead, events,
or locales is entirely coincidental.

Without limiting the rights under copyright reserved above, no part
of this publication may be reproduced, stored in or introduced into a
retrieval system, or transmitted, in any form, or by any means (elec-
tronic, mechanical, photocopying, recording, or otherwise), without
the prior written permission of both the copyright owner and the
above publisher of this book.

To Alisa Craig, Charlotte MacLeod, Barbara Mertz,
Barbara Michaels, and Elizabeth Peters,
all of whom have inspired me with their
brilliantly witty books and encouraged me with
their friendship.

Chapter 1

"WILD CHERRY WINE"

FADE-IN:

1   EXT. SHACK—DAY—MED. SHOT
LORETTA BIGGINS carries a basket of wash to the clothesline and begins to pin overalls on the line. CAMERA WIDENS and we see BILLY JOE JENKS watching her from behind the fence.

> BILLY JOE
> Looks like you done some growing up while you was stayin' with your kinfolks over in Oklahoma.

> LORETTA
> Reckon I did, though I can't see how it's any of your business, Billy Joe Jenks.

> BILLY JOE
> I always thought you was too big for your britches. Now I can see you've filled them out mighty nicely.

Loretta tosses her chin and returns to her chores. Billy Joe comes through the gate and saunters up to her.

2 CLOSE SHOT—LORETTA

Loretta's startled gaze reflects her sudden awareness that Billy Joe has matured, too.

3 RETURN TO SCENE

> LORETTA
> Seems you done growed some yourself.

> BILLY JOE
> Does this mean we'uns is too old to play doctor like we used to?

> LORETTA
> Why, Billy Joe! I'm shocked you could say something like that to my face. You know I'm a good girl. I'm saving myself for the man I marry.

> BILLY JOE
> (harshly)
> You mean Cooter Grimmley? I heard some talk at the pool hall about how your ma finalized it with ol' Cooter just last night.

Loretta sinks to the ground and covers her face with her hands. Her shoulders shake as she is convulsed with sobs. Billy Joe squats beside her and clumsily tries to comfort her.

> LORETTA
> (brokenly)
> Oh, Billy Joe, I cain't bear to think of Cooter Grimmley. He's so mean and

nasty. Pa wouldn't make me marry him, would he? I'd just die!

BILLY JOE

I'll take care of you, Loretta, honey. I won't let that Cooter get his filthy, hairy hands on you. You're too good and pure for that durn polecat!

Billy Joe wraps his arms around Loretta, who wipes away her tears and bravely lifts her face to smile at him. CAMERA MOVES IN as he kisses her. Loretta's face is pink as she pushes him away.

LORETTA

I've never . . . let anyone do that before, Billy Joe. It makes me feel kind of dizzy.

BILLY JOE

God, I love you, Loretta Biggins. You're the prettiest, sweetest, purest girl I ever known. My heart's about to burst with all this love I got for you.
(beat)
Kin you could meet me tonight down by the creek?

LORETTA

Pa'll tan the living daylights outta me if he catches me.

She stumbles to her feet, but before she can take a step, Billy Joe grabs her. CLOSE UP on their faces.

BILLY JOE

Will you be there?

LORETTA

Yes . . .

DISSOLVE TO:

Ruby Bee was scared she was going to explode right then and there, splattering the walls and ceiling of Ruby Bee's Bar & Grill with blood and flesh and splinters of bones. Her eyes were as big and round as a matching set of harvest moons. Her body felt as though it were expanding like a liver-spotted pink balloon, and pretty soon her skin would have to give.

It was a delightful sensation.

"Now, you just say that one more time," she commanded in a squeaky voice, her throat so tight she could barely swallow.

The woman, who'd introduced herself earlier as Carlotta Lowenstein, was accustomed to such an intently physical reaction, and on more than one occasion she'd wondered if she remembered the finer points of CPR. "Why don't you have a glass of water?" she said with a sympathetic smile.

"Why, do forgive me, Miss Lowenstein!" Ruby Bee gasped. "Here I am as dumbstruck as a turkey in a thunderstorm and I didn't even think to offer you a glass of iced tea or a beer! I am ashamed of myself. What can I fix you?"

"Tea would be fine."

Ruby Bee bustled around behind the counter until she managed to pour enough tea in a glass to make her feel a little more hospitable. As she put the glass down in front of her visitor, the barroom door opened and sunlight momentarily splashed on the rows of booths, jukebox, and tiny dance floor.

"Yoo-hoo!" Estelle Oppers called as she marched

across the room to the bar, her bony shoulders squared and her bright red hair styled in the way that always made Ruby Bee think about the Statue of Liberty. "Are we going to that flea market in Piccard or not? I thought you said you were going to pick me up at three, but it's a darn sight closer to—" She stopped as she noticed the young woman on a stool, the one on the end that she herself had a proprietary feeling about. "Excuse me, missy. I thought Ruby Bee was going to close on account of a flea market we were going to an hour ago."

"Hush, Estelle," Ruby Bee said without even looking at her. "This is Miss Carlotta Lowenstein, and she's a scout."

The final pronouncement was so melodramatic that Estelle waited for the fireworks to go off or the orchestra to start playing. When none of this happened, she wrinkled her nose and said, "As in Girl Scout?"

"I scout for locations," the woman explained. "I work for Glittertown Productions, Inc. We're a small, independent company from the Los Angeles area."

"Movies," Ruby Bee said reverently. "Miss Lowenstein works for a movie company."

"You do?" Estelle said, impressed in spite of herself. She took a harder look at the woman, who didn't look like one of those movie people, not with her neatly cropped dark hair and stocky body. Distorted by thick-lensed glasses, her eyes looked a little bulgy but intelligent. Her suit was nice enough, although it was wrinkled and one of the cuffs was missing a button. She wasn't unattractive, but she wasn't at all glamorous—and therefore was seriously suspect. "You're really from Hollywood?"

"Our office is in Burbank, but we've used some of the sound lots in Hollywood," Carlotta said. "Because we're small and work on a tight budget, we do a lot of work on location in some of the less expensive areas of the country. We finished up a film in Arizona at the beginning of the spring.''

"What's it called?'' asked Ruby Bee.

Carlotta took a long drink of tea while she considered her reply. The truth would not sit well. "It's not ready for release yet, and our executive producer likes to keep the titles to himself until the distribution's finalized. It's an in-joke of sorts.''

Ruby Bee and Estelle nodded, both secretly thrilled to be privy to a Hollywood in-joke, even if it was hard to figure out what was so dadburned funny about it.

"Well?'' Carlotta said as she finished her tea. "What do you think about your town as the location for our next production? If we can arrange to use the sites I mentioned earlier, and if we have the cooperation of the citizens, I'm prepared to fly back to the Coast and grease the gears.''

"What sites?'' Estelle demanded.

As usual, Ruby Bee butted in. "They need a shack and a barn, and Miss Lowenstein happened to drive by Raz's place. I can't imagine he'd object, even if he has to relocate Marjorie to the backyard. They also need a big house with pillars and bushes.'' She wiggled her eyebrows at Estelle, who was having no trouble reading her mind. "I'm sure the mayor would be honored to have his house in a movie, aren't you?''

"The mayor?'' Carlotta said doubtfully.

"Hizzoner Jim Bob Buchanon,'' Estelle cut in. "He owns that ugly supermarket across the street. Mrs. Jim Bob can be difficult to deal with, to put it mild-like, but I reckon she'll puff up like a soufflé when she finds out her house is going to be on the big screen.'' She was proud of tossing out the lingo so casually, but this movie woman was frowning as if her pantyhose were affecting her circulation. "Do you happen to need a beauty parlor?'' she added optimistically.

Carlotta just kept frowning. "Mrs. Jim Bob?"

Ruby Bee butted in once again. "It's one of those local traditions that's hard to explain. Her real name's Barbara Anne Buchanon Buchanon, she and Jim Bob being first or second cousins once or twice removed. In fact, you're going to run into a whole passel of Buchanons. There's Earl and Eilene, and their boy Kevin, who's betrothed to Dahlia O'Neill, whose granny is a Buchanon from the Emmet branch of the family. Raz Buchanon, as I mentioned earlier. Adele Wockerman was a Buchanon afore she married, and—"

"They marry each other?" Carlotta murmured. Her eyes were narrowed behind the lenses, and she wasn't sounding overly enchanted with the amount of inbreeding that everyone in Maggody took for granted. After all, it had been going on for a good hundred years, and no one was exactly clamoring for admission to the clan.

"Some of them," said Estelle. "You can recognize them by their chimpanzee foreheads and yellowish eyes. None of them's what you might call college material, but they have the right number of fingers and toes, and not one of them's been locked away in one of those hospitals for the insane."

Ruby Bee scooted the pretzel bowl in front of their guest and gave Estelle a thoughtful look. "What about Terdlow Buchanon? Didn't he end up in prison for whacking up his parents and trying to sell the body parts to the poultry plant in Starley City?"

"I reckon he did. And there's Maisie Louise Buchanon, who had nigh onto sixty cats locked in her house when they finally found her body at the end of the summer. Phewy!"

"We can't forget Robin Buchanon, neither. She was blown to smithereens at the edge of a marijuana patch up on Cotter's Ridge. Her bush colts were mean enough to pluck live chickens with their teeth.''

"A beer," Carlotta said, fanning herself with a clipboard. "A beer sounds quite lovely."

Estelle settled down on the adjoining stool, propped her elbows on the bar, and said, "So what's this movie about, Miss Lowenstein?"

"Please, call me Carlotta. The screenplay's still in the rewrite stage, but basically it's a contemporary version of *Romeo and Juliet.* Young love thwarted, that sort of thing."

"I see," Estelle said with a sage nod. She popped a pretzel in her mouth and tried to remember the plot. It'd been a good thirty-five years since she'd been in high school, and she hadn't paid all that much attention in class, having already decided on her career in the art of hair design. There was the balcony, and something about messages getting mixed up. She was almost sure the boy and the girl croaked in the end.

"What's it gonna be named?" Ruby Bee asked.

Carlotta was keenly aware of the potential danger, and once again paused to seek the safest path through the minefield. "At the moment, we're calling it *Wild Cherry Wine.* The director, Hal Desmond, wants to convey the essential timelessness of the plot by the utilization of the long-standing traditions of the region. It's an exploration of the interdynamics of a family unit that must seek equilibrium in the universal conflict of personal fulfillment versus basic survival."

Ruby Bee blinked, but she didn't say, "Huh?" Hollywood people were supposed to talk like that, she figured. "Who're the stars?"

Carlotta rattled off five names so quickly that neither Ruby Bee nor Estelle caught any of them. "I must make my calls," she said, still talking faster than a truck barreling down the interstate, "and start lining up the production crew and clearing schedules. We'll be here at the end of next week, and we'll need all the available motel rooms in town and a catering service. I'll be back with you on the details as soon as I do a preliminary with the production people."

"How long will it take to make this movie?" Ruby Bee said, not bothering to mention that all the available motel rooms (five of them, to be exact) were out back and the only caterer in town was standing three feet away with a dishrag in her hand.

"No more than two weeks, if we can do the exteriors without any weather delays." Carlotta put the strap of her bulky purse over her shoulder and picked up her clipboard. "I look forward to seeing both of you shortly," she said as she slid off the stool. "I'll be in touch."

"Are you going to need any extras?" asked Estelle.

"A few." Carlotta saw no reason to explain that the vast majority of scenes took place in bedrooms or in intimate clearings in the woods. All three of the previous productions had tiptoed along the delicate line between an R rating and an X rating, not because Hal had moral reservations but because the distribution money was better if the films could be shown at drive-in theaters.

She went out to the rental car and stopped to assess the potential establishing shots for the opening credits of "Wild Cherry Wine." The sign at the edge of town proclaimed a population of seven hundred fifty-five, but the sign was pockmarked from years as a target and splattered with bird droppings. She'd driven past a peculiar metal structure called the Voice of the Almighty Lord Assembly Hall, a hardware store, a pool hall with a cross-eyed drunk in the doorway, a line of boarded-up stores, and an antiques store complete with a red-necked rube in a rocking chair. After a delay at the single stoplight, she'd passed a supermarket as tacky as anything back home; a launderette with the improbable name Suds of Fun; and a small, red-brick building with a police car parked nearby.

Glittertown Productions, Inc., had experienced problems with law enforcement agencies on every production, the law about prevailing community standards being so vague. Only three months ago, lynchings had been mentioned in Flagstaff. Hal had sweated like a marathon runner until the last scene was done and the entire company could flee across the state line.

Carlotta went back inside Ruby Bee's. The two women broke off their spirited conversation as she said, "Do I need to clear anything with the police department? We might require traffic control for one or two scenes, and we always prefer to cooperate with the local authorities." As in bribing them ahead of time to circumvent expensive delays.

"Oh, no," Ruby Bee said quickly. "I am personally acquainted with the chief of police, and I'm sure she'll be tickled pink at the idea of a movie being made in Maggody. Why, it's the most exciting thing that's happened here since Hiram Buchanon's barn burned down, and that was a good twenty years ago."

"Two of the local teenagers were . . . courting in the hayloft," Estelle added.

"*Ciao,* then," Carlotta said and returned to the car, smiling to herself as she savored the delicacy of the phrase. She had a feeling the citizens of Maggody, Arkansas, were going to be more than a little taken aback when they learned how Hollywood, or at least her company, defined the word "courting" these days.

"Hiram Buchanon's barn, twenty years ago," I said into the telephone receiver. I settled my feet on the corner of my desk, rocked my chair back until it hit the wall, and gazed idly out the window. "That chicken house where the marijuana was being cured. The bank and Miss Una's house. Four fires in twenty years, Harve. Now we've had three more in the last month."

Harve Dorfer, the Stump County sheriff, exhaled noisily, and I could almost smell acrid cigar smoke. "I know, Arly, I know. But what in tarnation can we do about it? I sure as hell don't have the manpower to put a deputy inside every old barn and shack in this half of the county."

"The volunteer fire department from Emmet offered to open a branch office in town. I'm thinking about cornering the market in marshmallows and wieners." I held up my free hand to admire the black grime under my fingernails. "I went back to that last shack and took another look. For some crazy reason, I got it into my head that I was being watched. I looked over my shoulder once too often and ran into a tree."

"Haunted, is it?" Harve chuckled.

"It may be haunted, but it's also arson. Our problem is that it's going to be damn hard to prove it. I talked to the investigator at the state police barracks, and he agreed it was impossible to determine anything from a pile of ashes."

"Think we got us a nut case?"

"Three fires in a month," I said, sighing. "All abandoned structures of little or no value, and the damage confined to the immediate site. No one hurt, no families left homeless, no great loss to the landscape. But, yeah, Harve, I think we've got a nut case with a box of matches and no socially redeeming hobbies."

We chatted for a while longer, but neither of us had a theory worthy of repeating, nor did we have a devious scheme to find the nut and take away his matches. After we'd given up, I went outside and looked at the ridge beyond the east side of town. The mountainside was pale green. Although the nights were cool, the days were beginning to swell with early-summer warmth. The teenagers had begun to skip school to skinny-dip in Boone Creek, and the grown-ups to sit on their porches in the evenings to drink iced tea and monitor their neighbors.

There was no curl of smoke rising from the mountainside, however, and I went back into the PD to write up a tedious report about my investigation of the charcoaled shack that hadn't been inhabited for so long that no one in town remembered who used to live there. Or cared. I skipped over the part about sensing someone in the brush on the hill, but as I paused to think of a properly officious phrase, I felt the same circle of heat on my back, right between my shoulder blades. I resisted the urge to shiver and sternly told myself it had been a beam of sunlight cutting through the remains of the roof.

I finished the report, stuffed it in a drawer for later perusal, and decided it was quittin' time, so to speak. In that, I was not only the chief of police but also the entirety of the department; I was on duty twenty-four hours a day. It would have been a relentless burden had Maggody been riddled with violent criminal activity on a regular basis, but everybody tended to go about his or her business, licit or illicit, in a quiet and orderly fashion. Oh, I knew the owner of the pool hall bootlegged beer from an adjoining state, and every once in a while I suggested he desist. The rumor of a moonshine still on Cotter's Ridge waxed and waned, but I wasn't about to waste my energy combing the woods for it— or for the marijuana patches that were up there, too.

Instead, I dedicated a portion of each day to nabbing

speeders out by the skeletal remains of Purtle's Esso station. I followed the school buses in the afternoons to remind folks to stop when the flag shot out from the side of the bus and children scampered mindlessly across the highway. When I heard about the local teen-agers acting up, I went down to the high school and bawled out the offenders. I listened at least once a week to Raz Buchanon gripe about whatever was ailing him.

And mostly let the days slide by. I'd been doing so since I'd come back to Maggody to recuperate from life in the fast lane and divorce in the excruciatingly slow one. The transition from Manhattan to Maggody had been accomplished so easily that it alarmed me. Marti-nis to beer. Caviar to catfish. Nightclubs to nights alone in a tiny apartment above the antiques store across the road from the PD. Debating foreign policy to complain-ing about the weather.

I was becoming complacent, I lectured myself as I walked down the road to Ruby Bee's Bar & Grill for a comfortable supper and an update on the gossip, which was dished out as readily as the black-eyed peas. There was nothing to stop me from returning to Manhattan. The job at the security company would be there. Since I'd been the martyr in the divorce, most of my old friends would put me back on the invitation list.

But it didn't feel right; not yet, anyway. The confu-sion and pain of the divorce had worn down my edge, left me skittish and unsure of myself. I wore my hair in a bun and stored my makeup in the back of a drawer. I favored a khaki uniform over designer jeans and silk blouses. My nightly fantasies were works of art. I'd run home to mama, and for the moment I was content to be bullied and pampered and fed the best scalloped potatoes on either side of the Mississippi.

The parking lot was thick with pickup trucks, most of them with well-stocked gun racks in the rear windows and tool boxes in the beds. The Flamingo Motel sign flickered nervously; it looked as though the bird was about to lose another feather and the V CAN Y sign another letter. One of these days the symmetry would be completed and we'd be looking at V C N Y. Viable Connections in New York. Very Close; Not Yet.

The jukebox was wailing and the booths were filled with nuzzling couples or bellicose drunks. One couple appeared to be copulating on the dance floor, to the amusement of the spectators, since everyone in town knew the girl was carrying on with the boy's brother—and his uncle. Everyone also knew Joyce Lambertino was pregnant, Elsie McMay's daughter was visiting, the Missionary Society was in a tizzy over the upcoming elections, and that Chief of Police Arly Hanks would never catch herself a fellow if she didn't stop moping around and start listening to her mother, who happened to be the infamous Ruby Bee Hanks, proprietess. And not to mention allowing Estelle Oppers, owner and sole operator of Estelle's Hair Fantasies, to do something about that schoolmarmish bun and plain dark hair. An auburn rinse and a body perm had been suggested.

One of the neckless wonders at the bar staggered toward the men's room, so I appropriated his stool and waited until Ruby Bee noticed me. "What's for supper?" I inquired politely.

"How can you eat at a time like this?"

I glanced at the clock above the bar. "At a time like six o'clock, give or take a few minutes, I can eat. In fact, I cannot fathom not being able to eat at such a time, which isn't to say there aren't other equally appealing times."

"All you ever think about is eating and sleeping and making uncalled-for remarks." She shot me a pinched look, then moved down the bar to berate one of her regulars, who had dumped the pretzels and was now flipping them into the air like tiddlywink pieces. He quit immediately, because he and everyone else had enough sense to be intimidated by Ruby Bee, who was short and matronly and who could toss out a drunk without regard to his weight or his degree of compliance.

She returned and devoted great energy to wiping the spotless countertop. "I suppose you haven't heard the big news."

I thought for a minute. "Joyce's pregnancy? Elsie McMay's visitor? The fire up past the Pot O' Gold mobile home park?"

"Don't be smart-mouthed with me, young lady."

Devotion to scalloped potatoes forced me into humbleness. "What big news?"

"It's all over town. You being the chief of police, I'd have thought you took an interest in local happenings."

"I've been occupied with a fire bug, which is somewhat important to the community, unless we all decide to start smoking–literally."

"Seems I heard about that old shack burning down two nights ago," she said with a small frown. "But nobody's lived there for years and years. I am talking about the movie."

I didn't think she was referring to *The Towering Inferno,* so I arranged my features for maximum fascination and said, "What movie?"

"You mean Arly doesn't know?" Estelle said from behind me.

"She's been too busy to pay any attention to what every last soul in town's been buzzing over all day," Ruby Bee said, taking more swipes at the pristine counter.

"Why don't you just tell me," I said meekly.

They did, although it was a challenge to pick out the

snippets of fact from the fanciful ravings of two potential movie stars who were already imagining themselves strolling along the sidewalk of fame and accepting statuettes for best supporting actress.

"Is it really going to happen, or was the woman merely considering Maggody?" I asked.

Ruby Bee grew solemn. "It's really going to happen. She called a while ago and said she needed to fax consent forms. I had to tell her we didn't have any of those machines in town. She's reserved all the rooms out back and arranged for the cast and crew to eat here."

"What's the name of the production company?" I said, trying to come up with a reason why anyone (besides yours truly, that is) would come to Maggody voluntarily, especially a second time. "What other movies have they done recently?"

Estelle leaned forward and murmured, "We can't say one word about their last picture. We swore to keep it a secret."

"Good for you," I said. "How about pork chops, Ruby Bee? And peach cobbler with ice cream for dessert?"

She nodded, then gave Estelle one of their aren't-we-too-clever-for-words looks. "Sure, Arly. And how about a nice glass of wild cherry wine to go with that?"

They found this remark hilarious—shrilly, wildly, loudly hilarious. I was not the only one staring in bewilderment at them as the jukebox whined a lament of lost love and whiskied woes.

What fascinated him was the ease with which he could start the fires. The first time he'd used a pile of kindling and a match, then moved to a prudently chosen hiding place to watch as flames begin to lick the roof and curl through the windows. Rafters crashed to the floor. Walls collapsed, hurling armies of sparks at the cloud-choked sky. He felt as if he'd unleashed a maleficent dragon inside the primitive structure. The first fire had given him a sense of power he'd never felt before.

The second fire had been even more compelling. As he'd watched, he'd been overwhelmed with a strange sensation that abated slowly and left him flushed and damp with satisfaction. As the third one consumed his chosen victim, the sensation had been stronger.

The woman cop with the dark hair had come once with a grim man, and the two of them had squatted on the floor to scrape brittle black fragments into plastic bags. She'd returned later, alone. He'd almost laughed aloud at her obvious uneasiness, but of course he'd been very quiet. She could dig through the ashes as much as she desired, as long as she didn't try to stop him.

Chapter 2

6 INT. SHACK—EVENING

Loretta is sitting on the sofa as WE HEAR the doorbell. Zachery crosses the room and throws open the door to admit COOTER GRIMMLEY. He is wearing a coat and a bow tie and holding a hat.

> ZACHERY
>
> Well, if it ain't Cooter! Come on in and set right there by little Loretta.

> MARTHA
>
> I already told Loretta the good news. How 'bout a piece of apple pie and a cup of coffee?

Cooter stays by the door, staring at Loretta.

> COOTER
>
> I thank you kindly, Martha, but I reckon I'll pass on the pie. I came to see if my fiancée wanted to take a stroll and enjoy the cool breeze.

Loretta stares at the floor. CAMERA WIDENS as
Zachery crosses to her and pulls her to her
feet.

ZACHERY
(jovially)
'Course she does, Cooter. It's time you
two got to know each other better. Why,
you'll be hitched afore you know it.

COOTER
We shore will, won't we, honey child? By
this time next year, you'll be so busy car-
ing for a little baby that you won't have
time for a peaceful stroll with your husband.

LORETTA
I 'spose so. Ma, Billy Joe said he was coming by with some fresh okra from his
garden.
(beat)
Tell him I said it was real nice of him to
think about us.

COOTER
Billy Joe Jenks? He's just a dirt-poor,
white-trash kid. I grow plenty of okra to
share with y'all. I don't want to hear tell
of you even talking to that pissant excuse
for a farmer.

MARTHA
I'll keep 'em away from each other,
Cooter.

COOTER
You better if you want to keep your farm.
She's mine, and I ain't gonna stand for

him or anyone else taking what I aim to
take for myself. Now come on, Loretta.
We don't got all night. Not yet, anyways.

He takes her wrist and pulls her out the door.
Martha and Zachery exchange looks, but neither speaks.

DISSOLVE TO:

"But is it a sin?" Mrs. Jim Bob repeated, determined to
remain on her knees but increasingly aware of the
graininess of the floor. The windows of the Voice of
the Almighty Lord Assembly Hall were open, but the
air inside was as fusty and stagnant as the contents of
an old trunk.

Beside her, Brother Verber rumbled thoughtfully
while he tried to decide what to say. He knew he had
to say the right thing, that being defined as what she
wanted to hear, but nothing in his correspondence
classes from the seminary in Las Vegas had dealt with
the sinfulness—or lack thereof—of having your house
in a movie. He clasped his hands more tightly against
his white-bread soft belly and rolled his eyes upward
to stare at a cobweb on the ceiling. A drop of sweat
formed on the tip of his nose, and hung there with the
tenacity of a stalactite.

"Well?" she prompted him.

"It's a matter of conscience," he said piously. "In
that you, Sister Barbara, serve as the conscience of the
whole town and have never let even your pinkie stray
off the path of righteousness, I think it's safe to assume
that whatever you choose to do will be the Christian
thing."

Mrs. Jim Bob fought back a flash of annoyance as she

sat on the edge of the pew and dusted off her knees. "If I saw clearly what the proper thing was, I wouldn't have driven all the way over here to ask you, Brother Verber. I was planning to take a coffee cake to Eula, who's been so feeling poorly that she hasn't decided how to vote in the upcoming Missionary Society election. Then Ruby Bee called on me with this crazy story about a Hollywood company wanting to make a movie in town, with my house in it."

"It's troubling," Brother Verber said, aware he wasn't behaving like the spiritual dictator of his flock. He normally didn't have any problem telling folks what to do and when to do it (and usually made a practice of doing just that), but a recent episode with an inflatable doll and a sackful of dirty magazines had undermined his conviction in the sanctity of his own opinions.

Mrs. Jim Bob had lost a little faith in him, too, but he was still the shepherd and she but a humble lamb, so she figured it was only fitting that she give him a chance. "The problem is," she said through a smile so tight the corners of her mouth didn't move, not even one tiny millimeter, "that everyone knows what kinds of immoral things go on in Hollywood. Every last one of those people takes drugs, drives too fast, sops up liquor like a sponge, and commits . . . well, unnatural acts during the day. What if they were to start doing that sort of thing in my newly redecorated living room? What if they were to sneak upstairs to the guest room and commence fornicating on that ruffly pink bedspread that I had dry-cleaned less than a month ago?"

Brother Verber's mind strayed for a moment, but he managed to avoid any onslaught of tattletale sweat. "Right there with the sun shining through the window?"

"That is not the issue."

"No, of course it ain't." He banished the image from

his mind, wiped his forehead with his handkerchief, and did his best to concentrate. "What does Jim Bob say about your house being in a movie?"

"He asked how much they would pay," she said with a sniff. "I do not feel we can welcome immorality into our home for three hundred dollars, but Jim Bob seemed to feel otherwise." Her eyes narrowed as she remembered the last time she'd been obliged to confront Jim Bob with certain violations of the Ten Commandments. Some of them she'd rewritten for the occasion, but she felt her revisions were just as good, if not better, than the originals.

"Do they have any use for a religious setting?" asked Brother Verber. There was a variety of good works he could accomplish with that kind of money. Like a new television in the trailer that served as the rectory, for starters.

"I doubt it. The name of this movie is *Wild Cherry Wine,* and I think that says it all, don't you? I simply will not have strangers drinking alcoholic beverages in my living room." Her decision made for herself, Mrs. Jim Bob stood up, smoothed away the wrinkles in her skirt, and put on her white gloves. "I really must run by Eula's and see how she's feeling. My duty is to the members of the congregation, not to outsiders with their trashy Hollywood morals."

"Praise the Lord," Brother Verber muttered to her back as she marched toward the door. He waited until she was gone before allowing himself to ponder the wicked, lascivious ways of the outsiders, at least one of whom was bound to be a starlet with big breasts, a tiny waist, a firm derriere, wet lips, and sultry, smoldering eyes. He was so overcome by his vision that he thudded to his knees, entwined his fingers, and earnestly began to pray.

Dahlia O'Neil sighed as she and Kevin sipped cherry limeades in front of the Dairee Dee-Lishus.

"What's the matter?" Kevin asked, swallowing hastily so he could inquire about his beloved's obvious state of depression. Why, she'd shook her head when he'd suggested cheeseburgers and onion rings. Now all three hundred plus pounds of her quivered in distress, as if she were the goddess of a volcano about to erupt in tears. He would have dropped to his knees to entreat her to pour out her soul to him, but the parking lot was muddy and he was wearing new jeans.

"Ain't nothing the matter," Dahlia growled, her teeth clamped on the plastic straw. A gargly noise came from her cup as she sucked up the last few drops. "Nothing at all, so there ain't any point in you asking me over and over again. Take me home, Kevin."

"Home? But I thought we was going to drive out to Boone Creek and—"

"And what?"

She sounded so unfriendly that Kevin's mind went blank. This happened a lot, and according to some folks in town, it stayed that way more often than not, but this time Kevin was blinded with panic. His father had let him take the car, which he hardly ever did after Kevin had experienced a few mishaps (though no one had been killed). There was a blanket in the trunk, along with a cooler filled with soda pop and a package of vanilla sandwich cookies. He'd even brought a transistor radio so the night could be filled with music, the breeze with the heady perfume of honeysuckle, the sky with twinkly stars, and his arms with as much as he could hold of the woman he loved.

He turned on all his manly charm. "Ah, but Dahlia, my dumpling, the night is young."

"The night may be young, but your brain ain't been born yet," she said without mercy. Her cheeks bulged out, and several chins appeared as she lowered her face and glared at him like a bull getting ready to charge.

"But what did I do?" Kevin forgot about his new jeans and dropped to his knees.

She looked down at his teary eyes, trembling mouth, and undulating Adam's apple, and for a moment felt something akin to pity for him. "Nothing, Kevin."

"And we're still betrothed, even if you don't want to go out to Boone Creek to count the lightning bugs?"

The pity dried up real quick. "I told you that we're gonna behave like respectable folks now that we're betrothed. Last time you let the devil creep into your soul, it was about the worst week in my entire life, Kevin Fitzgerald Buchanon. If it ever happens again, you'll find yourself on your knees asking Raz's prize sow to be your awful wedded wife."

She refused to talk to him on the drive home, and climbed out of the car without so much as a peck on the cheek. The house shook as she stomped across the porch and through the door.

"Women!" Kevin said to himself as he backed out of the driveway, flattening a dozen chrysanthemums in the process, and drove back toward town. As he went past Raz Buchanon's place, he remembered the brutality of his beloved's remark. An ice pick stabbed his heart. He decided he needed some advice from someone who understood women. That ruled out his pa, and he sure couldn't go asking his ma about counting lightning bugs by the creek, but at last he thought of someone.

"Who does she think *she* is?" Hal Desmond barked from behind his desk. "Get me the last contract, Carlotta. She took three points last time. Why in God's name does she think she deserves six now? What's she done—grown another breast?"

Carlotta did not leap to her feet and dash into the front room of the office to find the contract under discussion. She was much too enured to these petty and petulent tirades, and less than impressed with them. Hal was red-faced, but what else was new? He was trembling so hard that his curly brown toupee was liable to slip off his head, but who cared? She, along with other distaff members of the production company, had seen him without the toupee or anything else, and none of them had found the result worthy of discussion.

Crossing her legs, she settled back in the chair and said, "Gwenneth's heard rumors that actors actually get paid salaries, as in scale minimum and more. I told you to keep her locked in the basement between pictures. You're the one who insisted on escorting her to the hot new placcs and displaying her at parties. An extra three points seems to be the price of having cleavage hanging on your arm, Hal."

Hal lit a cigarette and regained control of himself, which wasn't all that hard, since his tantrums were perfunctory. He was a producer and a director. He had an artistic temperament. He was the one who made it happen. He had a full head of expensive hair, a keen grasp of the industry, a Jaguar, a house on the beach, and a herd of lackies to jump when he snapped his fingers. Except for Carlotta, he amended with a grunt. If she weren't so damn efficient, she'd have been cinematic history a long time ago.

He blew a plume of smoke in her direction. "I took

Gwenneth to Marty—what's his last name? Anyway, I took her to Marty's to stir up some interest in the flick. I've got to go through Marty to get to the distributor, and I've got to get to the distributor if we want *Prickly Passion* to be shown in the passion pits of America."

"Did Gwenneth make it with Marty?"

"I don't know," he admitted. He would have run his fingers through his hair had it been possible. "I told her to, and I threw him a few stories about her undeniable prowess. Gave him the tape with the outtakes of her and Frederick when they were, shall we say, ad-libbing to excess? If she'll ad-lib like that with Marty, he'll persuade Cinerotica to pick up the film in a big way, and we might see some money for our effort."

"You're a pimp."

"Yeah." He jabbed out his cigarette and gestured at her. After a moment of thought about her schedule for the evening, she took a cassette of *Prickly Passion* from a shelf, loaded and activated the VCR, and went behind the desk to massage his fleshy neck. As she did so, she realized her fingers could not reach around it. A shame.

Outside, headlights streamed down the boulevard like lemmings heading for the sea.

"Why would anyone want to make a movie in Maggody?"

"I don't know," I said as I passed the box of greasy popcorn to Sergeant John Plover of the Arkansas State Police. "Why would anyone forget to clean the windshield before inviting someone to accompany him to the drive-in movie?"

"There're a lot of bugs between Maggody and here. How was I to know they were suicidal? But tell me more about this movie business, Arly."

I glanced at the totality of my social life. He was good-looking in a sneaky way, with shaggy blond hair, a crooked nose, a quirky smile, and a dimple that appeared when he was trying not to laugh. The dimple was on display at the moment. I retrieved the popcorn and said, "Some little company from California. Ruby Bee told me its name, but I didn't recognize it. It's not MGM or Disney. The cast and crew are slated to reside in the Flamingo Motel."

"That many, huh?"

I checked the screen to see if the giant carnivorous cricket had leveled Tokyo yet. "And they didn't demand cots and rollaways, so they can't be more than ten of them. I suppose they chose Arkansas because it's cheap and they can get away with nonunion labor."

"Choosing Arkansas is not inexplicable, but choosing Maggody is," Plover said amiably. It was his most irritating trait—this good-humored, easygoing amiability of ol' Sergeant Complaisancy. It carried us along from week to week, but I was increasingly aware that I knew very little about his inner convolutions. Maybe he didn't have any. A soul of silk, perhaps.

I was about to agree with his remark when my beeper went off. "I'd better call in," I muttered. "Ruby Bee's likely to have developed a hangnail or some such tragedy. Let me know if Cricko eats anybody."

I used the pay telephone outside the concession stand, and came back to the car with a scowl. Slamming the door hard enough to cause heads to pop up in backseats all around us, I said, "There's another fire between Maggody and Hasty. Harve wants me to meet him there."

"Does this mean we'll have to miss *Tanya Makes the Team?* Damn it, you know how much I enjoy sports stories." He was already putting the speaker on the stand and starting the engine, however, alleviating me of the necessity of making a comment about his sordid taste. After all, I was the one who savored the antics of nature's finest mutants. That in itself might have merited some introspection, but I was more concerned about the recent spate of fires.

"What do you know about firebugs?" I asked as we pulled onto the highway.

"Not much. You ought to talk to Merganser about it. He's done a couple of special courses with the FBI and knows more than anyone else at the barracks."

"He came out to investigate the last fire, but the shack was so dry that it burned to the ground before the fire department arrived. We both agreed it was arson, though. You can't blame faulty wiring when the place had no electricity."

"Maybe some derelict was holed up there and made a fire to cook," suggested Plover.

"Four times in the last month? You'd think he'd learn something about camp fire safety along the way." I stuffed my mouth with popcorn and thoughtfully chomped my way through it. "These fires are being set deliberately. Our nut case, as Harve so politely calls him, could be a derelict. He could also be a kid or a drunk from the pool hall or a real, live psycho. What frightens me is that he seems to be heating up rapidly. Eventually someone's going to get hurt, or the fire's going to spread and do serious damage."

All Plover could do was repeat his suggestion to talk to Merganser. We turned on the county road that led to Hasty, and had no difficulty finding the scene, in that roiling smoke deposited ashes on the windshield long before we caught sight of an orange glow above the treetops. Sheriff's department vehicles blocked the road, thwarting the growing line of trucks and cars filled with spectators.

We parked and joined the parade of pedestrians, some of whom had the foresight to bring coolers and folding aluminum chairs.

"What's burning?" Plover asked me.

"A barn," I said, trying to picture something I'd driven past a million times. "There used to be a house, but it was torn down years ago. The roof of the barn collapsed, and it wasn't much more than a pile of gray lumber and a home for mice and snakes."

"Evenin,' Arly," said a voice from behind us.

I looked back at one of the Maggody magpies. "Hi, Eula. What are you doing out here?"

"Lottie called me when she heard about the fire, and I thought I'd come take a look at it. Oh, there's Elsie and her daughter walking with Larry Joe and Joyce. I don't think it's good for Joyce to be exposed to smoke when she's"—Eula noticed Plover and lowered her voice—"in a family way."

"Don't worry about him," I said. "He's my gynecologist. You wouldn't believe some of the things he's seen. Tell her about the contortionist who—"

Eula fled. We wound through the crowd, went past the police line, and found Harve glumly watching the volunteer firemen hosing the fire, which by now consisted only of isolated sputters of flames.

"Any evidence?" I asked.

Harve plucked a cigar butt from his shirt pocket. Once he'd gotten it going, he said, "Not a damn thing. Some kid spotted the fire about an hour ago, but it took him another ten minutes to find a telephone. By the time the boys got here, all they could do was contain the damn thing."

Wade Elkins, the fire chief, joined us. His face was
streaked with soot and his curly dark hair dotted with
ashes, but he was still attractive, and he moved quickly
for someone who'd roused his troops, driven ten miles,
and battled the fire for most of an hour. "How many
more bonfires are y'all planning to have this month,
Arly? I'd like to see the end of a baseball game just
once."

"Sorry, Wade," I said, not sure why I was apologiz-
ing. "I know you and the guys are getting tired of our
fires. Maybe we can arrange for the arsonist to set
a few over in Emmet so you won't have to drive so
far."

"But then I wouldn't get to be your hero of the
hour." He winked at me. "I'm beginning to look forward to our little romantic, firelit trysts. Just you and
me and—oh, yeah—everybody this side of the Missouri
line."

Harrumphing under his breath, Plover tapped Harve
on the shoulder. "Where's the kid who reported the
fire?"

"You think he might have seen something?" I
said.

Harve shrugged. "Said he didn't, but you're welcome
to ask him again. He's the one in the plaid shirt."

I recognized Billy Dick MacNamara in the huddle of
high-school boys and pointed him out to Plover. "He's
a Maggody boy, lives with his mother out past the high
school. I questioned him once about some tools missing from the shop room, but it turned out he wasn't
involved."

"He was kinda stuttery when he called," Wade said.
"Took me a while to figure out what he was talking
about and where the fire was. There wasn't anything
left when we got here, so it didn't make a rat's ass of
difference."

I called to Billy Dick, who came over with a leery expression on his plump, round face. He was a bleachy kid, with hair so light it was invisible, and eyes that were pale to the point of being almost color-less. He moved clumsily, as though the ground were covered with a sheen of ice. "This is Sergeant Plo-ver," I said to him. "He's assisting the sheriff and me."

Billy Dick blinked at us, one at a time. In a high, uncertain voice he said, "It's s-scary, ain't it? My ma's all worried that someone'll b-burn our house down while we're sleeping." Every now and then he tangled with an initial consonant, but he was not difficult to understand.

"What time did you see the fire?" Plover asked.

"I—uh, I left my house at nine, so it was probably ten minutes after that. I drove real fast to the nearest house to report the fire."

Wade nodded. "I got the call at nine-twenty. Took us half an hour to organize and get here."

"This is a pretty lonely road," I said, "and it was late. Think, Billy Dick: Did you pass any cars when you drove out this way?"

"I wasn't paying much attention. I've been keeping company with a girl what lives in Hasty. I was thinking about her all the time I was driving—right up until I noticed the fire, anyway."

Plover's dimple appeared as he said, "Nine-thirty's late for a date, isn't it?"

Billy Dick scuffled his foot in the dirt. "Her p-parents had to go into Farberville on account of her great-aunt taking a fall in the bathtub. She was afraid to stay home alone."

"Oh," Plover said knowingly.

I ignored this display of macho bonding. "Try to remember if you saw any cars going in either direction, Billy Dick. Were you momentarily blinded by head-lights?''

He closed his eyes and sucked noisily on his lower lip until his chin glistened in the last of the firelight. I was about to repeat my question when he said, "Yeah, twice. Just past the low-water bridge there was a p-pickup coming toward me. I didn't see what color it was or anything. And right before I spotted the fire, there was a taillight going over the top of a hill. The other one must have been broke.''

"Well, then," Harve said, working the cigar butt from one corner of his mouth to the other in record-breaking time, presuming there was a record. "We got a truck that was headed for Maggody and a taillight headed for Hasty. It ain't much, but at least it's some-thing.''

Plover shook his head. "Unless the perp set the fire so that it would take a while to blaze up, and was back home watching the baseball game by nine o'clock. Or unless he was parked off the road and watched Billy Dick here drive by, then sedately went on his way.''

"Dammit, Plover," Harve said without anger, "it's my party and we're going to play by my theories, mostly 'cause that's all we've got. Arly, see what you can turn up about a truck coming your way. I'll put one of my boys on the Hasty end. A vehicle with a broken taillight might not be too hard to find.''

I nodded. "And I'll cruise the road tomorrow and look for a place where the perp could have pulled off far enough not to be seen.''

Wade yelled a few orders to his men, then grinned at me. "Maybe you ought to take me up on that offer to open a branch in Maggody. I'd be real pleased to stay at your place with you until we catch this guy. On your couch . . . or elsewhere.''

"So kind of you," I said, taking a wicked pleasure in Plover's faint snort. "If a fireman can't heat up the situation, who can?''

On that incredibly witty note, we disbanded.

Chapter 3

8   EXT. WOODED PATH—NIGHT—MED. SHOT

Loretta is sitting on a log. Cooter paces in front of her, his face tight with anger and his hands curled into fists.

> COOTER
>
> So you and that white trash went for a walk the other night, did you?

> LORETTA
> (miserably)
> Yes, sir, but that's all we did.

CAMERA MOVES behind Cooter as he steps in front of Loretta.

> COOTER
>
> So you're still a sweet little virgin, huh? Never seen one of these before, huh? Wouldn't know what to do with it, huh?

> LORETTA
> (brokenly)
> Yes, sir—I mean, no, sir. Billy Joe and I

didn't . . . He wanted to, but I told him I
had to wait until I was married.

CElig: COOTER
I'll find out if you're lying when the time
comes. If you are, I'll find ways to make
you miserable for the rest of your life.
(beat)
How old are you?

LORETTA
Fifteen, sir. My birthday's coming up real
fast.

COOTER
I don't care about any fool birthday. Fifteen's old enough to be learned a few
things. I aim to start the lesson right now.

LORETTA
Yes, sir. My pa said I had to do whatever
you told me to.

9   CLOSE SHOT—BILLY JOE
Billy Joe is hiding behind some trees, his expression tormented.

10   RETURN TO SCENE
Loretta and Cooter should be able to AD-LIB
through this. CAMERA MOVES between them.

Note: See script of *Prickly Passion,* scenes 1,
6, 11, 17, 29.

CUT TO:

"Needless to say, I had no intention of cooperating with
those Hollywood types," Mrs. Jim Bob informed Per-

kins's eldest, who was on her hands and knees, scrubbing the kitchen floor. "But I was under the misconception that they would simply take over the house and I would have no say in what they did."

She waited for Perkins's eldest to respond, but when nothing was forthcoming, she decided to call Lottie for a nice chat. She fixed a cup of tea, tucked a few lemon cookies on the edge of the saucer, settled down on the sofa in the living room, and dialed the number. To her chagrin, she was treated to a busy signal.

"Lottie Estes is the worst gossip in town," Mrs. Jim Bob said loudly so that Perkins's eldest could benefit from the opinion. "I merely wanted to let her know that I have been asked to take a small yet vital role in the movie. I protested, naturally, but the woman who called all the way from California pleaded with me to accept." She once again waited for a response—anything, even a primitive grunt of admiration—but Perkins's eldest seemed to be in one of her taciturn moods. "I shall donate the money to charity. It's the Christian thing to do, and I will feel much better about being involved with that kind of people if I know I'm helping to feed little heathen children in Africa or to do something about those disgusting homeless people."

Perkins's eldest took the bucket and went outside to dump the scummy gray water on the shrubs.

"Because," Mrs. Jim Bob continued, "it's vital that we share with the less fortunates and the heathens. It seems I'm to play the role of a kindly widow woman who gives shelter to an innocent girl in order to protect her virtue. I must say, I wouldn't have accepted a part in which I did anything less."

Jim Bob came through the back door, stealthily opened the refrigerator to extricate a beer, and went back outside to lie in the hammock and dream about movie stars. On his way across the yard, he nodded to Perkins's eldest, who was taking down sheets from the clothesline.

Mrs. Jim Bob took a deep breath. "I asked the woman, a Miss Lowenberg or something, the names of my costars, but I only recognized one: Anderson St. James. He was in one of my soaps for years, and I always thought he had a civilized air about him, even though the script called for him to act rather crudely to his wife. Do you recall him?" She took the ensuing silence as a negative. "Perhaps you wouldn't, since you don't have a television out in that disreputable excuse for a house. I was telling Eula just last week that I was amazed to hear you had plumbing."

Perkins's eldest accepted a few dollars from Jim Bob and trudged down the driveway, looking like she was thinking about something. It could have been about her next cleaning job, or it could have been the result of gas. Perkins's eldest took secret pride in being an enigma.

Mrs. Jim Bob lost interest in the Perkins residence. "I asked when they would send me a script. The woman, who claimed to be the assistant director, said not to worry about my lines, that I was obviously quick-witted enough to learn them in a Hollywood minute— whatever that is. I asked her which days I would be filming so that I could have my hair done, and she said it was impossible to decide ahead of time." She tightened her mouth for a minute as she faced an unpleasant reality. "I'm going to be forced to use Estelle. If I don't know until the last minute, I simply won't have time to run into Farberville to have my regular girl do my hair."

Jim Bob let the sunshine wash over him like he was

in a hot tub with a hot number. Life was verging on
perfect, even if his screwy wife was inside shouting at
the walls. A tidy sum for letting them use the house,
and as the owner, the right to be there to watch over
his property. And he sure as hell was going to watch
over Gwenneth D'Amourre. When that Hollywood
woman had called to say how grateful Miss D'Amourre
would be if he allowed them to use the house, why,
Jim Bob had been obliged to cross his legs to keep from
wetting his pants. He'd recognized the name immediately, in that he always managed to catch a movie or
two in the motel room when he was down in Hot
Springs for the Municipal League tomfoolery. *Tanya Makes the Team,* he thought with a lazy grin.
Gawd, she'd made the team all right, and done it damn
well.

He lowered his foot and pushed to set the hammock
into motion, then lapsed into a most intriguing fantasy.

"But I'm not sure if the turquoise taffeta is quite
right," Mrs. Jim Bob said to the doorway. "I suppose a
widow woman might wear something dark, although
there's no reason why it has to be dowdy. My navy
wool with the lace collar might be better. What do you
think?" She waited politely for a moment. "No, I guess
you're not the one to give wardrobe advice, are you? I
think I'll see if Lottie's stopped chattering."

This time the telephone began to ring, and Mrs. Jim
Bob decided to allow Perkins's eldest to work undisturbed.

✧ ✧ ✧

"But Raz," Ruby Bee said plaintively, having already
tried sternness and also a futile stab at reasonableness,

"Marjorie is a barnyard animal. She's supposed to be outside."

Raz loosed a stream of tobacco juice into a conveniently situated coffee can. "No, she don't care for it. The gnats get in her eyes and she gets all nervous and jumpity." He beamed at his pride and joy, who was snoozing peaceably on the sofa.

Ruby Bee tried not to wince at the sight of his stained stubbles of teeth and crumb-encrusted whiskers, or to allow herself to dwell on the miasma of the room created by equal contributions from the owner and his pet. "They can't use your house if there's a sow in it. Don't you want the money?"

"What fer?" He cackled. "I got everything Marjorie and me needs. We got us a color tellyvision, a VCR with a clicker, and a new icebox stocked with frozen entrées. Marjorie is particular about the brands. She gets all het up if the food don't match the picture on the box."

"Where are you getting all that money?"

Raz spat into the can, then hooked his thumbs on the straps of his overalls and swelled up like a bloated carcass in a pond. "I got my ways, Rubella Belinda Hanks, and they's none of your business."

"They're probably Arly's business," she retorted in her most snippety voice. "I heard someone's running a still up on the ridge again, not too far from Robin Buchanon's old place. Wouldn't be anyone in this room, would it?" When he flinched, she moved in (verbally—not physically) for the kill. "Now, if I'm busy cooking for these movie people, I won't have time to pass along my suspicions to Arly. But they won't come if you don't agree to let them use your house and barn, and they might not understand why there's a sow in the living room."

"I reckon I can run the hose and make Marjorie a nice wallow," he said sullenly. His cheek bulged, but he caught her glare and sucked it back in. "But only for a day or two, and they pay me in cash. I ain't gonna mess with some damn-fool piece of paper. Cain't buy corn with paper."

Ruby Bee lifted her chin and sailed into the fresh air outside the shack, feeling pleased with herself despite the worrisome possibility that she was aiding and abetting Raz Buchanon in the act of something that smelled a sight worse than his front room.

"Okay, here's the way it goes," Hal said. He was sprawled on the leather couch in his office, a cigarette between his lips and his unclad body glistening from a session in the sauna. Although he took sessions under a tanning lamp three times a week, his skin resolutely remained alabaster except for the sprinkling of freckles and moles. "The mother finds out Loretta's been sneaking out at night to let Billy Joe feel her up. She tells the father and he goes into a rage because they'll lose the farm if Cooter refuses to marry her."

Carlotta nodded as she found her notebook and a pencil, and sat down behind Hal's desk to listen to him spill his ideas as quickly as he spilled his seed. She would diligently record them, then throw them away and make whatever revisions she felt were needed to the script. Hal never remembered his suggestions, particularly when he had done several lines of coke.

"Zachery learns about the trysts," she said, trying not to look at him. When he was naked, it was difficult not to think of the menu at a luau. "Then what?"

"He'll drag her outside to spank her. Do these primitives have woodsheds? For that matter, do they have—what do you call 'em?—opposable thumbs?''

"I'll check on the availability of woodsheds.'' Carlotta scribbled a note in the margin.

"So he drags her wherever and orders her to drop her pants. He's going to spank her, but once he starts slapping those lily-white mounds and ogling the red marks, he—''

"Gwenneth won't go for this.''

"You'd be surprised,'' Hal said with short laugh. "She knows she'd better do what I tell her to do, so just get it down and quit interrupting. I've got to have total silence when I'm in a creative mode. I've got to flow. Okay, close up on him as he throws her to the ground and starts scrambling out of his pants. She leaps to her feet and runs—''

"With her pants around her ankles?''

"She leaps to her feet, kicks off her pants—I like it, I like it—and runs through the gate and across the road to where this widow lives. I am on a roll tonight, *n'est-ce pas?* Let me hear what we've got thus far.''

Carlotta read his scenario in a bored monotone, irritated because she was already late for her aerobics class. "And pounds on the door?''

"There she is, tears running down one set of cheeks and the other set rosy from the spanking, and the father bellowing for her to come back. The widow—give her a real hick name—the widow hustles the girl in and locks the door.''

"Okay, Loretta's in the widow's house.''

"Wait a minute; I'm losing the flow.'' He walked into the washroom, but continued talking between gusty snorts. "Are we gonna have a problem with this mayor's wife?''

"Probably. I promised her a few lines, but we'll have to tiptoe through the scene. Let's make sure we shoot it after we've used her house."

Hal came back into the office, a towel around his waist, and made himself a drink from the bar. "Are we ready to roll?"

"Everybody's agreed to the usual terms, and Fuzzy's willing to do the technical side." Carlotta hesitated for a minute, not sure if she wanted to prolong the conversation with her boss. At last her innate sense of responsibility overcame her distaste. "When I talked to him, he sounded tight, really tight. From what I've picked up, he's back on booze and his wife left him several weeks ago. He's on the edge, Hal. We might see if we can corral someone else until our boy either implodes, explodes, or regains consciousness in court."

"If you can find someone willing to work nonunion in a hellhole three thousands miles from civilization, do it," Hal said, displaying his typical compassion. "Tell you what, baby, you've got enough of my input to finish the scene and have it on my desk in the morning. I'm going to run a little powdery present by Marty's and lay on some more crap about setting up a meeting with the swish as Cinerotica. Gawd, I hate swishes. They're so damn arrogant."

After Hal dressed and stumbled away, Carlotta poured herself a drink and sat down behind her desk in the adjoining room to type up the scene. She toyed with the idea of Zachery raping the widow, but dismissed it (at least for the moment) and wrote out a charmingly steamy encounter between Loretta and Billy Joe in the widow's own bed. Out of mischievousness, she had the widow discover the two and demand coitus interruptus. The actor who would portray Billy Joe would be incensed, of course, which was why she devoted an inordinate amount of time frustrating him via the script.

She was typing briskly when the telephone rang, and she mentally debated the ramifications of ignoring it. However, she'd given her office number to a rugged young actor who'd attempted to sound interested in her rather than her proximity to Hal. "Glittertown," she said into the receiver. "Lowenstein here."

"I need to talk to you."

"Hey, Fuzzy," Carlotta said, disappointed. "We were just talking about you. Were your balls burning?"

"Naw, the penicillin took care of it. This is important. I ran over to Vegas yesterday. Took a room in one of those seedy joints out by the airport. Guess which soft-porn movie was available for a modest price?"

"I just write them, Fuzzy. Once they're made, I don't care if they're the feature at Rockefeller Center after the Rockettes flash their panties at the tourists."

"I think you'll care," Fuzzy said in a dark voice. "It was a new flick called *Prickly Passion,* starring Gwenneth D'Amourre and Frederick Marland." He paused for a minute, and she heard the tinkly collision of ice cubes. "I watched the damn thing. This well-endowed prospector finds a busty, half-naked woman wandering in the desert. He takes her back to his shack, and the two of—"

"Enough." Carlotta took off her glasses to rub her eyes and temples, then drained her drink. "Are you sure you didn't drink a quart of rotgut tequila, and watch the film in your dreams?"

"In *your* dreams, Carlotta. No, I even brought back the card with the times and prices of the movies. There were a couple of scenes we left on the floor, but I had plenty of time to recognize the prospector and the prostitute—and I'm familiar with each and every mole and freckle, including that little butterfly tattoo Gwenneth's so proud of.''

"Damn it, that means there was a pirated copy, and now there are apt to be thousands of illegal copies floating around. We're all contracted for a piece of the net. What are the chances this unknown distributor's going to send a check?''

"About the time we go ice skating on the corner of Hollywood and Vine,'' he said with a morose sigh. "So who filched the tape and sold it? What'd we have on the set—three of us and the five actors? Hal and I did the editing ourselves. The negative's in the vault. There's no way anyone else could have gotten a copy.''

"You know, Fuzzy, Anderson said something about seeing a version of *Satan's Sister* that contained some of the stuff we decided was too risky. It's beginning to look as though we have a full-time pirate in our midst. I'll see what I can find out before we leave for the next one.''

"Did Hal try to give me the boot?''

"Oh, good Lord, no. He was really sorry to hear about your marital problem, but he said he was thrilled to work with you again.''

"Like hell he did.''

"Would I lie to you?''

"Would the pope take a check?''

Carlotta was smiling as she replaced the receiver.

I was on the way out of Merganser's office when I ran into Plover. He suggested coffee, and we went into the break room at the back of the barracks. While he played host, I flopped down on an ugly sofa and said, "Merganser was helpful, in a terrifying way. We agreed it wasn't arson for profit, and it doesn't look as if anyone's trying to cover up anything. If it's revenge, no one's been harmed physically or financially. That leaves us with a nut case."

Plover handed me a chipped mug and sat down across from me. "How nutty?"

I tasted the coffee and decided it might be better used to repair roads. I put the mug on the floor and said, "The profiles vary. It could be a thrill-seeker, someone who craves the excitement of the trucks roaring in and the firemen dragging out the equipment. This one, most commonly, tends to be male and starts setting fires in his teens and early twenties. Problems at home, low self-esteem, lack of appropriate positive role models, possibly with a sexual dysfunction."

"That describes our witness," Plover said flatly.

"I know, and I'm going to talk to him later today. I'll verify his explanation for being on the road and discreetly ask where he was when the other fires were discovered." I paused as I recalled Merganser's second option. "Or it may be the work of a psycho who's been starting fires out of some misguided idea that he—or she—is under orders from unseen powers."

"Why has he surfaced in the last month? Why hasn't he been torching abandoned buildings all along?"

"Beats me," I said, reaching for the mug and then catching myself. "There's no one new in Maggody. I guess I need to check in Emmet and Hasty."

Plover raised his eyebrows ever so slightly. "Good idea, Arly. Perhaps the fire chief can help you with the investigation."

"What's that supposed to mean?"

Sergeant Innocent shrugged. "It means you can ask what's-his-name if anyone has moved to Emmet in the last two months. He looks like he'd know—especially if it was a female."

I tried to maintain a normal tone, but I didn't have laudable success. "And what's that supposed to mean? Wade's a nice guy. He's a county extension agent and contributes a lot of free time to the volunteer fire department. He's the one that keeps tabs on the equipment, makes sure the paperwork gets done, and supervises the training sessions."

"Did Merganser tell you that firemen have been known to start fires so they can be heroes?"

I stood up, kicking over the mug in my haste, and headed for the door. As I reached it, though, I stopped and attempted to sort through the anger and indignation swirling inside me like fierce red sparks. "I don't know what's bothering you," I said without turning around (and thus startling a baby-faced corporal so badly that he bumped into a wall). "All we do is go to the movies or have dinner maybe twice a month. What you do the rest of the time is your business—since I sure as hell have no part in it."

"I thought that was what you wanted."

I made myself look back at him. "I didn't say it wasn't, Plover. You're entitled to privacy, just as I am. For all I know, you've got a wife and three kids stashed somewhere, or an insatiable passion for some college girl."

"You're the one who's in a self-inflicted cocoon."

I thought of several devastating retorts, but I realized my face was flushed and my eyes were beginning to sting. I hurried down the hallway and out into the parking lot, willing myself to do so with no more than professional briskness. Chief of Police Ariel Hanks had places to go and witnesses to question. She did not have time to engage in a childish exchange with a man who fancied himself an amateur shrink.

She drove all the way back to Maggody and parked in front of the PD before she burst into tears. One tough cookie, that Chief of Police Ariel Hanks.

"A house across the road from Raz's place?" Ruby Bee said into the receiver. "There's nothing directly across, but Dahlia O'Neill and her granny don't live but a hop and a skip north of there."

"Fantastic," Carlotta said. "Can we use the house? We've had to do a few more revisions and add a character. She doesn't have to live in the immediate vicinity, but it would make the shooting go faster."

Ruby Bee didn't bother to tell her that everyone in town not only knew about the latest addition to the cast but also knew what she intended to wear and how she planned to have her hair fixed. "I don't reckon Dahlia's granny will mind, since she's down in Jessieville visiting kin. Dahlia can be right ornery, though."

"What'll it take? We can go one hundred dollars, one-fifty max. It's only two interiors, so we'll be done in no more than a couple of hours."

Ruby Bee wasn't sure how to break the news to this nice woman from Hollywood. She finally decided there was no tactful way to go about it. "Dahlia has her heart set on being in the movie. She's been moping around like a motherless calf ever since she heard about it, and poor Kevin's fit to be tied."

"There's no other house near the shack?"

"Sorry, honey, but the only other persons who live out that way are Perkins and his eldest, and I'd sooner cozy up to a grizzly bear as ask him."

Carlotta was also renowned for her flexibility. "Okay, we'll go with this Dahlia woman. Give me a quick rundown: How old is she, and what does she look like?"

Ruby Bee did so.

The ensuing silence crackled all the way from Hollywood to Maggody, and you could almost see people in New Mexico and Arizona gazing up at the telephone lines, asking themselves what in tarnation was going on. Ruby Bee was wondering if they'd been disconnected when Carlotta said, "Tell me you're kidding."

" 'Fraid not," Ruby Bee said sadly.

"Oh," said Carlotta in a faraway voice, which was not surprising in that she was in what most of Maggody considered nigh on to a foreign country, where folks ate raw fish and sat around naked in oversized buckets of boiling water.

Estelle came into the bar and grill and glanced curiously at Ruby Bee, who was clutching the receiver but not saying a word. Her expression was impossible to make heads or tails of, except that she looked perturbed.

"Is there someone on the line?" Estelle asked. When there was no reply, she went around the bar, poured herself a glass of sherry, and sat down on her stool to wait for further developments, such as a word being spoken into the receiver.

It was a good five minutes of toe-twitching tedium before Ruby Bee said, "Okay, I'll ask her. You sure about this . . . ?"

Carlotta was sure.

Wild Cherry Wine (REVISED 5/20)

9   CLOSE SHOT—LUCINDA
     LUCINDA, a hulking earth mother, is concealed
     behind a clump of bushes, and observing the
     scene with a curious frown. Her lips move si-
     lently and she blinks several times.

10   RETURN TO SCENE

A knuckle on the window brought me back with a yelp
of surprise. I wiped my eyes and looked up at a seriously unappetizing view, a.k.a. Kevin Buchanon's face.
It was so close that I could see the fading blemishes,
the emerging pimples, the smattering of blackheads
(coming and going), and even the craterish pores of his
nose.

"Arly?" he said through the glass. "Are you
okay?"

I rolled down the window an inch and said, "Yes, I
am just peachy. What do you want?"

"I was hoping you might see fit to explain about how
men and women get along with each other," he said,
fogging the glass as he moved even closer. "My
beloved's all sad these days, except when I mention
going to Boone Creek, and then she likes to whop me
up the side of the—"

"Stop, Kevin. Under no circumstances am I going to
attempt to analyze the unbreachable gulf between female sensibleness and male insufferableness. Not in my
worst nightmare would I dare to interpret your and
Dahlia's interactions. Go away. Better still, run away
from home and join the Foreign Legion. Maybe Dahlia

will feel more kindly toward you if you have a battle scar and some medals.''

I rolled the window up and backed out of the lot. After a moment of debate, I drove toward Emmet to see if Wade Elkins had any new theories about the firebugs.

It was all for naught, in that he wasn't home and I preferred not to hunt for him at his office. Just as well, I told myself as I drove home.

Chapter 4

15   CONTINUED:
Billy Joe and Loretta are grappling under the sheet as the door opens stealthily.

16   CLOSE-UP—WIDOW THIGPEN
Words cannot convey the level of shock on her face. However, she advances soundlessly, and we realize she is reliving memories of what has taken place in the bed in the past. A bemused look comes over her as she spies on the sweaty young lovers.

17   BACK TO SCENE

LORETTA

Oh, Billy Joe—is you sure this is right? I swore to God above that I'd save myself for my wedding night.

BILLY JOE

This ain't a sin, my darling Loretta. Mebbe there ain't no way to keep you from marrying Cooter, but he won't be the one

what takes your purity and hides it in his
black heart forever.

                    WIDOW THIGPEN
What all's going on—and in my own bed?
Loretta Biggins, I am sorely ashamed of
the way you're carrying on with this
white trash. No wonder your pa was
gonna whip you!

                       LORETTA
Widow Thigpen! I didn't hear you come
in.

Billy Joe flops back with a groan of frustration.
Loretta covers herself with a sheet and sits up.

                    WIDOW THIGPEN
I don't recall hearing Billy Joe Jenks come
in, neither.

                       LORETTA
I let him in through the window. I'm so
sorry, Widow Thigpen. When Billy Joe
gets too close to me, my body seems to
catch on fire like a pile of kindling.
                       (beat)
But it's a sin, ain't it?

CLOSE-UP on Widow Thigpen as a knowing
smile flits across her face.

                    WIDOW THIGPEN
I was young once, Loretta. I was in love
with the boy down the road, and more
times than I can count, we met under an
old sweet gum tree and made love like
we'd invented it.
                       (beat)

He was strong, and handsome as a movie
star. The first time I was scared, but I
closed my eyes and I never regretted it.

BILLY JOE
Then you'll let us stay in here?

LORETTA
No! It's not right, Billy Joe. I can't let Ma
and Pa lose the farm. It's jest not right.

Loretta begins to sob as Billy Joe and Widow
Thigpen exchange enigmatic looks.

DISSOLVE TO:

Frederick Marland rolled up the script and began to
slap his knee with it. "This is so very amusing, Carlotta. Gwenneth and I come within centimeters of
full engagement six times in the first fifteen scenes.
Do you think I've got a elevator button between
my balls? Going up, going down . . . going up, going
down."

He was slouched in the last seat in the van, his jaw
extended with the petulance of a toddler and his dark
brown eyes glowering as he unfurled the script and resumed reading it. Despite his tendency to regress, he
was handsome enough to be followed around malls by
giggly girls and a few young mothers pushing strollers
and telling themselves they should know better. He'd
agreed to let his sunstreaked brown hair grow for the
role, and the soft curls over his ears and on his neck
were those of a Renaissance cherub floating above a
Madonna.

Although he was in his mid-twenties, on cue he could
invoke an aura of adolescent innocence; within weeks

of his arrival in L.A., it had earned him a small part in a soap. Inevitably, the writers had wandered on to other sordid subplots, and his character had slithered down the drain. The experience had served him well, however, and his career was proceeding exactly as he'd planned.

In the seat in front of him, Gwenneth D'Amourre was trying to hold the script still with one hand and steady her cosmetics case with the other as the van bounced from pothole to pothole. "Oh, Billy Joe—is you sure this is right? I swore to God above I'd save myself for my wedding night." She looked up with a teeny-tiny frown. "Hey, Carlotta, did you make this rhyme on purpose? It's kinda sweet, you know? This is right; wedding night."

Gwenneth had prepared for the eight hours of plane and van. She wore a halter and shorts, and her baby-blue eyes were concealed behind the expensive sunglasses she removed only for the camera and bed. Very little was concealed behind the halter, but Gwenneth liked to give her fans a thrill when she sailed majestically through airports. Her lush golden hair (her term) cascaded down her lovely, supple shoulders like a tawny lioness's mane (as above), and she was adept at flipping it out of her face with a toss of her elegant (ditto) chin. Gwenneth's résumé was heavily peppered with adjectives, her private life with adverbs.

In the front seat, Carlotta had opted for the conservative yet comfortable attire of a blouse and khaki slacks. The remarks from the back rows of the van had caused her to lose her place in her notes, and her voice was sharp as she said, "Yes, Frederick, I do think you're controlled by nothing more than a tiny, shiny black button. No, Gwenneth, I did not notice that the line contains an internal rhyme. If you can't get it out without lapsing into that godawful singsong, I'll rewrite it."

"Well, I don't know," Gwenneth said thoughtfully, if not pensively. "Right, night. It sure does rhyme."

"Can't fool you, can I?" Carlotta muttered as she delved back into her notes, making check marks as she moved through them. The truck with equipment in the morning. Hal and Anderson on a late-afternoon flight, rental car reserved at the airport. Rewrite trailer scene to include the three-hundred-pound cavewoman. Locate liquor store. Carlotta drew a star by the ultimate item, glanced at the driver across the aisle, and gloomily drew a second star for good measure.

". . . the one what takes your purity and hides it in his black heart forever," said Frederick, his voice loud and incredulous. "Jesus H. Croissant, did Hal write this excrement?"

"Indeed he did," lied Carlotta.

Frederick mentally ran through the terms of his contract. "Maybe it's not that bad."

Fuzzy Indigo was driving the van, zealously aiming for each pothole in the road and wishing he had a flask in the pocket of his army surplus jacket. The scenery was friggin' unreal. Squalid houses, rusty trailers, ugly children, weathered chicken houses held together by barbed wire and spit. Ditches cluttered with aluminum cans, crushed paper cups, and a variety of distasteful things.

Fuzzy was by no means a perfectionist, but he was not immune to small displays of vanity. Although he was approaching sixty, he kept his skimpy gray hair combed across the creeping bald spot and long enough to slick back into a ducktail. He purchased only the trendiest fashions from secondhand clothing stores;

even his shoes, a size too small, were handcrafted lovingly from the skin of an endangered species. His wit was legendary in drunk tanks from Tacoma to Tijuana.

He was less successful in other areas. The jacket had not been cleaned since he'd appropriated it months ago from a dumpster. He'd given up shaving more than once or twice a week, and at those times he felt as if he'd donated a pint of blood. It was rare that he could complete a compound sentence, or after a particularly stupefying weekend, a simple one.

Behind rimless glasses, his eyes darted furtively as if he anticipated a dorsal assault, which he often did when he roamed the less chic streets of L.A. His hands gripped the steering wheel so tightly that veins were snaked across them like highways on a map, and a careful observer might notice similar lines throbbing across his temples.

Had he been a perfectionist in his profession, he wouldn't have agreed (once again) to work nonunion for a laughable fee and a cut of the net.

Fuzzy spotted a fresh lump of road-kill and veered toward it. His grin was humorless. Carlotta noticed it out of the corner of her eye and thought it maniacal. His gleeful chortle did nothing to alleviate her worry.

Directly behind him, Katherine "Kitty" Kaye was draped across her husband's shoulder, snoring softly and dreaming of more lucrative days and more glamorous evenings. Her feline face was as rough as suede from excessive sun-worship, and her body, once firm yet round, was angular. Twenty-five years ago her voice had been praised for its melodious range. Now it was coarsened by a three-pack habit. Carlotta always gave her as few lines as possible and relied on her expressive mouth and eyes. Kitty was a trooper, a veteran but not a victim of Hollywood.

Her husband, Buddy Meredith, was a character actor who'd appeared in countless movies and commercials. Neither his face nor his name was ever recognized, not even by the residents of the neighborhood where he'd lived with Kitty for more than twenty years. It was a nice face, however. The gap between his front teeth and the slight imperfection of his nose gave him a non-threatening demeanor, and his unfailing affability reinforced it. He was among the few in the industry who accepted gray hairs, wrinkles, discolored spots, and a thickening of the waist as the normal progression of nature.

As Kitty stirred, he smiled at her and lightly ran his finger along her high cheekbone to the crease alongside her slightly curled mouth. She'd once been beautiful, but he'd never been handsome. Even after more than two decades, he never quite understood why she'd agreed to marry a kid with a hick accent and a gap between his teeth.

"Maggody!" Fuzzy announced.

The five passengers looked up, and in an uncanny display of team camaraderie that had evolved during the production of several questionable flicks, groaned as one. As befitting her more extensive experience, Gwenneth outshone them all.

I knocked on Billy Dick's front door and waited impatiently as a curtain twitched in the window. He opened the door part way and regarded me without expression.

"I'm glad I caught you," I said. "I wanted to ask

you a few more questions about the fire the other night."

He came out to the porch and pulled the door closed. "Ma's taking a nap in the living room. She's still on the l-late shift at the truck stop, so she doesn't get home till dawn." He hitched up his baggy pants and gave me a mildly curious look. "What do you want to know, Arly? I already told you and the sheriff everything I saw."

I studied him, wondering why he sounded so casual when his forehead was damp with sweat and his eyes retreating into their sockets. "Just a few things, Billy Dick. What's your girlfriend's name and address?"

"Why do you want to know that?"

"I need it for my report." I took a notebook and pencil from my back pocket. "We can do this here, or we can do this at the sheriff's office. I'm going over there anyway, so it doesn't really matter to me."

"Her name's Trudi Yarrow, and she lives across from the gas station. Blue house, with a plastic birdbath out front. Her pa drives a red truck."

"Okay." I made a note. "You said she called you a little before nine, right?"

"Yeah, as soon as her parents left. Ma was at work, so I went on out to the truck and started for her house. I saw the fire, like I said, and stopped at the first house with lights on to use their telephone."

"To call the fire department in Emmet," I said with an encouraging smile. "Then what did you do, Billy Dick? Did you stay at this house, or did you go back to the fire immediately to wait there?"

"What d-difference does it make?" His eyes were barely visible in the fleshy sockets, but they weren't so much as blinking. His face reminded me of a scoop of vanilla ice cream beginning to melt.

"Probably none at all. I'm just trying to get a clear picture in my mind of the sequence of events."

To my surprise, he put his hands in his pockets and sauntered to the end of the porch. "I drove back to the fire and waited," he said without turning around. "I didn't see anybody until the volunteers came roaring down the road and tumbled out of their trucks. You'd have thought the White House was on fire, instead of some p-pile of rotted wood out in the middle of nowhere."

"Did you see any of the other fires?"

He looked over his shoulder at me. "I went out to have a look at that one last week. I was at the Dee-Lishus when some of the boys told me about it."

His voice was different, as was his entire posture, but I couldn't for the life of me figure out what was going on behind those colorless eyes. I finally put the notebook in my pocket and told him I'd be back if I had any further questions. As I drove away from the house, I glanced in the rearview mirror. He was watching me, and for some inexplicable reason, I felt as if he'd done so before.

"They're here," Eula Lemoy told Millicent Mc-Ilhaney, who was holding the receiver with her shoulder while she rolled out pie crust.

"They're here," Elsie McMay told Joyce Lambertino's niece, since Joyce was hanging over the toilet bowl and unavailable to take the call. Saralee grasped the implications of the terse message, and when the retching noises stopped, relayed it through the bathroom door.

"Gwenneth D'Amourre has hair like a burst of sunshine," Kevin began, then stopped when he caught the full wattage of his beloved's glare. "But it's kinda messy," he added hastily.

"One of them's an absolute hunk!" Tracy told Heather, using the pay telephone at the Suds of Fun Launderette. "If he so much as spoke to me, I'd fall over dead."

Jim Bob didn't tell anybody anything. He stood in the doorway of Jim Bob's SuperSaver Buy 4 Less across the road from the Flamingo Motel, his arms crossed and his tongue flicking faster than a grass snake's. He didn't notice the sweat dribbling down his back as he watched Gwenneth carry some little fool suitcase into one of the motel rooms. He wasn't sure, but he thought she'd gone inside #3.

"They're here," Mrs. Jim Bob told Brother Verber on the telephone. "I was planning to take some cookies to Lottie Estes, but I think I'd better stay home in case they drop by to see the house."

"They're here?" Estelle shrieked. She banged down the telephone without so much as a thank-you-for-calling and met Darla Jean McIlhaney's startled gaze in the mirror. "I do believe your hair's dry enough, especially in this heat, so you can run along now. That'll be five-fifty, including tax."

"They're here," Raz commented to Marjorie as they drove along the dotted line in front of Ruby Bee's Bar & Grill. Marjorie grunted unenthusiastically.

"Are they really here?" Larry Joe Lambertino asked the breathless student who'd burst into the shop room. "Or were you outside sneaking a smoke and now trying to slip into class without a tardy slip?"

"They're here," the student said, praying Mr. Lambertino couldn't smell the smoke on his breath.

"They're here," the dispatcher at the sheriff's department told somebody or other. Before the end of her shift, she'd lost track of whom all she'd told, and had called her cousin twice by mistake.

I drove out the county road, checking both sides for overgrown logging trails that led into the tangled brush and scrubby oak trees. I stopped a few times to examine promising openings, but they either went only a few yards or had no tire tracks in the dust.

I passed the remains of the barn and continued on until I came to a house several miles farther down the road. Billy Dick had said the first house with lights on, I reminded myself as I went to the door and knocked.

An elderly woman opened the door an inch and stared at me with the malevolence of a crow. "You selling something?"

I showed her my badge and asked if she'd been home the night of the fire. She curtly assured me she hadn't and slammed the door in my face. I drove to the next house, where no one was home. The only other house had a blankness that suggested it was uninhabited, and a quick look through the window confirmed it.

Making a note to stop at the middle house on my way back to Maggody, I drove into Hasty and found the blue house across from the gas station. The birdbath was there; the truck was not. I knocked on the door several times, and was about to leave when I heard rock music from the backyard of the house.

I tracked it down to a transistor radio next to a stack

of magazines and a beach towel. The girl on the towel was prone, her bottom covered by a skimpy patch of material and her back bared and shining like a well-oiled lettuce leaf.

"Trudi?" I said as I approached.

She lifted her head. "Who are you?"

"Arly Hanks, the police chief in Maggody. I came by to ask you a few questions about the night of the fire."

"I don't know why." She fumbled with the top of the bikini until it was hooked, sat up, and put on sunglasses. Her face was basically flat, and her mouth sagged above a chin that seemed to slide into her neck. Sullenness had already created permanent lines between her eyes, and the discernible protrudence of her forehead hinted at an alliance with the Buchanon clan.

I moved to the shade under a persimmon tree and took out my notebook. "You called Billy Dick MacNamara at nine o'clock?"

"I did what? You'd better stay out of the sun, lady, or get yourself a hat."

I repeated my question and waited as she took a cigarette from a pack concealed by the towel.

"You've got it about as wrong as it gets," she said, blowing smoke at me. "I wouldn't call creepy Billy Dick if he paid me, and neither would any other girl in the county. Talk to my brother, Willard the Weirdo. He and Billy Dick are real big on some stupid game where they sit around and pretend they're dwarfs. It makes me want to puke."

She stubbed out the cigarette and flopped down on the towel. Confused, I stood there for a moment, then went to the back door and knocked.

The boy who appeared was as unattractive as his sister. I estimated his age at thirteen or fourteen.

As I took in his slight build and faintly crafty features, it occurred to me he might do the role of dwarf quite well. Not the rollicky, roly-poly kind that belts out, "Heigh-ho, heigh-ho," but the gnarly kind that lives underground and creeps out at night to create trouble. Then again, it wasn't Willard's fault that someone in the lineage had cohabited with a Buchanon. I tried to take a more charitable attitude as I asked him if he was Willard.

"I'm Willard. What do you want?" he said, attempting to sound belligerent.

"I need to ask you some questions. Did you talk to Billy Dick MacNamara the night of the fire?"

"Yeah," he muttered. "I called him about the map at nine o'clock, and he came over to help me get it fixed." He caught my blank look and added, "It's a map of the tunnels leading out of the dungeon of Balthazar Castle. We take turns being the dungeon master in a role-playing game, okay?"

"Were your parents here?"

"They left to see if my great-aunt was gonna die from some fall." He glanced at his sister, then lowered his voice. "My pa made me promise to stop playing the game. I'm not supposed to call Billy Dick, so it was the first time all week I had a chance to talk to him. Somewhere in the tunnel there's a dragon capable of burning up everything in sight. If that happens, this game's over, and we've been in it for more than a month." He gave me a tight smile. "Then we'll switch being dungeon-master. Billy Dick's still pissed over an earlier game, when he was attacked by an army of trolls after he'd lost his cloak of invisibility. They had him for supper and sucked his bones for breakfast."

I had to remind myself that I was at the back door of an ordinary house in Hasty, a goodly distance from the dungeon beneath Balthazar Castle. The sun was shining, and rather than the gnashing of trolls' teeth, rock music was drifting from a transistor radio. "That's fine, Willard," I said. "All I need to do is confirm that Billy Dick was on his way to your house when he saw the fire."

"Well, he was. He got here after ten and stayed for a couple of hours, working on the map. I can show it to you if you want."

"No, I'll take your word for it. Why did your father make you promise to stop the game?"

"He says it's foolishness to pretend you've got magical power and can defeat monsters. I say it beats the hell out of living in Hasty, surrounded by pea-brained jocks and fat sluts like my sister."

"Are your parents here now?"

"No, and you got no reason to talk to them." He went inside and closed the door.

Trudi did not move as I went past her. A robin perched on the edge of the birdbath watched me as I maneuvered around a truck, pulled out onto the empty road, and headed back to Maggody, rehashing Trudi's condemnation of Billy Dick and her brother's of her. The occupants of the middle house on the road had not returned, and the wizzened crow was not in her yard.

Traffic seemed heavier than usual as I parked in front of the PD, but I wrote it off as a hot sale at the supermarket and went inside to check for messages. The dispatcher at the sheriff's office sounded irritated as she told me to hold my horses while she sorted through the unholy mess LaBelle had left at the end of the shift.

"Here's one," she said at last. "Somebody name of Wade Elkins wants you to call him. Oh, and some sergeant from the state police, but I can't rightly make out the name." Papers rustled for a minute. "Well, ain't this something?"

"Ain't what something?" I said, allowing a little irritation of my own to taint the line. As I listened to her relate some garbled message about someone being here, I realized I could smell a minute trace of smoke. I hung up the receiver and walked (okay, crept) to the doorway that led to the back room.

The back room was smaller than the front, and its only redeeming feature was that I didn't have to go in there very often. There was a scarred wooden table that was covered with all the idiotic paperwork that came at me on a regular basis. On the wall, the county survey map was curling at the corners. The lone chair was laden with manuals and ancient newspapers.

I made sure that the coffee pot was turned off. The metal cabinet that housed the radar gun, the .38 Special, and other toys of the trade, such as my box with three real bullets, was as I'd last seen it.

Wrinkling my nose, I told myself that I was imagining the smell, that I'd had arson on the brain too long. However, as I started back, I glanced into the metal trashcan. In the bottom was a small pile of feathery white ashes. I bent down and poked my finger into one; it immediately disintegrated into drifting flakes. A dozen blackened matches ringed the ashes, as if someone had struck them methodically, one by one, and dropped them into the trashcan.

I asked myself why someone had burned a piece of paper and a bunch of matches in my trashcan, but nothing much came to mind. I was back at my desk before it occurred to me that this mysterious someone had come into the PD while I was gone, started a fire, and left without leaving a courteous note explaining the purpose of the visit.

Neither door had been locked, naturally. I'd been gone most of the afternoon, but I hadn't kept anyone informed of my plans. Most days I'm in and out, depending on my mood. I have visitors on occasion, Raz Buchanon being the most frequent, but he was hardly the type to leave such a peculiar calling card.

I was shaking my head and making all sorts of unattractive faces when the front door opened. I looked up into the eyes of a Greed god. A middle-aged Greed god, but that was perfectly all right with me. Dark hair with a touch of silver, milk chocolate brown eyes, a nose carefully sculpted, a friendly smile exposing teeth as evenly aligned as markers in a military cemetery. The rest of him wasn't bad, either, particularly in an Italian silk suit that had been tailored down to the last stitch.

"Well, hello," he said in a deep voice that did nothing to mar the package.

"Hi," I squeaked. Sad, but true.

"Is the chief in?"

I couldn't tell him the truth—that the only thing the chief was in was the throes of a torrid pubescent fantasy. I managed a nod.

His smile broadened as he approached the desk. "And might I see him, if it's not too much trouble?"

"You can't see him because he's a she."

"Is he, now? That's intriguing." He sat down in the chair across from me and silently studied me as if I were a unfamiliar tidbit on a dinner plate. He wasn't appalled by what he was seeing, but he wasn't prepared to take a bite until he knew what it was.

"I'm the chief," I said at last. "Arly Hanks."

"I don't think I've ever heard the name Arly before," he said. "Is that a local tradition?"

"It's Ariel." Gawd, I love it when I'm articulate and witty, each phrase exquisitely turned, each inflection and gesture meritious of an Oscar award.

He put his hand on his chest and cocked his head. " 'Go make thyself like a nymph o' the sea; be subject to no sight but thine and mine.' That kind of Ariel?"

He got my Oscar. "Yes," I lied, seeing no reason to admit that I'd been named after a photograph taken from an airplane. It now hung over Ruby Bee's bed, the contour of the bar and grill outlined in ink. Although her spelling was faulty, she'd thought the word had a nice ring; her mother had held similar thoughts about an outbreak of measles fifty-odd years ago. Spots and shots—a family heritage.

"Then I'm delighted to meet you, Chief Hanks," he said, standing up and extending a manicured hand.

I was getting up my nerve to extend my own when the door banged open.

"They're here," Plover said. He stopped as if he'd run into an electric fence. "But I guess you know that, don't you?"

It had been easy to get into the PD through the back door. Ridiculously easy. If he'd had to worry about her returning while he stood there, sending flaming arrows at the wadded paper in the trashcan, maybe that would have increased his sense of danger.

He'd found the gun but had left it on the shelf. A bullet could miss its target. His weapon was fire. He could control fire, make it obey him, make it crackle and explode and ultimately suffocate the stars.

Had she been frightened when she found his message, or was she too stupid to understand that he was
showing her that he was smarter than she would ever
be? If she missed it this time, he'd be forced to show
her again and again until she humbly acknowledged the
truth.

Chapter 5

WILD CHERRY WINE (REVISED 5/20)

19   EXT. WIDOW THIGPEN'S HOUSE—DAY
Billy Joe stops in the yard and gazes morosely
back at the bedroom window. He then puts
his hands in his pockets and heads for the gate.
CAMERA WIDENS to include LUCINDA, who's waiting by the fence.

> LUCINDA
> Well, don't you look like what the cat spit
> up!

Sighing, Billy Joe joins her at the gate.

> BILLY JOE
> I ain't in the mood for your jokes. What
> do you want, Lucinda?

> LUCINDA
> No luck with Loretta, huh?

> BILLY JOE
> I'm tormented. I can't sleep at night

thinkin' of Cooter Grimmley and what he aims to do to my angel.

LUCINDA

Mebbe I can help you all so you can be together.

BILLY JOE
(brokenly)
That'd be swell, Lucinda. Why don't I visit your trailer tonight so's we can figure out how to save Loretta?

LUCINDA

Lucinda'll take care of you, you poor baby. You can come at midnight . . . or as many times as you want.

She puts her arms around him and gently kisses him.

DISSOLVE TO:

Ruby Bee was almost hidden behind the stack of towels in her arms, but she was eager to make her guests feel right at home. She couldn't precisely remember who all was staying where, so she decided to start at #2 and work her way around.

Since she couldn't knock, she kicked the door smartly, and when she heard it open, said, "I'm Ruby Bee. I brought you all some fresh linens."

"Put them on the bed," she heard Carlotta say in a distracted voice. "Fuzzy's telling everybody he saw it, damn it. He even mentioned the butterfly tattoo on her butt."

Ruby Bee blinked into the terry-cloth barrier. "I beg your pardon, but I'm not—"

"He wouldn't know a butt from a butterfly," a male voice interrupted, relieving her of the necessity of further response. "You, put the towels down and pop on out of here like a champagne cork. Listen, baby, did you ask Fuzzy if—"

"Hal," Carlotta said, "this is Ruby Bee Hanks, the owner of the motel and the adjoining restaurant. She's agreed to do breakfast and dinner whenever we want, and to pack sandwiches for lunch. Ruby Bee, this is Hal Desmond, the producer and director of *Wild Cherry Wine*, and the CEO of Glittertown Productions, Inc."

"Oh, right, yeah," Hal said in an unconvincing attempt at contriteness. "Glad to have you on the team, Aunt Bea."

Ruby Bee put down the towels and opened her mouth to correct him. However, she couldn't get it out (or much of anything beyond a gurgle) when she looked at the man on the bed and determined real fast that he was buck-naked.

Carlotta took the top towel and tossed it at him. "Cover yourself up, for pity's sake," she said. "She's going to think we're making a documentary about walruses."

Once he'd covered his privates with the towel, Ruby Bee took a better look at the fellow who was so all-fired important. He did bear a passing resemblance to a walrus, she thought with a wince. His face, on the other hand, made her think of Marjorie, what with his squinty little eyes and thick, wet lips. Raz would have been offended by the comparison.

"I'm real pleased to meet you," she said from a safe distance.

"Join the club. Now, if you'll excuse us, Carlotta and I are discussing the distribution of the last flick."

Before she could catch herself, Ruby Bee heard herself blurt, "Does it have a name yet?"

"At wrap it was *Prickly Passion,* but now—who the hell knows?" Hal curled his lip at Carlotta, and his crackle of laughter could have sliced a ripe tomato. "Or cares?"

He began to toy with the towel. Ruby Bee snatched up most of the pile and fled out the door before he—well, exposed himself like—well, not like anyone she'd met before. Of course, she amended as she stopped to catch her breath, there was Burl Buchanon and his raincoat shenanigans, but everybody kind of got used to it, and before too long his family remembered a conveniently distant cousin in the Canadian wilderness.

She went on to #3 and knocked on the door, but no one answered and she figured it was Carlotta's room. Now that she'd come across Carlotta in the same room with a buck-naked man—and not acting the least bit perturbed—maybe the gal didn't deserve any towels.

Directly across the expanse of gravel was #4. Ruby Bee held her head high as she marched right over and knocked on the door.

"It's open!" yelled a male voice.

She'd had quite enough exposure for one day. "I brought you some extra towels," she yelled back, "but I'll just wait until you're decent!"

"That could take decades, considering the business we're in!"

Ruby Bee was still mulling that over when the door opened. The man was normal-looking and dressed in regular clothes. He gave her a smile. "I'm Buddy Meredith, madam. Please allow me to relieve you of this unconscionable burden."

"Haven't I seen you on television?"

"You and millions of other oblivious fans," he said, although nicely and with a little twinkle. "Most recently you might have seen me attempting to persuade you that my detergent is better than yours. It isn't, though; they just pay me to say so."

"You're the Wite & Brite man," Ruby Bee said, suddenly feeling woozy as she stood face to face with a celebrity. He was so close she could have touched him—not that she'd have dared. "I tried it once, but I was a might disappointed with it." She realized what she said and blushed all the way up to her roots. "Not that it was your fault, Mr. Meredith. It was on sale, and I had a coupon, too."

"Please come in," he said with an eloquent flip of his hand.

Trembling, she entered the temporary abode of an honest-to-goodness television star. Two men were sitting on the nearer bed, a mess of cards and dollar bills scattered on the bedspread between them. One of them looked to be the other's grandfather, but it seemed the younger one, who was vaguely familiar, was old enough to drink whiskey and gamble. In the afternoon, too. She mutely held up the towels as an offering.

"This is our star, Frederick Marland," nice Mr. Meredith said, "and this is our production man, Fuzzy Indigo."

She was about to say howdy when she heard her name being hollered from the parking lot. Battling back a growl, she managed a polite smile. "I'm pleased to meet you, Mr. Marland," she said to the handsome young man who was reputed to be a star even if she couldn't quite put her finger on where she'd seen him. "And you, too, Mr. Indigo. Welcome to Maggody and the Flamingo Motel. You be sure and call me night or day if—''

"My goodness, Ruby Bee," Estelle gasped from the doorway, "I've been looking everywhere for you."

She stood there, blinking worse than a condemned man in the electric chair, until Ruby Bee took pity on her and introduced her to the three men. She wasn't the least bit surprised when Estelle pranced over to Mr. Meredith and said, "Ain't I seen you on television?"

"He's the Wite & Brite man," Ruby Bee said briskly. "I recognized him right off. Now, why in heaven's name were you out there bellowing like a sick cow? Don't you know the Flamingo Motel has paying customers that would appreciate a little peace and quiet?"

"We've got what some might call a situation in the kitchen," Estelle shot back.

"Ah, a situation," Frederick Marland said, mimicking Estelle's high-pitched voice and undeniably twangy accent. He did something to his face so he looked about sixteen years old. "Gee, I ain't seen a situation since Ma knocked over the butter churn and Granny slid right off the porch into the lilac bushes."

Reminding herself that he was a famous celebrity, Ruby Bee opted to ignore him and pulled Estelle over to the door. "What are you talking about?" she whispered.

"Kevin is what I'm talking about."

Over Estelle's shoulder, Ruby Bee watched nice Mr. Meredith sit down on the bed and begin to shuffle the cards. Famous Mr. Marland was still looking ever so proud of himself for being a smart-mouth. The third man, the one who reminded her of a wino she'd seen in a Little Rock bus station, was staring at the wall, his lips moving just a little bit and his hand shaking enough to splatter the bedspread with drops of whiskey. He was a real odd fish, she thought before she returned to the business at hand, which was trying to figure out what Estelle was so antsy about.

"What about Kevin?" she said, still whispering.

"You know how you left Dahlia in charge of the bar and grill while you came out here to meet the movie stars before anyone else had a chance? Some of us had to change clothes before we could come over, but you just—"

"What about Kevin?"

"Well," Estelle said slowly, making it clear Ruby Bee was going to suffer long and hard for upstaging some, "he found out that Dahlia's supposed to kiss one of these here actors—when she's doing her role, naturally. I guess she didn't see fit to tell him beforehand, maybe on account of him being the jealous type. He upped and ordered her to give up her part. She didn't take kindly to being ordered to do anything, especially by Mr. Milquetoast hisself, so at the moment she's throwing pots and pans at him while he's scuttling around the kitchen like a gimpy cockroach, pleading with—"

Ruby Bee shoved the towels into Estelle's arm and took off for the kitchen. All the way across the parking lot she kept thinking how Estelle had wasted all that time rambling like a free-range chicken instead of getting right to the point—the point being that the kitchen was now a battlefield along the lines of Little Big Horn.

As she went into the barroom, she heard a crash that liked to give her a heart attack. Dahlia was shrieking so loudly that all the customers had given up trying to make conversation and were sitting there like they were in church. None of them looked bored, though. Every now and then there was a lull; Ruby Bee figured that Kevin was attempting to beg for his life, if not for her crockery.

She shoved open the kitchen door in time to see a pie pan sail across the room. A cookie sheet followed, as did a second pie pan. Dahlia was huffing and blowing so hard her face was scarlet, and her hair, recently styled by Estelle to look neat if not inspirational, was going every which way. She was sucking in air so loudly Ruby Bee wondered how there was any left.

"Dahlia O'Neill, you stop right this minute!" she ordered. "You, too, Kevin Buchanon—wherever you are!"

Dahlia had her fist wrapped around the handle of a glass pitcher. "Jest show your face, Kevin Fitzgerald Buchanon! Jest show your filthy, male-chauvinist face!"

Ruby Bee grabbed the lip of the pitcher and held on. "I said we're not going to have any more of this! Didn't you hear me, missy?"

Dahlia's thick white fingers relented, and Ruby Bee snatched the pitcher to her chest and retreated a few steps. As she did so, Kevin's face rose from behind the counter in the middle of the room. In contrast to Dahlia's scarlet complexion, his face was whiter than the towels in #4 and almost as nubby with beads of sweat.

"I was just trying to reason with you, my sweetness," he bleated.

"No, you was trying to tell me what I can and can't do."

"But we're betrothed. You don't have any call to be kissing some man so that everybody in America can see you doing it."

Dahlia put her hands on her hips and gave him a snooty smile. "Sez you."

"But I'm your fiancé," Kevin continued, "and I'm the one what ought to say whether or not you go kissing some fellow. How'd you feel if I was to go smooching with Miss D'Amourre or that other actress?"

Ruby Bee considered butting in, but instead busied herself assessing the damage to the kitchen (not too bad, mostly unbreakables scattered around) and sopping up the conversation so she could repeat it later. After all, everyone in town took a genuine interest in the couple, particularly since they'd been accused of fornicating on a porch swing a while back. Ruby Bee had never believed one word of that.

"Miss D'Amourre wouldn't smooch with you if you was the last man on earth," Dahlia countered icily. "I have dreamed of being a movie star since I was little, and now I have the opportunity. If you got objections, Kevin Fitzgerald Buchanon, you can tell them to those lightning bugs you're so fond of counting out by Boone Creek!"

She nailed him with a salt shaker, then stomped out the back door, letting it slam behind her like a firecracker. The two remaining occupants exchanged looks; then Ruby Bee shrugged and told him to start picking up the pots and pans that were littered about like artillery shells (which, in a sense, they were).

"I don't understand women," Kevin said sadly. "Sometimes you'd think they were from another planet way out there. What am I gonna do?"

"Clean up this mess before I lose my temper and start throwing things at you," Ruby Bee said. "I reckon my aim's a darn sight better than Dahlia's." She went back into the bar, intending to continue back out to the motel units to distribute towels, but what she saw was enough to stop her cold.

Estelle was cozied up to the bar with nice Mr. Meredith, hanging on his every word like he was begging her to marry him. In one of the booths, Frederick Marland was surrounded by high-school girls, all tittering and begging for his autograph. Next to them, Fuzzy Indigo was gaping at Raz Buchanon, who appeared to be telling him something difficult to digest.

And in the last booth, way at the back, where it was almost too dark to read the menu, Jim Bob Buchanon was making cow eyes at the blond actress with the well-endowed body. Ruby Bee couldn't see if either of them was saying anything, but she figured there was some basic communication going on under the table.

She was still trying to take all this in when Carlotta and a decently attired Hal Desmond came through the door, muttering to each other, and flopped down in yet another booth. Somehow he looked different, and it took Ruby Bee a minute to realize he was wearing hair.

Ruby Bee couldn't decide if she was irked that half the town had swooped in like salivatin' turkey buzzards, or pleased that business was picking up. She finally reached for her apron, and was heading toward the booths when the door opened and in marched all sorts of folks, including Elsie McMay, Lottie Estes, Joyce Lambertino, a dozen more high-school girls, and the dispatcher from the sheriff's office. Shortly thereafter, Ruby Bee was so busy she found herself wishing Dahlia were there to help.

For the longest time, I felt if we'd all been frozen in time and space, because nobody seemed to have anything to do or say. I finally cleared my throat and said, "Good afternoon, Sergeant Plover."

"Yeah," he said without moving his jaw. It was a rather classic cop mannerism; I'd seen it countless times on *The Late, Late Show.*

"I'm Anderson St. James," my visitor said. He held out his hand, and after a minute Plover had the grace to shake it briefly. "I dropped by to introduce myself to the chief of police and beg for cooperation during the next two weeks."

"I doubt you'll have to beg," Plover said. He looked at me as if I were a two-bit hoodlum in a Chicago alley. "I had a note from Merganser. He sifted through that last site and found a few rags that had been soaked in gasoline. You'll get the report in a few days."

"I knew it was arson," I said, keeping an eye on his itchy trigger finger. "Thanks for coming by. Tell Merganser I'll get back to him as soon as Harve and I have discussed the report."

Plover stomped out the door. His car shot out of the gravel lot, the engine roaring, and I'm quite sure he was exceeding the local speed limit as he disappeared down the road. And to think he had sworn to uphold the law, tut-tut.

"Testy chap, isn't he?" Anderson St. James murmured as he sat back down in the chair and resumed his visual dissection. "I do hope my presence doesn't cause any problems for you, Chief. I really am the official ambassador for the company, calling on you to assure you we'll do everything we can to make our stay pleasant for all."

"The entire town's looking forward to it," I said, opting not to discuss my personal affairs. Plover and I were going to have to discuss them, though, I told myself with a small sigh. "Why are you the official ambassador, Mr. St. James? I've been hearing a lot about a woman named Carlotta, who seems to be making all the arrangements.''

"Please, call me Anderson, and if we get to know one another on a higher plane, Andy. Carlotta will be by tomorrow to run through the shooting schedule with you so you'll have an idea where we'll be each day.'' He gave me a facetiously despondent look. "Each night I suppose we're stuck in the motel, unless some of the good citizens take pity on us and offer to show us the nightlife in the adjoining towns.''

"The Dew Drop Inn in Hasty? The third shift at the poultry plant in Starley City? I don't know how to break it to you''—I took a breath—"Anderson, but there's not much to do anywhere around here.'' I realized I was on the verge of simpering as he continued to watch me through these divine eyes, and I abruptly thought of several things to do in the immediate vicinity . . . of my apartment. I'd be calling him Andy-baby by the end of the day if I didn't get myself under control.

He smiled as if he'd read my mind. "Perhaps we'll find a few divertissements. Would I risk being accused of bribery if I offered to buy you a martini in the establishment down the road?''

"It's strictly beer and pretzels,'' I mumbled with all the poise of a junior-high girl being asked on her first date. However, I made it to my feet without disgracing myself, and managed not to squeal when he slipped his arm through mine and escorted me out of the office. I was almost surprised we didn't step out onto the streets of Manhattan.

Brother Verber was engaged in an argument with the Almighty, although it was pretty much one-sided. He'd taken the telephone off the receiver so he could concentrate on a message from Upstairs, but he was beginning to think he wasn't getting through.

"I don't mind making sacrifices if I know I'm doing it in the name of righteousness," he said, trying not to sound too eager about offering to make sacrifices because you never knew what might be suggested. "It's a sinful place, what with beer and dancing. I've been told they dance so close they look like they're in the midst of a perverted sexual ritual. But I won't look, and I won't touch a drop of alcohol. I need to find out exactly how wicked these Hollywood folks are so's I can prepare my sermon."

There wasn't a divine nod, but there wasn't a rumble of thunder, either. Brother Verber peeked outside warily, just in case there might be a lightning bolt with his name on it. When nothing happened, he hitched up his trousers and set off for the den of iniquity known as Ruby Bee's Bar & Grill.

"I'm not at all sure what the protocol is in this situation," Mrs. Jim Bob said loudly to Perkins's eldest, who was last seen dusting in the bedroom next door. She pulled free a few tendrils of hair so it wouldn't look as if she'd just that minute come home from the beauty parlor. But was the green silk dress too much? She didn't want the movie folks to think she'd gotten all gussied up for them, but she didn't want to be mistaken for a common cleaning woman, either.

She decided to leave off the mink stole but to stay in the green and let them assume she always dressed as befitting her position in the community. "When you get done in there," she continued loudly, "run the vacuum around the living room once more and put on the tea kettle. They may think they'll be offered whiskey, but they might as well get used to Christian behavior in this house.''

It was getting late in the afternoon, and she knew some people called it the cocktail hour, especially Californians and other heretics. While she studied her image in the mirror, she wondered just how sinful it would be to offer them sherry. She went so far as to dial the number at the rectory, but it seemed Brother Verber had chosen to disregard his duties in order to talk to someone else, and in her hour of need.

"Is that bottle of cooking sherry still in the cabinet under the oven?" she yelled to Perkins's eldest. She interpreted the lack of response as an admission of guilt, but being charitable, said, "If you been tippling, get down on your knees and confess aloud to myself and the Almighty. I can't promise you won't be damned for all eternity, but I won't fire you, and you can make up what's missing from your wages." She waited graciously for repentance to ring through her house like Christmas bells, but while she was waiting, she noticed a smudge on her collar and began to unbutton the dress.

Perkins's eldest was in seventh heaven, or fifth or six, anyway. On the stool to her left, the best-looking man she'd ever set eyes on was talking to Arly Hanks. On the stool to her right, Estelle Oppers was jabbering away to another movie star. The director fellow had bought everyone a beer or the refreshment of choice, which meant her glass of diet soda pop was courtesy of Hollywood. Behind her, Eula and Lottie and Joyce were squeezed into a booth with famous Miss Kitty Kaye, and before too long Brother Verber came slinking in to stand by the door and gawk. The whole barroom was humming like a room chock full of sewing machines.

She herself wasn't talking or jabbering to anyone, or even letting on that she was drinking in the scene, because, as mentioned earlier, she considered herself an enigma.

Chapter 6

When the noise at Ruby Bee's grew intolerable, I decided I'd had enough beer, music, smoke, and pleasant if not piercing conversation with an incredibly handsome movie star. Said movie star gallantly offered to walk me home, and I graciously consented, although I suspected he was more interested in my badge than my body. I could almost hear Ruby Bee advising Carlotta to send an attractive man to the PD to mollify the chief, who had a reputation for being mulish. Estelle had probably thumbed through the glossies and selected the perfect candidate. I didn't have to read their minds to know all this; I'd read their smirks when they'd kept a furtive surveillance on the two of us all evening.

"We're here," I said two minutes later, the delay the result of a ponderous chicken truck. "I live above the antiques store."

Anderson had the decency to appear disappointed, although I was aware of his profession. "But I'd envisioned a leisurely stroll along the river. Are you sure you don't live in a charming cottage amid the rustling pines and the babbling brook?"

"I'm sure I live in a cramped apartment at the top of

the stairs, where the rats rustle and my mother calls in the middle of the night to babble." I disengaged my hand, which had found itself in his, and murmured something inane about having to break up bank robberies in the morning.

He murmured something inane in response, but somehow or other I wasn't going up the stairs; on the contrary, I was in the process of being nuzzled very efficiently and enjoying it very much when Kevin Buchanon shouted, "Fire!"

I spun out of the embrace and located Kevin, who was straddling his bicycle across the road. He was pointing at my window. I jerked my head around. The flickering light made the panes look as if they were made of stained glass.

"Holy shit!" I started for the stairs.

Anderson grabbed my arm. "You can't go up there! Call the fire department!"

"Nobody messes with me," I growled. I yanked my arm loose and went storming up the stairs, my face as hot as the flames inside my apartment—the flames burning up my paltry treasures and trespassing in my sole sanctuary from the omnipresent madness that was Maggody. I banged open the door. Smoke washed over me, stinging my eyes and gagging me, but once I'd wiped away the tears and stopped coughing more hoarsely than an entire TB ward, I realized the fire was limited to a pile of rags on the linoleum floor.

I grabbed a glass and splashed water from the tap onto the mini-inferno until the flames gave way to noxious gray smoke. I then stumbled to the window, opened it, and went back to the landing outside the living room to suck in some fresh air and do my best to stop shaking.

Roy Stivers, my landlord, lumbered around the corner and squinted up at me. "You okay, Arly? One of those Hollywood fellows rapped on my door and told me to call the fire department. Caught Wade on his way out the door, thank God. He said they'll be here as soon as they can.''

Anderson bounded up to the landing, his mouth tight and his perfect hair a tiny bit ruffled. "That was a crazy thing to do.''

"I suppose so, but I wasn't about to twist my hands and imagine everything I own being reduced to barbeque while the volunteer fire fighters were pulling on their pants.'' I rubbed my face, as much to erase the anger as the soot. "It charred the linoleum, which wasn't all that attractive, anyway. I was thinking about replacing it.'' I tried to laugh, but it sounded wheezy.

"How'd it start?'' Roy called up, no doubt thinking of the store below that was crammed with antiques. They weren't Louis XIV's, but they were valuable enough to allow him the luxury of expensive whiskey, first-edition volumes of poetry, and periodic sojourns to unknown destinations.

"Did you leave a cigarette in an ashtray?'' Anderson asked.

"Hell, no,'' I said, aware the anger had not been erased. "For starters, I don't smoke, and I don't have any ashtrays. I didn't flip a match into a pile of rags before I left, either. This was set intentionally.''

He put his hands on my shoulders as if to keep me from flying off the landing in a rage, which was not impossible to imagine. "Who would do such a thing?''

I looked down at the flock of vultures *(Falconiformes incendiaristes)* that had surged out of Ruby Bee's to check the action. The locals were jostling for position, pointing, squawking, and hoping for a real live melodrama in the making. Ruby Bee broke through the line and came across the road, her hands wrestling each other in the folds of her apron. The Hollywood people were in a huddle under the Flamingo sign, their faces garish in the pink light.

Other lights came down the street as the volunteer fire department arrived in three pickup trucks. As I stood in the rectangle of light from the living room, I felt as though I were on a stage, exposed and vulnerable—and missing my copy of the script. "Would you please tell the man in the first truck that the fire is out?" I said to Anderson.

I continued to study my audience as he went down the stairs. On the other side of the street, sunk in the shadows beside the PD, stood a figure. He melted away, but I was pretty sure I'd caught a glimpse of the pale, round face of Billy Dick MacNamara.

Once it was clear that the show was over, the others melted away, too, although in a rowdy babble. I went inside to see if the smoke had dissipated, and I was flapping a towel and cursing steadily when Anderson joined me.

"It's not quite as classy as a Beverly Hills mansion," I said, "and you'll have to excuse the smell. I'm fresh out of room deodorizer and incense." I flung the towel in a corner.

"You're quite as classy as the women who live in the mansions," he said as he moved around the room, gazing at my choices of literature (lurid), cheap prints (French Impressionism), and the stacks of paperwork (tedious) that trailed me home from the PD. "And you're real."

I kicked the sodden rags out of the way, then squatted down to examine the charred depression in the floor. It was a good two inches deep; if I filled it with fresh water, the cockroaches could spend their nights at the pool. Blackened matches were scattered around it; the firebug had left his signature for me, just in case

I missed the connection. "Real what?" I said as I stood up. "Real foolhardy?"

"Possibly. You certainly didn't consider the danger when you charged upstairs as if it were San Juan Hill." Anderson sat down on the sofa and gave me an inviting look.

I decided to ignore it and began to collect the rags in a tidy pile. "As I said, no one messes with me. What's maddening is that I know who set this fire, but I don't have any proof. I can confront him with a lie, but it's not a crime to lie unless it impedes an investigation. A first-year law student would have him out in ten seconds flat. The worst thing is that the damn kid was in here—in my apartment."

My head jerked around as I searched for other signs of his vile intrusion. Nothing seemed to be missing, but his pudgy white hands could have touched my things, twisted and turned them, moved them a centimeter or two, all the while leaving a trace of oil mingled with sweat on everything I owned. If he chose to return when I was asleep, he could do so. My skin began to itch, and the beer in my stomach turned sour.

"You'll get him eventually," Anderson said soothingly. "Why don't you sit over here and let me wipe all the black streaks off your face? You look as if you applied blackface in a most inept fashion, and we don't want any accusations of racism."

I sat down, albeit warily, and allow him to clean me up to his own satisfaction. Before I realized what was happening, several strategic bobby pins had been removed, and my hair tumbled down my back. He disengaged the remaining ones, arranged my hair over my shoulders, and sat back with a bemused smile.

"Sometimes it doesn't work," he said. "Some women need their hair tightly restrained, their glasses on their noses, their collars buttoned. It works every time in the movies, but in the real world there's not always a seductress waiting to be unshackled.''

I opened my mouth to point out I was no seductress, shackled or unshackled, when he leaned forward and kissed me. It was right out of the last chapter of my more lurid novels, and I heard myself remembering snippets of purple prose that could curdle milk.

''Why is it no one messes with you?'' he said as he nibbled my ear. ''Because you won't let them?''

I let him mess with me for a moment longer, then retreated and said, ''That's right, Anderson—I won't let 'em. You'd better go now. I'm going to borrow a fan from Roy and try to get rid of the stench.''

''What about your testy trooper?'' he asked. ''Do you keep him at arm's length?''

The mention of my testy trooper chilled me. I could almost see him sitting across from us, his feet flat on the floor, his arms crossed, and his face radiating disapproval from behind mirrored sunglasses.

''I don't keep him anywhere,'' I said coldly. ''Furthermore, it's none of your damn business. I don't know if you make a practice of trying to find yourself a local bed and breakfast when you shoot a—''

''Back down, Arly. I don't make a practice of anything. I was attracted to you because I found you a cryptic combination of sophistication and . . . naïveté. No, that's not the word. I have no idea what you are, but I'd like to find out. Even though I live in La-La Land and associate with some remarkably shallow people, I hope I'm something more than a stereotype.'' He stood up and walked to the door. ''You know, I've never stayed in one of those bed and breakfast places.''

''Neither have I,'' I said with a small smile.

Millicent McIlhaney waited until Darla Jean came back into the kitchen with the mail, then said, "Last night you were hanging all over that movie star like he was honey and you were a fly. I'm surprised you don't have sticky fingers this morning."

"Maybe I do." Darla Jean breezed right on through the room, dropped the mail on the sofa, and went upstairs to her bedroom to call Heather Riley. While the phone rang, she bunched her pillows under her head and got comfortable, because she had a lot to talk about and Heather had been at her cousin's house in Lisbon (Arkansas, that is—also the possessor of a Paris and a London, and even an Omaha) the previous evening, a.k.a. the Fateful Moment. "You're gonna die when you hear who I met last night," she said.

"Frederick Marland," Heather said archly. "I already heard all about it from Traci, and about ten other people after that. He held your hand and you turned to cornmeal mush. You asked him for his autograph, and—"

"I did no such thing! I am too mature to act like some silly little kid. Traci sure ain't, though. She was flapping those cheap eyelashes so hard one of them came loose and fell onto the table like a dead spider."

"She didn't tell me that," admitted Heather, who actually did want to hear Darla Jean's version, because Traci said there had been something going on under the table that wouldn't exactly please Darla Jean's boyfriend when he heard all about it. "So you got a date with him, huh?"

Darla Jean glared at her stuffed poodle, who'd done nothing to warrant the hostility. "Of course not."

"He's not picking you up this evening?"

"He's not picking me up this evening," Darla Jean said coolly. He wasn't, either. She was supposed to knock on his door after supper, and all she was going to do was give him a ride to Farberville so he could pick up some fancy kind of suntan lotion that he couldn't find at Jim Bob's SuperSaver Buy 4 Less.

"How old do you reckon he is?" Heather continued, knowing perfectly well what the plans for the evening were. Traci wasn't a candidate for queen of the honor society, but there wasn't anything wrong with her hearing. "I heard he's playing a teenager, but Angie said she could tell he dyes his hair. He's probably *thirty* years old, Darla Jean, not to mention being a Hollywood movie star. You're going to get yourself in trouble if you start fooling around with someone like that."

"I am not fooling around with anybody!"

Heather didn't bother to point out that it was common knowledge that Darla Jean and her boyfriend were fooling around out by Boone Creek so often the squirrels and coons were tired of watching them. "You just better be careful," was all she said.

Raz Buchanon found what he was looking for, and with a cackle took it back to the living room, where Marjorie was lying on the recliner. "I knew I could find it iff'n I looked hard enough," he said as he loaded his cheek with shreds of tobacco and settled down on the sofa. "I'm sorry you had to wait all this time, but my collection goes back twenty years."

Marjorie waited patiently.

"But I knew it weren't that long ago," Raz went on, "on account of it weren't near a month of Sundays ago when it happened. Once I laid eyes on the feller, I was dead sure he'd been on the cover of one of these here newspapers, right there in the same issue with the article about how that woman in Brazil birthed a baby with two heads that spoke different languages, one being an alien tongue."

Marjorie blinked in amazement.

"Now, you jest hold your horses and I'll find the article." He shook his head as he passed over the photograph of the two-headed baby, but he wasn't about to rile Marjorie by getting distracted by the miracles of modern science. "Here it is! It sez that"—his lips moved slowly but surely—"the woman was killed in one of those ritual murders they favor in Hollywood. You kin see in this here drawing where they wrote all over the wall in blood." He showed it to Marjorie, who snuffled in disbelief while he laboriously worked his way through the next paragraph. "It sez the feller was making a movie in the desert, and he come home to find his wife all covered with blood and about as dead as you kin get. It was jest like a few years back when those wild-eyed hippies took to killin' famous movie stars."

Marjorie turned ashen at the very thought.

I parked in front of Billy Dick's house. The truck was gone, and I was hoping he was busy looking for shacks to burn as I knocked on the door.

After a few minutes, a woman in a faded housecoat opened the door. Her gray hair was messy, and she had the vaguely bewildered look of someone who'd been asleep. Billy Dick must have inherited his soft bulkiness from his father, because she was short and undernourished. Her eyes were as pale as his, though, and as disturbingly blank.

"Mrs. MacNamara, I'm Arly Hanks," I said.

"I know who you are."

"I'm still working on that fire last week, and I wanted

to ask Billy Dick if he remembered anything more about the truck he saw by the low-water bridge.''

"He's gone off somewhere. Said he'd be back before suppertime so he can take me to work."

That was the good news. The bad was that she wasn't inviting me in for a cozy chat, and, in fact, was looking a little bored with the conversation.

"Do you mind if I come in and wait?" I said, doing my best to look so exhausted I might crumple before her eyes and thus require all kinds of action on her part. "I was up most of the night trying to clean up after the fire in my apartment."

"I heard about that. I suppose you can sit for a few minutes, but I don't expect Billy Dick for at least an hour." She held open the screened door and gestured for me to come into the living room. The walls were as drab as her housecoat, the furniture shabby, the few knickknacks coated with a veneer of dust. The television was on, but the sound had been turned down. She switched it off and moved away from it, a guilty look on her face.

I sat down on the edge of the sofa. "How long have you lived here, Mrs. MacNamara?"

"Goin' on most of a year, I suppose. The house belonged to a cousin of mine, and when he died, he left it to me. Billy Dick and I had been living in Farberville, out in a trailer park on the east side of town, and it seemed like a good idea to move somewhere and start fresh."

"Start fresh?"

She sank down on a chair in the corner, her hands in her lap, and looked at the worn carpet. A scrawny tan cat came around the corner of the doorway, hesitated when it saw me, then glided across the room and leaped into her lap. She stroked it listlessly while she decided what—if anything—to tell me. When she at last spoke, her voice was so low I had to lean forward to hear her. "My husband passed away when Billy Dick was twelve. It was hard on both of us, not only losing him but having to make ends meet on a waitress's salary."

"How'd Billy Dick feel about moving to Maggody?"

"He never said anything about it. He's busy with his own doings, and he doesn't ever say much. Ever now and then I ask him, but he just gets mad and stomps out the door."

"I guess it helped when he found a new friend."

Mrs. MacNamara flinched, and unless I was overly sensitive, the quick look she gave me was hostile. "I guess it did, even though I don't cotton to him playing silly make-believe games with a boy so much younger. Billy Dick didn't have a lot of friends in Farberville. He's always preferred to keep to himself mostly, just like his pa and me. We worried a sight more about paying bills than we did about wasting money in fancy restaurants or at the picture show. My husband—well, he had an ailment that kept him from working all the time and holding down a steady job. He'd work, but then he'd have a bad spell and get fired."

In Maggody, an unspecified "ailment" was the accepted euphemism for alcoholism, and I would have bet all three bullets that my theory was correct. Mrs. MacNamara had the dispirited look of someone who'd waged a futile war for a long time. She hadn't been able to control her husband, and it sounded as though she no longer controlled her son.

I doubted she knew anything of his activities. "I've got some more people to talk to," I said, rising. "Please tell Billy Dick that I stopped by and that I'd like him to call me either at the police department or at my apartment."

"I'll tell him, but I can't promise he'll call."

"Thanks." I went outside, relieved to be free of her

potentially contagious drabness, and drove toward Farberville and the state police barracks. I wanted to talk
to Sergeant Merganser one more time.

"Did you hear what Fuzzy told Carlotta?" Gwenneth
said as she dribbled coconut oil onto her arm and began to rub it into her skin. Even a cruddy little swim-
ming pool would have been better than the edge of the
motel parking lot, but she and Kitty were bored out of
their coiffures after less than twenty-four hours in Maggody. Sunbathing seemed better than vegetating. Both
women were on aluminum lounges, and wearing what
most of the locals would describe as Band-Aids and little pieces of string.

Kitty lit a cigarette and blew a ribbon of smoke into
the sky. "From the mouth of the seriously inebriated?"

"I think it means something," Gwenneth said. She
regarded her companion from behind her dark glasses,
then flipped her hair back and sighed gustily (lustily
would come later, in front of the camera). "Fuzzy
swears he saw an unauthorized cut of *Prickly Passion*
in a motel in Vegas. When Hal had me in his room last
night to rehearse my lines"—she rolled her eyes, even
though Kitty couldn't appreciate the effect—"he admitted as much and said someone had pirated a tape."

"Well, hell," Kitty said, then paused while she oiled
her basically bare breasts. They weren't of Gwenneth's
caliber, but they were better than standard issue and
twice as expensive. "If that's true, we won't make
nearly as much on the distribution. Buddy and I are
currently in an uncomfortable situation, and we were
counting on our five-percent cuts to ward off the
wolves baying at the Jaguar."

The sunglasses fell off Gwenneth's delicately tilted

nose, as she jerked upright. "Five?" she said shrilly. "Five? You and Buddy got five? Hal swore up one leg and down the other that everybody was getting three. That son of a bitch! I'd like to take his toupee and shove it—"

"Good afternoon, ladies," Ruby Bee said as she came across the parking lot, a tray in her hands and a determined smile on her face despite the quantity of naked flesh on display in her parking lot. These Hollywood people seemed disinclined to clothes, she thought uneasily. "I brought you all some iced tea. It must be hotter than an oven out here on the gravel."

Gwenneth got the sunglasses back in place and rewarded the woman with a dazzlingly white smile. "Aren't you a sweetie! I was just telling Kitty that I'd pass up a day of shopping on Rodeo Drive for a glass of tea." She held out her hand, and Ruby Bee hastily put a glass in it.

"Thanks," Kitty said, her voice as gravelly as the parking lot. "I didn't have a chance to meet you last night when Hal ordered us—I mean, invited us to have a few beers at your bar and meet the locals. I'm Kitty Kaye."

"Oh, I know who you are," Ruby Bee said, trying not to gush but gushing all the same. "I saw every last picture you made back in the fifties. I used to try to fix my hair just like yours in case Humphrey Bogart came knocking on my door. It must have been heavenly to be kissed by someone like that, even if you had to do it 'cause it was in the script."

"It had its moments," Kitty murmured. "It's very kind of you to remember me. I can't count the number of times I've been accused of being dead, even to my face. Before we leave, you and I will pose for a photograph, and I'll autograph it for you personally. Buddy will, too, if you like."

"Oh, Miss Kaye," Ruby Bee breathed reverently, imagining the framed photos on the barroom wall, just like in those fancy Noow Yark restaurants.

Gwenneth frowned at a freckle on her arm. "Who's Humphrey Bogart?"

Kitty and Ruby Bee exchanged looks that bordered on unspoken condemnation. Ruby Bee started to explain, then realized it'd be presumptuous to think she knew better than Miss Kitty Kaye, who'd kissed him in the fifties.

"Later, darling," Kitty said. "So, Mrs. Hanks, what kind of excitement can we anticipate in Maggody?"

"I'd be happy as all get out if you'd call me Ruby Bee, and you, too, Miss D'Amourre. The only folks what call me Mrs. Hanks are the pesky fellows from the ABC." Ruby Bee could hear herself prattling like one of those ventriloquist's dummies, but she couldn't seem to stop. "The ABC's the Alcohol and Beverage Control. They have to inspect my license twice a year and snoop around to see if I'm serving minors."

"Those dirty-faced men who dig for diamonds?" Gwenneth asked, although she appeared more interested in the circle of oil she'd drawn around her belly button.

Ruby Bee wondered if this blonde wasn't several logs short of a rick, but she didn't say a single word, and after a moment, Kitty Kaye yawned and said, "Where is everybody?"

Gwenneth's yawn was more restrained. "Carlotta and Hal went to check the sites. The boys are holed up in that last room, playing poker and doing their best to run through the entire liquor supply by dusk. Anderson said he was going to take a walk, although I cannot imagine why he'd do such a seriously sweaty thing like that." She sat up and held the iced tea glass until Ruby Bee retrieved it. "I, for one, am ready for a martini. Do you suppose dear Buddy could be flattered into making me one? He's the only one who merely allows the gin to gaze longingly at the vermouth."

Kitty handed her glass to Ruby Bee, who'd sprouted roots in the parking lot on account of being in such proximity to Hollywood movie stars. "Thank you ever so much, Ruby Bee," she said with a nod. "I do believe, Gwenneth, that I'm going to hunt up my hubby and lure him into our room. We don't have any scenes quite like yours, but he does enjoy our rehearsals . . . as much as Hal must enjoy his rehearsals with you."

"Hal is such a pig," Gwenneth began, then stopped and shielded her eyes with her hand. "Oh, shit! Here comes that horrible man from last night! He's sleazier than the janitor at Cedar Rapids High School."

Ruby Bee looked over her shoulder. Jim Bob was bearing down on them like a garbage truck, and carrying a bottle in a plain brown wrapper.

Gwenneth started to rise, but Kitty caught her wrist and in a voice so low Ruby Bee nearly missed it, said, "Remember what Hal said, dear. We must be at our loveliest, mustn't we?"

"Oh, shit," Gwenneth repeated, but without emotion.

Ruby Bee was downright amazed when the blonde transformed herself into a coy little Kewpie doll and went so far as to wiggle her fingers at the approaching figure. Kitty murmured something and fled into #4. Although Ruby Bee thought of a few biting remarks to make to Hizzoner, she settled for a sniff as she went past him on her way to the barroom.

"Oh, you are such a sweetie!" she heard a giggly voice say.

Despite her best efforts to hear anything else, she didn't. She wasn't all that perturbed, however, since she'd pick a whole passel of interesting tidbits, includ-

ing a reference to someone's husband (she couldn't wait
to see Estelle's face when she was presented with that),
hints that had sounded scandalous, and a sort of flimsy
theory concerning the upcoming movie to be made in
Maggody.

All of it would have to sit on the back burner for the
time being. It was getting close to happy hour at Ruby
Bee's Bar & Grill, and she figured the crowd would be
larger than the evening before.

I opened the door of the PD, and for the first time
ever, I did so cautiously. I don't know what I expected—a sheet of fire, a bomb rigged to the doorknob,
or someone waiting in the back room. I found none of
the above. As far as I could tell, the only person to have
set foot inside was the postman, who never bothers to
ring once.

I was filing the mail, with the largest percentage going into the metal wastebasket, when the door opened.
I had to bite back a gasp, which was pretty damn silly,
but I did and glanced up with a facsimile of a smile for
the couple.

The woman held out her hand. "I'm afraid we didn't
have a chance to meet last night, Chief Hanks. I'm Carlotta Lowenstein, and this is Hal Desmond, the producer and director of *Wild Cherry Wine,* and the head
of Glittertown Productions. We're hoping you have
some time to run through the shooting schedule."

"Okay," I said as I shook her firm, dry hand. "Nice
to meet both of you."

"I'm sure it is," Hal said. He sat down in the chair
across from my desk and snapped his fingers at Carlotta.

"Do you have an ashtray?" she asked me.

"I'll get a saucer," I said. She seemed pleasant enough, but unlike Anderson St. James, Hal Desmond wasn't winning any Oscars in my PD. I fetched a particularly chipped saucer, handed it to him, and resumed my seat on the far side of the desk.

Hal took out a pack of cigarettes, tapped one out, and lit it, all the while regarding me with reptilian curiosity. "So you're the chief of police. How'd that happen?"

"It happened," I said with a shrug. "How'd you happen to choose Maggody?"

"Carlotta did that, didn't you, sweetheart?"

I might have recoiled from his sardonic tone, but she didn't so much as raise an eyebrow. "One of the actors suggested the area. I rented a car in Springfield and cruised through every hamlet until I found the perfect site to shoot the film."

"It's quaint," Hal said, flipping cigarette ashes on the floor. "I can't deny its essential quaintness. In fact, I'd say its quaintness is unparalleled."

"Perhaps," I said, having no idea if we'd been praised or slapped across the face.

He didn't seemed concerned with my minimalistic response. "And the citizens. Now we're really talking quaint, aren't we, Carlotta? We've had the good fortune to meet some of these very quaint people, and I am at a loss for words to convey how exceptionally quaint they are. If I can capture only the epidermis of their quaintness, I'll be the toast of the Cannes Film Festival. Don't you agree, Carlotta?"

"Right, Hal." She glanced at her clipboard, then smiled at me. "Hal and I have been running by some of the specific sites we've lined up. One gentleman was eager to assure us he would keep his sow outside while we there."

"Fuckin' quaint," Hal said, shaking his head. "It's so fuckin' quaint I told Carlotta here that we ought to bang out a few revisions and utilize the situation, which has incredible undertones of rural depravity. Sometimes those of us in the industry lose touch with the real people."

"Raz Buchanon isn't real," I said.

"Good," Carlotta said with a wry laugh.

Hal held up his hands, his thumbs meeting and his fingers erect to form three sides of a rectangle, and framed my face. "You've got good cheekbones—not anything to alarm Hepburn, but not bad. If we did something with the hair . . . You ever do any acting in high school? Think you might be interested in a screen test?"

Carlotta looked as if she might hurl the clipboard at him, and her voice was icy as she said, "Hal, this is the chief of police. She already has a career—in law enforcement."

He tilted his makeshift camera back and forth, winked at me, then let his hands drop. "A director has to be on the lookout. I personally discovered Gwenneth D'Amourre, you know. She was—what, seventeen or eighteen? A sweet little thing fresh off the farm, but I could see the potential, and that's what counts. When Gwenneth came over to my personal booth at the Polo, wiggling like she had an eel up her ass, I knew I had a star within my reach."

Carlotta scribbled a note on the clipboard, but I doubted she was recording his words of wisdom. I settled back in my chair and stonily watched him.

"Same thing with Frederick Marland," Hal continued, his hand jerking so much that cigarette ashes drifted down like dandruff. "Not that he wiggled like that. He took the more forward approach of sitting in the reception room of the office for—I dunno—maybe two, three weeks, every day, just like a brass lamp. You gotta admire that kind of perseverance, and I finally took pity on him and let him into my office. His accent was worse than the rubes who live around here, but I looked at his body and I thought P-O-T-E-N-T-I-A-L. Then I thought, Hal—what've you got beyond potential? Two kids, both saddled with hick accents. So I signed 'em both up, took the hayseeds out of their mouths, lined 'em up with a speech coach and an acting coach, straightened their teeth, dressed 'em up in the right clothes, and created the hottest pair of actors in the industry today."

I suspected I was supposed to clap. "I don't think I've heard of either of them," I said sweetly.

Carlotta stepped on Hal's foot. "The first two films have had limited release," she told me, ignoring his yelp. "The third should be out this fall, after we've concluded the distribution negotiations. I'm sure Chief Hanks has more important things to attend to, so let's run the schedule by her and get back to the motel before our cast and crew start killing each other."

"You know something," he said as he rubbed his foot, "you've got a real attitude, Carlotta. One of these days I'm gonna have to do something about it."

She looked down at him. "Only if I don't do it first."

It was more exciting to be in her apartment during the day, when at any moment she might return. The previous night had been too easy, but he'd wanted to make it clear he could start a fire anywhere, not just in shacks on dark, deserted roads.

He opened the drawer in the night table, but it contained nothing of interest. Aware that his footsteps might be heard below, he walked soundlessly to the dresser. Inside the second drawer he found what he wanted, although he could not have explained the sudden urge to touch a woman's clothing, to let silky underthings ripple through his fingers like water.

Not water, he corrected himself. Water was the dragon's poison. He fingered a red slip edged with lace. This was better, he thought as he used it to wipe the sweat off his face, then stuffed it in his pocket.

He tucked a small present under the remaining items, and smiled as he imagined her expression when she found it. She would know he could come and go as he pleased. Would she begin to realize he was nearing the moment when he could seize his rightful power from the dragon?

Chapter 7

24   INT. BIGGINS'S HOUSE—LORETTA'S BEDROOM—NIGHT

Loretta is undressing in front of the mirror, gazing at her image.

> LORETTA
> (softly)
> Oh, Billy Joe, if only Pa would let us be together.

WE HEAR a distant church bell, followed by a tap at the window. CAMERA WIDENS to include Billy Joe, who gestures for Loretta to unlock the window. Covering her breasts with folded arms, she crosses the room and does so. Billy Joe opens it and vaults over the sill.

> BILLY JOE
> I had to see you, my love. I saw you and Cooter Grimmley right there in his living room. He may live in a fine, big house, but he's still a filthy sumbitch.

> LORETTA
> Hush, Pa'll hear you. He and Ma are sitting

in the other room. I think I'd better put my clothes on.

She reaches for her shirt, but he catches her wrist, pulls her other arm back, and stares longingly at her breasts.

LORETTA
(continuing)
Billy Joe, don't do that. No, you got to stop. I cain't think when you does that to me. You're making me . . . excited.

BILLY JOE
Am I? Lemme see about that.

LORETTA
No! Please stop. Pa's not ten feet away on the other side of the door.

CAMERA MOVES behind him as he backs her up to the bed and eases her down, all the while AD-LIBBING endearments and caressing her.

BILLY JOE
(distractedly)
I got a plan, Loretta. We can get away from this filthy town and start a new life together. You'd like that, wouldn't you? Then I could do this . . . and this . . . all the time.

ZACHERY
(off screen)
Loretta, what're you doing in there?

LORETTA
You got to go, Billy Joe!

Billy Joe reluctantly stands up and starts for the window.

BILLY JOE

I'll figure out a plan. I'll get a message to you . . . somehow or other.

DISSOLVE TO:

Carlotta frowned at the crowd on the far side of the dirt road, but she was used to it and was doing her best to ignore the gawkers with their cameras, coolers, picnic baskets, and aluminum chairs. Fuzzy was inside the shack, in theory setting up the equipment, but he'd been in there so long she was beginning to worry that the crazy old coot had done something to him—or vice versa.

Hal was pacing in the weedy yard, a cigarette in one hand and a copy of the script in the other. He was dressed just like everybody thought a Hollywood director was supposed to dress: sunglasses, a battered canvas hat, a loud pink shirt, a khaki safari jacket, and plaid shorts. The only items causing dissension among the spectators were the black socks that clung to his calves like bark.

He was acting just like everybody thought a Hollywood director was supposed to act, too. He'd nearly bitten Joyce Lambertino's niece's head off when she ventured too near the fence, and she'd skedaddled back to Joyce, bawling. When he reached one side of the yard, he reeled around and took off lickety-split like he'd been shot out of a cannon. It was a most satisfying scene for all concerned.

Carlotta consulted her shooting schedule. There were eleven interiors in the Biggins's family home. Although they'd considered doing some of the exteriors while the weather was good, she decided to wait a few days until the locals lost interest and drifted back to whatever dreary things they did on a daily basis. Anderson was getting chummy with Chief Hanks. Perhaps she could be cajoled into blocking off the road during some of the less-clad encounters. She made a note to remind Hal to make a lot of comments about artistic integrity and symbolism—and to stop capsulizing the film as "the Clampetts do *Romeo and Juliet* in the nude."

Gwenneth and Frederick drove up in the van. When they disembarked, the buzzing stopped. It might have been due to their selection of clothing, in that Frederick was wearing ragged overalls that seemed to call attention to his privates. His bare chest was resplendently muscular and thick with curly brown hair.

Gwenneth was wearing cut-off jeans so tight that most of the crowd couldn't figure out how she got into them, or if there was any way she could get out of them short of surgery. Her shirt, on the other hand, was nigh onto gossamer, and Kevin Buchanon, who was right up front, realized he could see her nipples just as clear as day. It was enough to make him dizzy and send his Adam's apple into a frenzy.

Jim Bob was feeling a bit overheated himself, as his eyes dwelled on each lovely breast, then slid on down to strip the rest of her naked. From what she'd said the night before, when they'd again gotten real cozy in the last booth, he might get his wish. He wondered if she liked to wear a black lace teddie and a matching garter belt. He wondered if he could buy them in Farberville. He did not wonder what his wife would say if she could read his mind, because she was sitting in the living room, dressed like she was going to church, and beadily awaiting the movie company. She was doing this because he'd said they were coming right soon. Later he'd explain that they misinformed him.

"Put your eyeballs back in your sockets," Eilene Buchanon said to her husband, her voice more tart than a green persimmon. "You look like a bullfrog."

"You're embarrassing me," Millicent McIlhaney said to her husband, sounding just like Eilene if not more so.

"If you disgrace me," Dahlia muttered to her betrothed, "you're going to find yourself stuffed in this here mailbox."

"I ought to call the Woman's Commune in Bugscuffle and arrange a demonstration," said one of the hippie women who ran the Emporium. "I cannot believe in this era that some sexist Hollywood pig would encourage such flagrant misconception of a woman's worth based on physical attributes."

"Right on," said the other one, ogling the dude in the overalls. She doubted she had any misconceptions about his physical attributes, but she was willing to explore the thesis.

"Like, wow," said the bearded wonder who lived with them. Neither responded to him, but they rarely did.

"I am gonna pass out," Heather Riley whispered to Traci. "Doesn't he have the cutest buns you've ever seen? Wouldn't you like to see 'em in the moonlight on a blanket alongside Boone Creek?"

"What'd Darla Jean say about last night?" Traci whispered back.

For a brief moment, Heather took her eyes off the attraction across the street and wrinkled up her face like a Pekinese. "Nothing. The first time I called, she was real nasty and said I'd woken her up. I waited a whole hour, about to pee in my pants the entire time, but then she said she had to take in the laundry or she'd be grounded and then she banged down the phone before I could get in one word.''

"So you don't know what happened?''

Heather shrugged and resumed her analysis of Frederick Marland, who might be as old as thirty but was holding up real well. The fantasy that ensued was enough to make her gulp like she was swallowing cracker crumbs.

"They are too married," Ruby Bee said to Estelle with a snooty smile. "I heard Miss Kaye say she was going to fetch her hubby from that poker game.''

"It matters not to me, Miss Marital Almanac. I have better things to do than sneak around the parking lot and eavesdrop on other people's conversations.''

Carlotta, who'd heard none of this but could have written wittier dialogue in her sleep, frowned at Gwenneth and Frederick. "Where are Buddy and Kitty? I told Anderson I didn't need him until eleven, but unless poor little Loretta wants to whine to the wall, we need her doting parents.''

"I knocked on their door," Gwenneth said, "but nobody answered.''

Hal joined them. "Is this a business or a corporate picnic? Let's get with the program, people. Everybody has a copy of the schedule, fer crissake. I could understand if one of these pinheads missed a call, but those two have been in the business since—since—I don't know.'' He glowered at Carlotta. "Didn't you bother to check with everyone last night before you guzzled beer half the night?''

"I confirmed the details with everyone," she answered evenly.

"Well, go call that goddamn motel and tell Aunt Bea to kick them out of bed!''

"Do you honestly believe there's a telephone inside

there? Is it in the billiard room, or hidden under the ferns next to the Jacuzzi?''

"Then go get them! Take my car! I cannot sustain my creative flow with all these delays." He stalked across Raz's porch and went inside. The slam of the door was a perfect punctuation mark; from across the road came a smattering of applause.

"I saw them in the barroom last night," Gwenneth contributed, wishing that the dreadful mayor person would stop staring at her so hard she was apt to pop the button on her shorts.

"They were there until about ten," Carlotta said. "Kitty and I watched all the local widows fight to sit in Buddy's lap. You were preoccupied with a bit of lap-sitting, yourself."

Gwenneth pursed her lips into a pretty pout. "Hal said we had to make nice with these people until we had a wrap. I was doing what I was told."

"And we know why you do what Hal tells you, don't we?" Carlotta said with the faintest hint of venom.

"Do we?"

"Can it," Frederick said, not at all interested in the exchange. "I am beginning to sweat, and I'd like to do something more lucrative than be leered at by high-school girls. Gwenneth, my precious young nympho, let's go inside and block what we can until Buddy and Kitty get their buttocks here."

Carlotta started for the van but spotted Ruby Bee and Estelle nearby and went over to them. "Good morning. Ruby Bee, did you happen to see Buddy Meredith or Kitty Kaye this morning?''

Ruby Bee paused for a moment so everybody could appreciate how the assistant director was asking her a question concerning the whereabouts of famous celebrities like Miss Kaye and the Wite & Brite man. "I don't reckon I did. I took breakfast trays to everybody's doors like you requested. Now that I think about it, the tray in front of #5 was still sitting there when I locked up to come watch the movie bein' made."

"I saw it, too," Estelle said, a little miffed that Carlotta hadn't said a word to her or even bothered to smile. "It didn't look like it'd been touched. If you want, I'll drive back and knock on their door."

Before Carlotta could respond, the door of Raz's cabin flew open. Gwenneth marched across the yard, her face rigid and her breasts bobbing indignantly, and came through the gate. "There is a pig in there," she told Carlotta in a steely voice. "That person says he'll put it outside, but it's lying on the sofa. He chews tobacco and he spits. Furthermore, he scratches as if he were infested with lice. My skin is absoluting crawling."

"What are the others doing?"

"I need to lie down somewhere clean and cool," Gwenneth went on with a martyred sigh, allowing the spectators to appreciate her delicate sensibilities. "Truly, Carlotta, I am simply going to burst into tears if you force me to go back inside there."

"Talk to Hal."

"I cannot communicate with him. He and Fuzzy are drinking an unknown substance from jars, and Frederick is watching them with that nauseatingly superior smile of his. I just know the place is swarming with spiders and fleas—and that pig is disgusting!" Two silver tears trickled down from behind the dark lenses of the sunglasses.

"Would you like to sit for a spell in my station wagon?" Estelle asked solicitously.

"Yeah, do that," Carlotta said. "I'm going to run back to the motel and pick up Buddy and Kitty."

Estelle was pretty darn impressed with herself as she took Miss D'Amourre's arm and led her to the station wagon. She knew that everybody was watching how she had a real famous movie star in tow, and Ruby Bee could fume all she wanted, since her car was parked way down by the highway.

"So there've been five fires?" Anderson said. We'd broken into Ruby Bee's Bar & Grill (the key's on the ledge above the door), and were drinking coffee in the back booth. Yes, the dark one, even in the morning. Sunlight was not allowed to violate the ambience of the barroom. "Are you positive the one in your apartment was set by the same person? The style's quite different."

"It was a message," I said with a sigh. "I know who's setting them, and he knows that I know—if you follow that. The investigator at the state police barracks is going to see what he can find out about Billy Dick MacNamara's history in Farberville. I won't be surprised to learn he's been in trouble before, or at least suspected of being involved. In the meantime, all I can do is try to catch him with matches in his hand."

"Can't you get assistance?" Anderson said, taking my hand in his, although not, I assumed, to determine if I was holding a book of matches.

"I talked to the sheriff, who squawked and snorted as he always does, then lapsed into his lament about his shortage of manpower. He has a point. We can't stake out every old building in the county on an indefinite basis."

"Can you tail the boy at night?"

"I can try, but I doubt it'll do any good." I smiled at him, trying not to let myself linger too long on his lovely eyes and talented lips. "You like this, don't you?

A little real-life drama after all those years of cinematic fantasy?''

To my surprise (okay, dismay), he let go of my hand and leaned back against the partition. ''There's something I need to tell you,'' he said in an odd voice. ''Or then again, maybe I don't. It has to do with my wife.''

The door opened, and Carlotta came across the barroom. She was dressed neatly, but her hair was not its usual tidy cap, and her bloodless fingers were clutching the clipboard as if rigor had set in. ''I'm glad I found you, Chief Hanks. Kitty and Buddy missed their call this morning, and I'm afraid there's something wrong in #5. Do you know where Ruby Bee keeps a second set of keys?''

I was still reeling from the word ''wife,'' and her agitation wasn't helping. ''Why do you think there's something wrong?''

''The breakfast tray hasn't been touched, and no one answered when I pounded on the door. Have you seen either of them, Anderson?''

''Not since early last night. They were here when I went back to my room.''

''Maybe they went into Farberville,'' I suggested. I should have been struggling to my feet while trying to remember where Ruby Bee kept the keys, but I actually wanted her to go away so that Anderson and I could continue our conversation. Married, huh? No big deal. We weren't in the midst of a torrid affair. And not necessarily destined to be so. On the other hand, Plover's complacency was wearing thin, and it wouldn't hurt to give him something to think about, presuming he noticed.

Carlotta shook her head. ''They have no transportation. The van and the rental car are both at the site. Do you mind finding the keys?''

I went behind the bar and opened the drawer below

the cash register. It was a miser's nest of stubby pencils, pens, string, rubber bands, receipts, invoices, IOU's, and more than a dozen keys, ranging from shiny ones to rusty, old-fashioned ones that probably locked buggy doors.

"Did they say anything last night?" Carlotta asked Anderson.

"Buddy was having a great time with the locals," he said slowly, gazing at the dim room as if he could replay the evening in his mind. "He told me he'd grown up in a town like this and still got a kick out of the colloquialisms and rural rituals. He had the accent down pat."

I grabbed all the keys that weren't out of the question and went across the dance floor. "They're unmarked, but some of them are likely to be the ones for the motel room doors."

We hurried out to the parking lot. As we approached #5, I spotted flies buzzing above a tray covered with a napkin, and abruptly I felt as uneasy as Carlotta obviously did. Anderson had pointed the couple out to me the night we'd had beers. Neither of them looked especially spacy. Had Gwenneth or the one called Fuzzy taken a hike, I wouldn't have thought twice about it.

I handed all but one key to Carlotta and tried it. We'd gone through most of them when the lock clicked. I opened the door a few inches, but none of us made a sudden rush through the door.

"Buddy? Kitty?" Carlotta called hesitantly.

I bit my lip as I pushed the door all the way back and ordered myself to step into the room. There were two suitcases in the corner, and a shirt draped over the back of a chair. The swaybacked bed was made neatly enough to pass inspection. A couple of liquor bottles were on the dresser next to glasses and an ice bucket.

"That's her purse," Carlotta whispered from behind me.

I swallowed several times. "Maybe they went across the road to the supermarket, or went for a walk."

"Not them," Anderson said, also behind me and envincing no desire to come any farther. "They knew the schedule. The budget's too tight to waste time. Hal's watch doesn't have a minute hand; it has a dollar sign."

I opened the curtain and took a harder look at the room. They clearly weren't here, and if there'd been a struggle, it had been of a genteel variety. "I guess I'd better check the bathroom," I said under my breath. No one offered to save me the trouble, so I walked across the room and tapped on the door. "Anyone in there?"

My voice was on the squeaky side, but it was loud enough to be heard through the plywood door. I glanced back at Anderson and Carlotta, who looked as if they were waiting for me to step on into the lion's den.

Gritting my teeth, I opened the door.

Brother Verber picked his way along the bank of the creek. With each step, his shoes sucked in the mud and threatened to send him into the shallow, scummy water of Boone Creek. He sat down on a log and wiped his forehead and neck, then wasted a few minutes trying to figure out how much farther it was to Raz's cabin.

Everybody else either had driven there and battled to find a place to park, or had walked up the road. He could have approached that way, too—if he didn't mind everybody knowing his business. The problem was, his business was spiritual guidance. His duty was to lead an unsullied Christian life. Therefore his goal was to sneak up from the flank and have a quiet gander at what the Hollywood folks were doing inside the cabin, and in broad daylight.

He mopped a little more, then stuffed his handkerchief in his pocket and stood up. Waving irritably at the cloud of gnats (God's own little creations, but annoying just the same), he trudged along until he came to the backside of Raz's barn.

An emaciated hound barked at him as he made his way up the bank and into the shade of the barn. The ground was littered with broken glass, cans, wads of paper, and tendrils of wire that tried to snake around his legs. He moved to the corner and peeked around it to assess his chances of making it to the back of the shack without being spotted by some vigilant member of his flock. He could hear car doors slamming and folks greeting each other, but, perhaps due to his preliminary prayers to that effect, the cabin and scruffy growth around it blocked out the view of the road.

The back door opened. Raz came outside, spat in the dust, and turned back to speak to someone inside. Shortly thereafter, Marjorie strolled through the doorway, gave Raz a sullen look, and plopped down in a fresh-looking puddle of mud in the middle of the yard.

"It ain't that bad," Raz said. "You got a nice spot, and the sun's shining. No, don't you go and give me that look, Marjorie. I dun told you how we didn't have no choice, unless you want to start dining on them budget frozen dinners. I cain't have Arly sniffing around up past Robin's cabin and stumbling onto the still." He went back inside.

Brother Verber warily eyed the sow. Like the pesky gnats, it was one of God's own creations, but it weighed quite a bit more and had evil pink eyes. Drool hung out of its mouth like a silver ribbon, and its snout was wet.

Then again, he'd never heard anybody tell of a death by sullen sow, so he reckoned it hadn't ever happened.

He stayed by the barn, however, and was real glad he had when one of the actors came outside, went over to a window, and knocked on the pane. Which didn't make any sense to Brother Verber. If the boy wanted in, why'd he go out in the first place?

He was scratching his head when there was movement inside the room. The actor fellow opened the window, then closed it and stood there with his arms crossed. A minute later the first half of the process was repeated, but this time a voice inside said, "No, sweetheart, over here by the mirror. Carlotta drew the chalk mark for you; all you have to do is find it."

Brother Verber caught a glimpse of white flesh as someone inside the room crossed in front of the window. He wasn't one hundred percent sure he saw what he thought he saw, but it was enough to make him start sweatin' like a hog (not a fair analogy; the part of Marjorie not in the mud was dry).

The window was closed from the inside. The actor turned around, but Brother Verber had anticipated it and had retreated prudently. He held his breath and waited several minutes, just to be on the safe side, before he peered once again around the corner of the barn.

The actor fellow tapped on the window—for the third time, mind you—and opened it. With the ease of a panther, he climbed over the sill and disappeared into the room. Brother Verber would have given the contents of the collection plate to starving orphans to be in that room, but he settled for sneaking along the fence to the back of the house, then edging across the porch to the open window, the sill of which was five feet off the ground.

He got centered under it and was about to take a peek

when he heard a man say, "I got a plan, Loretta. We can get away from this filthy town and start a new life together. You'd like that, wouldn't you? Then I could do this . . . and this . . . all the time."

This . . . and this? Brother Verber didn't know what they all were doing, but it seemed to involve a lot of heavy breathing and moaning—two sure signals that Satan was on the loose in Maggody. The thing was, he needed to know for certain that his suspicions were right, and the only way to do it was to take a look for himself, even if it meant going eyeball-to-eyeball with Satan.

Brother Verber straightened up inch by inch, and kept going until his eyes were a fraction above the sill. Lights glared from several spots. The camera was in the middle of the room; the man hunched behind it wore a fatigue jacket. Another man stood behind him, a cigarette between his lips, a canvas hat on his head, a jar in his hand, and a bored expression on his face. The action was on the bed.

Some folks might have ducked in order to avoid being confronted by Satan's handiwork (and in broad daylight). Brother Verber couldn't have moved if he'd been stung in the rear by a yellow jacket, or even a hornet. The stain under his armpits was spreading like an oil slick, and his nose was pressed so hard against the rough wood that he'd be obliged to doctor it later with ointment.

Satan was outdoin' himself.

The actor on the bed stood up, exposing even more of the handiwork and thus giving Brother Verber a particular physical problem that he was grateful no one was around to observe.

Before he could get ahold of himself, figuratively speaking, the actor took a step toward the window and said, "I'll figure out a plan. I'll get a message to you . . . somehow or other."

The bare-breasted woman fluttered her fingers in farewell.

"Cut," said the man in the hat.

The woman sat up and reached for a shirt. "This mattress must be filled with beer cans. I'm going to have horrible red marks all over my butt."

"Poor little butterfly," the actor said in a smirky voice.

"Come along, my lust bunnies," the man in the hat said. "At least we've got one scene wrapped."

The man behind the camera fiddled with a knob, then said, "Well, we would if it hadn't been for the pop-eyed pervert in the window."

Brother Verber wondered to whom they were referrin'.

Chapter 8

Sergeant Plover was the first to arrive in the parking lot, although the dispatcher had promised to have the sheriff and his men on the way as soon as she tracked them down at a convenience store outside of Starley City. I was waiting by the door of #5, doing my best not to think about what I'd seen in the pink-tiled bathroom not fifteen feet behind me. I'd told Anderson and Carlotta to wait in Ruby Bee's, and they'd gone so briskly that dust still hovered.

"Are you all right?" Plover asked me as he strode across the gravel.

"On the queasy side, but on my feet," I admitted. "You'd better take a few breaths before you go in there. The bathroom looks as if it's spattered with paint. The window's open, so there are a lot of flies." I swallowed several times, fighting back the image of eyes frozen with terror and a mouth contorted with pain. "It's really bad, Plover."

He winced. "You stay here and direct traffic. The boys from the barracks should show up within a few minutes."

I wasn't about to charge back in there, so I crammed

my fists in my pocket and waited for what felt like the better part of a year. It was as quiet as dawn in a cemetery, I realized. The vast majority of those who generally cluttered up the town were at the movie site, no doubt expressing their opinions and praying they'd be "discovered" by a real-life Hollywood director, who obligingly would propel them into stardom. There was very little traffic; on a normal morning, subcompacts converged on the SuperSaver, pickups on Ruby Bee's, and RV's with out-of-state license plates and exotic decals on Roy Stivers's antiques store.

Plover returned, his face ashen. "You're right—it's really bad," he said. "Who was she?"

"An actress named Kitty Kaye. I didn't recognize her, but Ruby Bee told me she'd made a lot of movies in the fifties. She was married to Buddy Meredith, another of the actors. They were sharing the room."

"Where's he?"

A symphony of sirens and flashing lights disrupted the peculiar serenity. The sheriff's vehicles began to descend on us, along with the technical team from the state police. An ambulance followed mutely. I waited until the sirens whined into silence, then explained how Carlotta had returned from the site to look for the couple, who were supposed to be at Raz's cabin.

"She came to the PD?"

"No, I was in Ruby Bee's, drinking coffee with one of the actors who wasn't needed this morning."

Plover's mouth tightened for a moment, and he gave me a look with Siberian overtones. "It was fortunate that she found you, wasn't it?" He turned around and went to the vehicles, leaving me to guard the scene all by myself.

The sheriff was chewing on a cold cigar stub as he joined me. "We'd better round up all the Hollywood folks. Where are they, and how many of them are there?''

I did a tally. "Eight, altogether. Two of them were with me when I . . . found the body, and they're inside Ruby Bee's. With the exception of the missing husband, the rest of them are at Raz Buchanon's shack, under the benign supervision of most everybody in Maggody and a decent contigency from nearby towns."

"Guess we'd better fetch 'em," Harve said. He eyed the door, then made a face at me and said, "What am I going to have the privilege of lookin' at, Arly? The dispatcher said you were a might sputtery about the details when you called."

"A woman, who's been cut with something very sharp. Blood on the floor, the walls, the fixtures, the ceiling, and whatever I've missed. The word 'whore' written in blood on the mirror above the sink." My stomach twisted, and I had to hold Harve's arm to steady myself. "It's straight out of some dreadful slasher movie."

"Tell ya what, Arly—you look like you need to hunker in the bunker for a spell. Go over to the barroom and have yourself a cup of coffee. We'll use that as a command post for the time bein', so you might want to get back to the dispatcher and give her the telephone number. I'll send somebody else to fetch the Hollywood folks. We'll just tell them there's been a little accident."

"A little accident, Harve?"

"Then again, I could send a deputy up there with the siren blaring and the lights flashing. He could jump out of the car, flip on the bullhorn, and broadcast to everybody east of Cotter's Ridge that a woman was brutally murdered in #5 of the Flamingo Motel. He could tell them how she was all cut up and that her husband mysteriously disappeared before the police showed up. No,

let's make that before Chief of Police Arly Hanks
showed up. Then he can invite everybody down to
look for themselves, and we make a bundle selling tickets at the door.''

"You've got undeniable talent, Harve. I'll see if I can
arrange for you to appear at the Stump County Im-
prov.''

He gave me a sober look. "It's gonna be a gawdawful
mess, no matter how much we try to clamp a lid on
it.''

"It's already a gawdawful mess," I said as I headed
for Ruby Bee's.

"This is outrageous," Mrs. Jim Bob said to Perkins's
eldest, who was running the vacuum cleaner around
the living-room carpet and couldn't hear a word over
the roar. "Jim Bob was quite sure they intended to utilize the house this very morning, despite the fact Carlotta told me that they wouldn't be here until
tomorrow, or even the next day. Carlotta's the assistant
director, for your information, and she seemed very
efficient—in a brusque fashion. I did my charitable best
not to be offended that the real director didn't call on
me, but she said he was in his room doing revisions on
the script. She said he works in creative spurts and was
real sorry he couldn't come by.''

Perkins's eldest zeroed in on a ball of lint behind the
divan.

Mrs. Jim Bob looked at her watch for not the first
time in the last five minutes. The house was reasonably
cool, but she was beginning to feel a bit damp, dressed
as she was in her blue satin dress, modest slip, girdle,
and stockings (pantyhose being the work of the Devil).
She took off her white gloves and placed them on the

coffee table, where she could get to them real quick when the movie crew arrived.

"What's more irritating," she continued over the noise of the vacuum cleaning, "is that every last soul in town is out gallivanting around. Lottie didn't say one word to me about having errands, but it's possible she has an appointment with some doctor and didn't want to mention it."

She graciously lifted her feet as Perkins's eldest worked her way around the front of the divan. "I must say I'm surprised Brother Verber is not in the rectory. He usually devotes his mornings to his sermons, which I think is a very Christian thing to do, don't you? That way he's also available should any sinners feel the need for a counseling session, or even for a dose of prayer for the wickedness of their ways. I must say, some folks in this town are courting eternal damnation, including some in this room who miss church on a regular basis."

She settled her feet back down and frowned at Perkins's eldest's backside. "But he doesn't answer the telephone, which is vexing. Where do you suppose he's at? Never mind, I think I'll have a cup of tea." She headed for the kitchen, the gloves in her hand just in case.

Perkins's eldest finished, unplugged the vacuum cleaner, and carried it toward the hall closet, wondering (but only vaguely) what all Mrs. Jim Bob had been shouting about.

Darla Jean McIlhaney took the sheet off the line and folded it carefully, despite the fact that she was thinking hard about the previous evening—which had stretched well past midnight. If her parents had caught her sneaking up the stairs, she'd have been grounded until her hair turned gray and her teeth fell out.

But her pa had been snoring like a brush hog, and her ma hadn't popped out into the hall, carrying the alarm clock and acting like Darla Jean was a naughty little kid. Thank God.

She knew Heather was pissed at her, but she didn't give a rat's ass 'cause she had more important things to worry about. Like what had happened between her and Frederick Marland. And if there was anyway anybody could find out, as long as the two of them didn't tell.

Short of someone noticing her ma's car at the motel, she felt pretty sure she was safe. Maybe. She dropped the sheet in the basket and sat down in the grass to sniffle and sigh.

I called the dispatcher, and then took coffee to Carlotta and Anderson, both of whom were too stunned to do anything except stare at the scarred Formica.

"The sheriff sent a deputy to bring back the others," I said.

"This is going to turn into a media circus," Carlotta said with a grimace. "Once it gets out that the formerly renowned Miss Kitty Kaye has been murdered on location by a knife-wielding maniac, we'll have a parking lot full of reporters. Those tabloid leeches love this kind of thing; they'll suck everyone in town dry."

Anderson's hand shook as he took a sip of coffee. "And what a wonderful time they'll have once it's known I was in the next room. I don't think I can handle it, Carlotta. If I knew where Buddy was, I'd do my damndest to join him." His voice was no longer melodious; it was flat. His features seemed less sculpted, and his perfect hair was mussed, most likely because he was running his fingers through it every other word.

"There won't be any way to finish the movie," Carlotta said in an equally flat voice. "We might as well donate the money to the town to erect a statue of Hal. And we're not talking a couple of thou—"

"Damn it! What about me?"

I frowned at him. "What about you?"

The two looked at each other. I couldn't tap into this unspoken conversation, but I was picking up on mutual wariness and a great deal of calculation. "Well?" I said irritably.

"Go ahead and tell her," Carlotta said. "Odds are we'll make the nightly news, and they won't mind digging through the old files to see what they can find about every one of us. I'm going to get a beer before all hell breaks loose."

Anderson took his sweet time selecting his words, but eventually he looked up and said, "It happened a year ago. I was on location doing a movie, a Glittertown epic that sank more quickly than the *Andrea Doria*. After the wrap, I drove home with a bottle of champagne. My wife's body was in the bathroom. She'd been slashed to ribbons, and there were profanities on the wall—written in her blood."

For the second time in less than an hour, I felt as though I'd been clipped by a chicken truck. "I didn't see anything about it in the newspapers," I managed to say. "I'm sorry, Anderson."

"The police decided to keep the gorier details from the media. They were concerned that it might give our resident loonies ideas. Southern California has a lot of them, some of whom are always on the lookout for inspiration. One of the tabloids picked it up, but the police insisted it was a simple burglary gone awry. A Charlie Manson-style murder is newsworthy; a house-

wife who interrupts a burglar is fairly standard stuff in
L.A. It was buried in the back of the newspaper, alongside the usual quota of gang shootings and domestic
fatalities.''

"Did they ever arrest anyone?"

"They pulled in a few of their favorite psychotics,
but they never found the guy. After a couple of weeks,
they told me they doubted they'd find him unless he
killed again.''

"There was only one person?"

"That's what they thought. He did a very thorough
job all by himself.''

"And you found the body? That must have been—"

"It certainly was," he said with a thin attempt at a
smile. "Pamela and I had been married for a long time.
Things weren't always blissful, but we were working
on it.''

I was searching for something to say when the door
opened and Hal Desmond strode into the room. "Yo,
Carlotta, make a note. We're going to rewrite twenty-
four, and then use this fat guy as comic relief later in
the woods scene. You are going to expire when you
see the footage. It's like we've added the clown in that
Shakespearean play with all the faggots. Now, what's
this shit about an accident? Somebody break a finger-
nail?"

All sorts of other people came in, sparing Carlotta
from an answer, although I did see her obediently make
a note on her clipboard. Plover barked at Hal to sit
down and shut up, and when he had everybody settled
in adjoining booths, gave them a terse explanation of
what we'd found in #5.

Gwenneth shrieked and collapsed against Frederick,
who put his arm around her and muttered a few curse
words. Hal glared at Carlotta as if she were responsible
for any delays that might occur. The only one of the

company who seemed unperturbed was Fuzzy, who took off his glasses and cleaned them on his shirt, then settled them back into place and waited with an unfocused expression.

Hal was the first to recover. "Jesus, I hate this! This is friggin' terrible. Poor Kitty and I have been close, close friends for years. God knows I loved that woman, I really did. I was the one who brought her out of retirement and put her back on the screen where she belonged. Where's Buddy? How's he taking it?"

"We don't know where he is," Plover said. "We're hoping one of you might have a suggestion. As far as we know, he's on foot. We would like very much to locate him so we can inform him about his wife."

"You don't think he had anything to do with it?" Carlotta said. "They were devoted. She refused to do any films that didn't have a part for Buddy."

"Yeah, they really were a great couple," Gwenneth added, having regained consciousness nicely. "Just yesterday Kitty and I were sunbathing out there, and she was—"

"Right," Hal interrupted. "Look, officer, we're all really shook up about this. She and all the members of our team are like family, if you know what I mean. As the father figure, I've encouraged them to bring their problems to me, and lemme tell you—nothing was ever too large or too small for Hal Desmond to take care of, from parking tickets to DWI's." He wiped his eyes and gave us a mournful look. "Kitty was one classy dame, maybe the classiest I've ever met. I know she'd want us to continue shooting *Wild Cherry Wine* as a tribute to her, so if we're finished here, Carlotta and I have some heavy-duty revisions to do on the script."

Plover's jaw dropped, and behind him the other officers gaped as if Hal had sprouted horns. Having been exposed to the man, I wasn't nearly as shocked. Appalled might be a more apt description.

"I don't think we're finished, Hal," Carlotta murmured.

Hal shrugged, his palms turned up as if to check for rain. "Hey, no problem. We do need to get a handle on what's likely to be a media madhouse. There's no way we can make the film if we've got reporters crawling on us like—like—I don't know, fleas or something. We chose this town because we didn't want a lot of publicity during the shooting. Glittertown prides itself on being on the road home before anyone notices we've even arrived."

"We noticed," Plover said weakly. I could see he was struggling to be a stainless steel cop, but was not succeeding in the face of Hal's outlandish behavior.

Taking pity on him, I stood up and said, "Harve, why don't you send out whatever patrol cars you've got to search for Meredith? Carlotta may have photographs of him. Sergeant Plover and I will take the initial statements, and I'll report to you when we're done."

Harve recoiled as if I'd pulled my .38 on him. "To me? Hell, Arly, I ain't got the time nor the expertise to deal with this. I had a Grab 'n' Go robbery about an hour ago, the clerk and two customers shot. Last night we had a nasty domestic spat that landed the poor woman in the hospital, a stabbing out behind a bar, and a report of Nazis in some widow's attic. You and Plover can have this one all for yourselves." He avoided looking at me as he fired up a cigar butt. "But I'm gonna do everything I can to help. I'll send everybody I can out to look for the missing person, and maybe I can ease the burden by putting a man on the arson case—for a day or two."

"Arson?" Gwenneth squealed. "If we're not stabbed

in the bathroom, are we going to be burned to death in our beds?''

Frederick patted her arm. ''Where there's smoke, there's fire, and you certainly smoke in bed.''

''Didn't know you smoked,'' Fuzzy said, then hiccuped and grinned at me like a drunken leprechaun.

Carlotta offered to fetch a photograph of our missing person. Anderson was drawing circles on the tabletop with his finger, and Gwenneth was hissing at her leading man.

I wanted to apply my foot to Harve's fanny, but I doubted it would do anything more than bruise my toes. ''All right,'' I growled, ''a man on the arson case for three days. More if I need him.''

''You bet,'' he said blandly. He shooed his men out the door and kept on going.

Plover was still on the dance floor, studying the Hollywood people as if they were members of a new and potentially dangerous species. I went over to him and said, ''Shall we interview them as a group, or drag them off to the dungeon one at a time?''

''Beats me. These people are unreal, and nothing in my training's going to help. Two of my men are dusting for prints, the photographer's taking shots of the body—and that guy wants to know if we're finished so he can revise his script! Does this sort of thing happen on a regular basis when he makes a movie? Seems like the actors might be reluctant to work for him—''

''Calm down,'' I said. ''Is the coroner here?''

''Yeah. He took a preliminary look at the body and, with some prodding, said it's likely she's been dead for as long as twelve hours.''

''She and Meredith were here until ten o'clock, and then left for their room. So we're talking between then and midnight, more or less. Station a man in the motel parking lot, and we can take statements in my office.''

When he didn't answer, I glanced up at him and realized he was staring over my shoulder, an unfathomable expression on his face. "What's wrong? Do you have an idea about this mess?"

"No," he said slowly, "I was just trying to sort out these characters. Let's start with the girl in the shorts, shall we?"

He wasn't referring to Carlotta.

"Where do you get off saying I can't go inside my own establishment?" Ruby Bee demanded, her cheeks the color of the exterior walls and getting rosier by the word. "I own the building and I pay taxes every year like a law-abidin' citizen."

"Sorry, ma'am," the trooper said. Because of the mirrored sunglasses, she couldn't judge his eyes, but he didn't sound like he was aiming to burst into tears anytime soon.

"Then you can just tell me what all's going on at the motel. I own that, too, and I have a right to know why all those police cars are back there. And if that's not an ambulance, then I'm not standing here in the parking lot being denied admission to my own establishment!"

"The area stays blocked off until I'm told otherwise," the trooper countered. "I'm under orders not to divulge anything else, ma'am."

Despite his disguise, Ruby Bee pegged him. "You come by on Fridays at noon, don't you? You and that man with the unfortunate warts on his hands, both of you real fond of having a couple of beers and the blue-plate special?"

"Yes, ma'am. Don't tell my wife, but you make the best fried chicken in the whole damn county."

"You planning to come next Friday?"

"Yes, ma'am."

"For chicken, scalloped potatoes, butterball beans, okra, biscuits and gravy, and a wedge of peach cobbler with vanilla ice cream?"

He nodded, looking downright miserable for someone in such a fine uniform and mirrored sunglasses.

"Well, then," Ruby Bee said, bearing down on him, "I think you'd better tell me what's going on inside my establishment and out back in the motel. Otherwise, come Friday you can have yourself a burrito in a cellophane wrapper at the supermarket."

Kevin was sorely disappointed when all the Hollywood folks packed up and left, as if they'd finished the movie without allowing his betrothed to be a star. From the grim look on her face and the rumbling deep in her throat, he could tell she wasn't entertaining happy thoughts, herself.

They were sitting on her porch, watching everybody straggle down the road with their picnic baskets and coolers, most of them subdued, since no one had a clue why the deputy had sent the Hollywood folks away. Lottie Estes had gone so far as to knock on Raz's door to ask him, but he didn't answer. As she and Eula walked toward her car, they'd agreed that thus far watching a movie bein' made was on the boring side. Well, the girl had been dressed like Daisy Mae, and the director had used a lot of un-Christian-like language, but for the most part, they'd wasted half the morning staring at the front of Raz's shack.

Heather and Traci were disappointed, too. They'd been hoping there would be a crowd scene requiring teenage girls, which is why they'd both gotten up early to spend more than an hour spraying and moussing their hair. The light breeze stirred nary a hair on either head; a hailstorm would have met with an equal lack of success.

"You wanna see if Darla Jean wants to go to the Dee-Lishus?" asked Traci.

"She could have taken down all the laundry in the county by now," Heather said. "Now, let's not jump on her and demand to know what happened between her and that hunk. We'll be real casual about it. Don't even mention Frederick Marland's name—okay?"

Traci solemnly vowed not to say a word.

Millicent McIlhaney was having to drag her husband back to the car, in that he was still overwhelmed by being in the presence of Hollywood folks. As they caught up with the girls, she tapped Heather on the shoulder. "Did you and Darla Jean enjoy the picture show last night?"

"Yes, ma'am," Heather said promptly.

"What time did y'all get back from Farberville?"

Heather glanced at Traci, who was being no help whatsoever. "I dunno. We went for ice cream and ended up sitting there for the longest time, talking about the upcoming junior class picnic."

"I'm glad to hear you had a nice time," Millicent said as she urged Earl into motion. "Real glad."

"Thank you, ma'am," Heather said. She didn't jab tongue-tied Traci in the ribs, but she thought about it.

Back on the porch, Kevin decided to risk it all. "That was kinda funny how they left like that, wasn't it?"

"Funny as in ha-ha, or funny as in Mrs. Wockerman listening to aliens through her hearing aid?" Dahlia said with an ominous look. "What kind of funny are you referring to?"

Kevin wished he knew.

On another porch on the opposite side of town, Billy Dick MacNamara handed Willard Yarrow a bottle of grape soda pop and sat down on the top step beside him.

"My parents are going to the hospital tonight," Willard said. "Trudi's got a date with some jock. You want to come over and play the game? I'll get some chips and stuff."

"What's his name?"

Willard blinked. "The jock? I dunno. He's hairier than a summer groundhog, and his head kinda rests on his shoulders. I snuck up on 'em once when they were sitting in his car. Trudi's darn lucky it was me instead of Pa, 'cause he would have whipped her silly and packed her off to reform school."

"What were they doing?" Billy Dick asked.

"Oh, you know," he said, taking a drink to hide his discomfort. "Hey, I worked half the night on my map, and I've got a real good idea how to get by the dragon and find the diamond mines of Exedor."

He prattled on about magic potions and the sword bought from the gnomes with the last of the gold stolen from the griffin, but Billy Dick wasn't listening.

"Listen, please," I said after Plover and I'd agreed on the procedure, "all of you need to wait in your rooms out back. Sergeant Plover will station a man in the parking lot to make sure you're not disturbed, and we'll escort you one at a time to the police department just down the road."

Hal slid off a stool and came across the room. "Arly, sweetheart, let me run this by you."

He handed me a piece of paper. I scanned it quickly, then read it aloud for Plover's edification. "Mrs. Katherine Meredith of Van Nuys, California, was found dead in a motel room during a vacation to the Ozarks. The police have determined that she slipped and fell while bathing. She is survived by her husband, B. Meredith. A private ceremony will be held in Van Nuys."

Hal was waiting eagerly. "Not shabby, huh? No one's going to make the leap from Mrs. Katherine Meredith to Miss Kitty Kaye, and B. Meredith's hardly a household name. You just type this up for the local paper and run off copies in case someone comes snooping from outside."

"Slipped and fell while bathing?" I said.

"I know, I know. It's an understatement, but it's still cinema verité, if you follow me. You're not going to tell me she didn't slip and fall at some point while this maniac was attacking her, are you?"

Carlotta joined us. "You don't want a horde of reporters any more than we do. Unless something along the lines of World War III starts today, the media may decided to grab this one and run with it until they drop. Kitty was a very sexy leading lady in the fifties, and her films are in the classics section of every video rental store in the country. Her autobiography sold well ten years ago, and a few years back there was a Kitty Kaye festival at one of the theaters in L.A."

"Kitty was a class act," Hal cut in, wiping at more of those invisible tears. "You know, Carlotta, somewhere in the credits we ought to stick in a dedication. Figure something out and let me look at it."

Plover found his voice. "You want us to say she slipped and fell in the bathroom?"

"It sounds better than saying she was attacked by a

local psychotic," Hal said, lighting a cigarette. "It's your neck of the woods. You want everyone in the country to think you're a bunch of murderers, feel free. It's not going to do much for the tourist trade, though."

I grabbed Plover's arm and propelled him to a corner. "It's not outrageous," I muttered. "Carlotta may be right about the zillion reporters descending on us. We're going to have a tough enough time sorting through this without television vans surrounding the PD and reporters screaming at us. At this point, only these people and the guys in the parking lot know what took place inside number five. I think we ought to hush it up, at least for a few days."

We argued for a while, but he finally relented and we left the barroom, content in the knowledge that no one else knew that Kitty Kaye had been murdered.

Chapter 9

24   CONTINUED:

> LORETTA
>
> O my Gawd . . . that was Preacher Pipkin! He must have seen everything! What if he says something?

> BILLY JOE
>
> He's a filthy pervert, that preacher man! If he hadn't run away like a yeller-striped skunk, I'd have punched him so hard he'd be harking the herald angels.

> LORETTA
>
> But what are we gonna do, Billy Joe? What are we gonna do?

> BILLY JOE
> (harshly)
>
> We're gonna get out of this town somehow. You just wait for that message, you hear?

CUT TO:

"My real name," Gwenneth D'Amourre murmured, nibbling on her scarlet lipstick. "What if it *is* my real name?"

She was in the chair opposite my desk, and Plover, always a gentleman, had dragged in a chair from the other room and was straddling it, his arms on the top of the back and his chin resting on them. The attentive gleam in his eye was unnerving me, although its recipient seemed to be undisturbed by it.

I tapped my pencil. "I need your real name for the record. I may still clap when Tinkerbell nears death, but I have this sneaky suspicion that D'Amourre is a stage name."

She glanced at Plover for help, but when he gazed back blandly, she took a last bite of lipstick and said, "Wanda Sue Thackett. It didn't seem to ripple, you know; it gurgled like dirty old bathwater going down the drain. Hal thought up my new name, and I think it's totally terrific."

"Me, too," I said as I wrote down the gurgly one. "Your current address?"

She rattled off an answer that included an apartment number. "It's very close to Beverly Hills," she added.

"And you're originally from . . . ?"

"Chicago."

"Age?"

Apparently this was a bit of a poser. I waited silently while she decided how gullible I was. The remark about Tinkerbell was probably a factor. "Twenty-two," she said with a hopeful look, then sighed. "Okay, twenty-four, but all my promo stuff says twenty, so don't spread it around."

"How long have you been associated with Glitter-town Productions?"

She wiggled in the chair, then resorted to counting on her fingers. "Well, there was *Satan's Sisters,* in which I played a whattaya call it—a novice, a beginner nun. Frederick was the handsome young priest. My father makes me join the convent, and at first I have to toil in the fields, but then—"

"We don't need the plot," I said quickly.

"It was very artistic, and one of the reviews said I looked celestial. Anyway, my second film was *Tanya Makes the Team.* In that one, I was a cheerleader who's willing to do anything she can to help her team win the championship."

Plover began to cough, and when he couldn't stop, flapped his hand at us and stumbled into the back room. I was surprised when I heard the door slam, but he was old enough to come and go as he pleased. I looked at Gwenneth. "And then?"

"Frederick's the quarterback, and Buddy's the kindly old coach who's lost his nerve. I decide to—"

"No, that's not what I meant. You've done other films?"

She crossed her legs and gave me a pitying look. "I am becoming a major force in the genre, and I'm in demand all the time. Last spring we did *Prickly Passion* in Flagstaff. Now, there's a nice town, with all kinds of shops and a great pool at the motel. I just soaked in the sun with . . . Kitty." She took a tissue from her purse, daintily blew her nose, and then took out a compact. Once she'd powdered her nose and carefully relined her lips in scarlet, she said, "I'm sorry, but I kinda had a crush on Kitty, if you know what I mean. She was real sweet to me and gave me a lot of advice about how to handle some of the animals in Hollywood. You would not believe the things that have been whispered in my ear about two seconds after I've been introduced to some guy in a silk shirt and alligator shoes."

"And *Prickly Passion* was the last movie before this one? That was in the spring. You've done three movies with the company, and this was to be the fourth, right? I'm not clear how long you've been associated, though."

"About a year," she said.

"This is the fourth movie in a year?"

"We're all professionals. Hal arranges the finances, Carlotta does the preproduction, Fuzzy rolls the camera, and we make the damn thing." She took an emery board from her purse and began to file her nails.

"Tell me what you've been doing since you and the others arrived in Maggody two days ago," I said, trying not to react to the scritchy sound that always makes my teeth ache.

"We got here in the afternoon. I didn't notice what time because I don't wear a watch. I used to wear one, but it left this horrid white mark on my wrist and I—" She realized I was not enthralled. "Anyway, Carlotta and I are sharing number three, the one on the end next to Hal's room. We all had dinner in the barroom. Since there wasn't anything for the cast to do yesterday, Kitty and I took our scripts and went out to the parking lot to sunbathe."

"And last night?"

"Last night was the same. After the meeting, we had dinner in the barroom. I asked for a fresh shrimp salad with vinegar and oil on the side. I ended up with tuna fish."

"Wait a minute—what meeting?" I asked. I noticed I'd penciled in her dinner order, and crossed it out.

"The production meeting. Hal, Carlotta, and Fuzzy confirmed all the sites yesterday, which is why there wasn't anything for the rest of us to do except sun-bathe," she explained. Scritch, scritch.

"Buddy Meredith and Miss Kaye were at the meet-ing?" She nodded. "And then had dinner with the group at Ruby Bee's, right?" She nodded again. I made a note, then gave her my full attention, wishing Plover were back to help me ascertain the veracity (or lack thereof) of her statement. "What happened after din-ner, Miss D'Amourre?"

"I had a conversation with a gentleman named Jim Bob something. We discussed my career, of course, and he talked about some store he owns and how I could have a ten percent discount. I perked up until I realized he was talking paper towels and canned vegetables."

"And Meredith and Kaye?" I persisted.

She blinked at me for a long while. I couldn't tell if she was composing a lie or simply trying to remember what the two had done. "I think they stayed at the bar until about ten, but I may be wrong. Jim Bob was be-having like an octopus, if you catch my drift, and I had my hands full preventing him from having his hands full. I finally got tired of being mauled and went back to the room at eleven or so."

"Did you glance at the window of number five?"

Once again I was treated to a series of blinks and a blank look. "I think it was dark. Yeah, it was dark."

Plover reappeared before I could twist the thumbs-crews any tighter. He studied Gwenneth for a minute, then shook his head slightly and said, "If Miss D'Amourre has finished, I'll take her back to her room and pick up our next interviewee."

"I am simply exhausted," she said, on her feet more quickly than toast popping out of a toaster. "I had to get up really early to do my hair and makeup, and it took forever for Carlotta to help me squeeze into these shorts. I had to lie down on the bed and wiggle so hard I thought I'd pass out."

Plover nodded like a benevolent father confessor. "And how did the filming go this morning?"

She took his arm and herded him toward the door. "Very well, actually. We wrapped the scene on the first take, although for a minute it looked like we'd have to do it again. It's quite a strain for me to reflect genuine emotion over and over again, if you know what I mean."

"I certainly do," said Father Trooper.

The door closed.

I wasted a little time drawing little daggers that pierced Wanda Sue Thackett's name, not a technique I'd learned at the police academy but nevertheless obscurely satisfying. I then had to recopy my notes on a clean sheet of paper, since I had no desire to be categorized as a possessive, immature, unprofessional chief of police.

Les Vernon, one of Harve's deputies, parked out front. I hastily threw away the decorated (desecrated) paper and was busily scribbling notes when he came inside.

"Hey, Arly," he said as he sat down in the seat previously occupied by the illustrious Wanda Sue Thackett.

"How's it going, Les? Heard any dirty jokes lately?"

He had, and obligingly told them, but they weren't worth repeating and I'd already heard them, anyway. "Harve says you want me to poke around on this arson case," he said when the merriment died down.

I ran through what we had, then told him I was pretty much convinced Billy Dick MacNamara was our firebug, either alone or with Willard Yarrow as his apprentice. He agreed to check out the latter and to talk to the

elusive people who lived on the road near the scene of
the fire. When I suggested he tail Billy Dick when it got
dark, he politely countered that he was off at six and
planning to be at the bowling alley at six-thirty for a
tournament.

I doubted I could cajole Harve into assigning me a
second man. I sent Les on his errands and idled away
a solid five minutes wondering why it was taking Plover
so long to walk Wanda Sue Thackett a short way down
the road. She sure as hell hadn't shown any signs of
any sort of physical handicap; she was bursting out all
over with health, especially in the T-shirt area.

However, when he finally showed up with Carlotta,
I gave him a cool smile and settled her across from me.
We ran through the preliminary stuff: Carlotta Lowenstein, aged twenty-five, from Oakland, a degree in film
production and a year with Glittertown Productions.
Her residence may or may not have been near Beverly
Hills. Her account of their time in Maggody concurred
with Gwenneth's: the first evening in the barroom, the
next day inspecting sites, another evening drinking with
the locals, and the attempt that morning to get down
to business at Raz Buchanon's place.

"This is so bizarre," she said, shaking her head. "First
Anderson's wife, then poor Kitty. It's like there's a curse
on the company."

I gave a Plover a brief explanation of her reference
to Anderson's wife's murder, then chewed on my pencil while I formulated questions. "While they were in
Maggody, Meredith and Miss Kay never said or did anything that seemed odd?"

"Nothing. They were having a grand time, as far as I
could see. The script's less than demanding, and both
of them are pros. *Were* pros, I guess."

"What do you know about their relationship?"

"They've been married at least twenty years. According to her autobiography, they met right after Meredith moved to the Coast. Eyes locked across the room, hearts beating as one, the whole thing straight out of one of Kitty's early movies. But I've never heard any dirt about either of them, and I certainly don't think Buddy would tweak her nose, much less do something so vicious."

"And you don't have any idea where he might be now?" Plover inserted, most likely just to hear his own voice.

"No," she began, then stopped and frowned at a fly splat on the wall above my head.

I gave her a minute, but she finally shrugged and looked down at her clipboard. Before I could continue, Plover said, "If Kitty Kaye was so revered, why did she choose to work for Glittertown?"

"Was so revered thirty years ago," Carlotta corrected him. "Once actresses reach a certain age—and it's not much—they're offered only minor character roles. A few remain big names, but women like Kitty are replaced with women like Gwenneth, who will fizzle out in the same fashion. That's why I opted for the production end of the industry. It's safer, and although the money's not as astounding, the work's steady and the potential is there."

"Why did you choose Glittertown?" Plover said before I could jump in.

The two of them seemed to be communicating in the same way she had with Anderson, and once again I was excluded. I was not amused.

"For several reasons," she said thoughtfully. "The experience is good. I do almost all of the preproduction chores, except for financing and distribution. Hal's version of his reputation exceeds him, but he can bully himself into the right places to kiss the right asses."

"You actually wrote *Tanya Makes the Team?*" Plover said, sounding oddly awed.

She nodded. "To the last touchdown. Hal claims he does the writing, but I do most of it and allow him to take the screen credit. When I've pulled together enough cash, I'll start my own company and try another genre."

"Other than sports stories?" I said, admittedly to hear the sound of my own voice in my own office.

"Something a bit more *noir,*" she answered smoothly.

I decided to get back to the task at hand. "Have there been any problems within the group? Squabbles or bad feelings?"

Carlotta returned her attention to the fly splat on the wall. "Well, this is the fourth film with Frederick and Gwenneth. She's beginning to annoy him, and he needles her whenever he can simply to retaliate. He knows he has to put up with her because of his share of the profit, which is more lucrative than you'd suspect, and she does whatever Hal tells her to do. They're both new and, for the most part, unknown. Gwenneth's limited by a lack of talent, but Frederick's career might take off before too long."

I made a notation about Gwenneth's lack of talent. "What about Fuzzy?"

"He's been fired by every studio on the Coast. He takes whatever work he can get to sustain his haze. He's actually a fairly good cameraman when he's sober, so in addition to everything else I do, I pat him down before we start, confiscate his flask, and watch him like a pit bull until we quit for the day."

"Was he in Ruby Bee's last night?"

"After we ate, he said he had something to do and

left. Perhaps he'll be able to remember what it was, or perhaps not. He earned his nickname.''

I made a note to search his room for bloodied clothes. ''And you left at what time?''

''I'm not sure. About eleven or so, maybe earlier,'' she said, for the first time in the interrogation sounding a shade flustered.

''Did you and Gwenneth go to the room together?''

''I . . . ah, I went for a walk. There are times when I literally loathe the sight of these people, and this was one of them. I wandered around the parking lot and along the road. I returned to my room after an hour or so.''

It was challenging to envision this competent young woman with a knife in her hand, but it was equally challenging to think of anything she might have done the previous night worthy of a lie. Maggody is not known for its nightlife. The animal life at the pool hall wouldn't have interested her, and watching people struggle at the self-service pump couldn't have entertained her for long.

''I took a walk,'' she said, rising, ''that's all. I really must get back to Hal before he has some kind of creative seizure over the delay and the revisions. Obviously we'll have to delete Kitty's role, but I can handle that. I don't know what to do about Buddy's role. Our budget's too tight to sit for several days; the meter's running. I don't suppose you've heard anything . . . ?''

''Nothing,'' I said. ''We're operating on the premise that he and his wife returned to the room at ten o'clock. Meredith hasn't been seen since then, and according to you, has no transportation. He could have hitched a ride into one of the towns, or headed into the woods for some reason.''

''He wouldn't hurt Kitty,'' Carlotta said firmly. ''I think he was married once before, or merely entangled, but he was obsessed with Kitty. As I told you earlier, there's never been a rumor about either of them, and in this industry, that's damn amazing."

"Who next, Chief?" Plover said as he opened the door for Carlotta.

I considered the remaining members of the company: Hal, Fuzzy, Frederick, and Anderson. I decided I couldn't face the first three on an empty stomach, and that I needed to interrogate Anderson without Plover's presence, since he was behaving so childishly every time I glanced elsewhere. The two were waiting for a response, so I finally put down the pencil and said, "Let's grab some lunch at Ruby Bee's and tackle the others after we eat."

"There are approximately a thousand people at Ruby Bee's," Plover said. "We might end up eating breakfast, and only then if we make reservations."

"We agreed to keep the entire area off-limits. Who let her open up?" I said, resisting the urge to snatch up the pencil and snap it.

Plover asked Carlotta to wait outside, and as he turned back, his face was pink. "I did. It seems she knows every last detail of what happened in number five. Hell, she may know more than the rest of us. When I escorted Miss D'Amourre back to the motel, Ruby Bee grabbed me and explained the situation."

"The situation?" I said, mystified.

"The situation in which, if she wasn't allowed to open for lunch, she would tell everybody in town about the vicious murder and Meredith's disappearance. The television station in Farberville was mentioned, as was the minor expense of calling Little Rock to talk to the nice boys and girls at the *Gazette*."

His face was pink, but mine was heading for cerise. "How'd she find out?" I sputtered.

"She wouldn't tell me, but she wasn't bluffing. I told her she could open. The motel's cordoned off, but the parking lot in front of Ruby Bee's Bar & Grill was full by the time I left."

I almost apologized to the man. I'd been mentally accusing him of snuggling up to Gwenneth—when he'd been too busy being blackmailed by my mother.

"The way they do it is they finish one scene and race to the next location without even taking a breath," Jim Bob said. He stayed in the doorway, just in case his wife got too riled up, and he was regretting—seriously regretting—having come back to the house for lunch before he went to the supermarket.

"And the director told you that he would be here this morning?" Mrs. Jim Bob vowed to herself that if he took so much as one step inside the living room, she was going to hurl the crystal candy dish at him, even though it was piled with pastel mints and liable to make a mess on the pristine carpet.

"That's what he said," Jim Bob said as he edged backward. "But from what I heard at the store, they were over at Raz's and all of a sudden upped and went back to the motel."

"From what you heard at the store?"

Her tone was so icy that it was giving him goose bumps. Jim Bob edged on around the doorway into the kitchen, where he was safe from one of her beadiest, unblinkingest stares to date. "Yeah, at the store," he said loudly. "I'm going to fix myself a sandwich real quick and get back to work. The soda pop distributor's coming by in an hour or so. I need to do some figurin' before I order." He opened the refrigerator, but he was keeping at least one ear cocked, and he could hear a storm brewing in the living room.

"I called the store," came the first chilly wind.

"I must have been in the back. One of pipes in the break room busted, and I couldn't have employees going home every time they needed to pee."

"The girl who answered the phone looked back there for you. She assured me that she searched the entire store, including the employees' break room."

It was getting downright frigid now. Jim Bob eased the refrigerator door closed, tiptoed across the kitchen, and let himself out the back door before a glacier started down the hall. A sandwich from the store deli wasn't nearly as appealing as a leftover meat-loaf sandwich, but it would do in a pinch, and if this wasn't a pinch, he didn't know what was.

"There is no meat loaf," Mrs. Jim Bob said, aware of his penchant and taking a small amount of pleasure in her announcement. "I told Perkins's eldest to have it for her lunch. I am increasingly concerned about her. She's been positively moody lately, and I hope it's not because she's burdened by a heavy conscience."

She paused a moment to rest her voice, and then, in a spurt of Christian charity, said, "Have yourself some of that green bean casserole and a chicken leg. Now, I know for a fact that Perkins's eldest was seen drinking beer at Ruby Bee's, and making pathetic attempts to ingratiate herself with those Hollywood folks, although it's difficult to conceive of any reason why they'd be interested in someone so common. It's surely more dignified and proper to await them in one's own home rather than risk being seen in a place like that."

She took a sip of tea, which made her feel even more munificent. "Oh, go ahead and have that piece of pecan pie on the bottom shelf. I was thinking Brother Verber might come by, but he'll have to settle for store-bought cookies. Maybe I'll just call him to find out why he's been neglecting his duties.''

Having done her Christian duty to forgive him his most recent trespasses, she picked up the receiver and dialed.

Plover and I decided to dine on delicacies from the Dairee Dee-Lishus. Once he returned with greasy cheeseburgers and cherry limeades, we retreated to the back room to sit at the table.

"This Anderson St. James may be our man," Plover said as he unwrapped his burger and lifted the bun to study the few shreds of pale lettuce and a translucent slice of tomato.

I mimicked his motions while I considered his re-marks. "Why do you say that?" I asked ever so casu-ally.

"Pretty queer coincidence, his wife and then Kitty Kaye.''

"But he didn't murder his wife. He was on location and came home to discover her body. He wasn't even in town.''

Plover chewed this over for a while, then said, "The police never caught this so-called maniac. What if St. James came home, murdered his wife, and then notified the authorities?''

"The police there are so incompetent they failed to notice the wounds were still oozing and the body warm? Is that your assessment of a police department blessed with state-of-the-art equipment and training?'' I stuffed the cheeseburger in my mouth and chomped furiously. "This has onions, damn it. I told you I didn't want onions."

"Scrape 'em off," said amiable Sergeant Plover.

"I ought to scrape you off," I mumbled through a mouthful, not sure whether I hoped he heard me. I pushed the food aside. "Look, I'll call the L.A.P.D. and see what I can find out about the murder last year. There may well be a connection of some sort, but you seem awfully eager to nail Anderson St. James. There's been no suggestion that he has a motive."

"Thus far, no one has a motive—according to them, anyway. Gwenneth and Frederick squabble, Hal Desmond takes credit for Carlotta's writing, and Fuzzy drinks, but all of them are in it for the money. Murder's inconvenient because it screws up the schedule. Maybe it's a psycho off the highway who aspires to be in the movies. Maybe it's your pimply firebug."

I glumly picked up the cherry limeade and took a sip. "No, I can't see it. I'm convinced he's guilty, but he's been careful not to start any fires that might endanger someone. It's a big leap from burning down a shack to slashing a stranger like that, and that still doesn't explain what happened to Meredith."

"What about the fire in your apartment?"

"Merganser told you about that, did he? How loquacious of him, especially when I asked him not to say anything."

"I was wondering about that, too," Plover said, staring at me over the expanse of a poppyseed bun.

Although there was no smoke, things were beginning to warm up in the back room. I headed for the telephone in the front. "There're a lot of things about me that you don't need to know, Plover," I said from around the doorway.

"That you don't *want* me to know might be more accurate," he said mildly.

"That I don't want you to know." I picked up the receiver and began what I knew would be a tedious attempt to catch the right detective at the right precinct in a city of numerous million people.

"If you don't stop grinning like a mule eating briars, I'm gonna shake you so hard your hair uncurls," Estelle said, advancing across the kitchen.

"Keep it down," said Ruby Bee. She realized she was retreating and told herself to hold her ground before she got backed up against the sink. "It's an official police investigation, and I am under orders not to breathe a single word to anyone about what all happened." Losing her resolve, she dodged around the center island. "I got a whole roomful of hungry customers, and I got better things to do than play games with you. I told you: I crossed my heart and hoped to die."

"I am not some stray grannywoman out of the hills, Rubella Belinda Hanks. We have gone through thick and thin together, and not one time—not one last living time, mind you—have I refused to share a confidence with you. Remember when I heard about Lottie's gallbladder operation? Did I act like Mrs. Mystery and not repeat everything I'd heard, including what she said in the operating room while being anesthetized?"

"And her teaching home ec to innocent high-school girls," Ruby Bee said, smiling just a tad before she caught herself. "This just ain't the time to discuss it, Estelle. Dahlia can't hardly handle the bar, much less take orders from the booths and fix trays for the movie stars to have in their rooms."

The waitress under discussion trudged into the kitchen, her lips pursed in a tight circle and her cheeks puffing in and out. She slammed down a stack of orders, exhaled noisily, and went back through the door, moving so heavily that pots rattled in the cabinet and the soup simmering on the stove sloshed gently.

"What's ailing her?" Estelle demanded.

"It's this movie thing," Ruby Bee said as she opened the oven door to peek at the cherry cobbler, which was bubbling perfectly as usual. "She was all fired up about her role, but now that Miss Kaye's been murdered, Dahlia's afraid the movie people'll pack up and go home without—"

"Murdered? Miss Kaye was murdered?"

Ruby Bee banged the oven door. "You heard me, even though you weren't supposed to. I swear, you've got more ways of worming things out of folks than a robin hopping around in the wet grass. I guess there's no point in not telling you what that deputy told me, but we can't tell another soul."

"I solemnly swear," Estelle said soberly, then scooted around the corner and grabbed Ruby Bee's arm. "But I think this is a real opportunity for us, don't you? You and I are going to be the ones to take trays to the movie stars and maybe hear them talking to each other about what happened. That nice Mr. Meredith may be married, but he was right friendly at the bar the other night, and I figure he might—"

"Hush," Ruby Bee ordered. She could smell the cobbler, but she could smell something else that was liable to have Arly kicking up stumps. Again. She thought about saying as much to Estelle, but the cobbler was done and the soup was boiling and all sorts of folks were bellowing in the barroom. "Help me dish up these orders," she said briskly. "Let's get through the rush hour, and then we'll settle down over sherry and discuss the case."

"Because I'm busy reading this," Darla Jean said, her face hidden behind the cover of a confession magazine. She was lying on her bed, the pillows squashed behind her head. The magazine trembled as she flipped to the next page. "This is what I want to do, so there's no reason for you all to hang around in the doorway staring at me like I'd turned pea green or something."

"Oh, come on, Darla Jean," Heather wheedled, "I'll buy you a soda. If you're afraid to go to the Dee-Lishus, I'll see if I can get my ma's car and we can go someplace in Farberville."

"Why would I be afraid to go to the Dee-Lishus?"

Heather made a face at Traci, who wasn't being any help. "I just thought you might not want to run into Dwayne."

The magazine stayed in place. "He's my boyfriend, ain't he?"

" 'Course he is," Heather said, her mouth as dry as cotton.

"Then why should I be afraid to run into him?"

Withering under Heather's glare, Traci licked her lips and said, "Because of your date with Frederick Marland, Darla Jean. Dwayne might not like that."

"It wasn't a date. I gave him a ride into Farberville, that's all. He bought suntan oil at the drugstore on Thurber Street, and we came right back." She lowered the magazine just enough to look at them, and it wasn't anywhere near a friendly look. "You got problems with that?"

Heather and Traci assured her that they didn't, but once they were walking along the road, they agreed that they did, since Heather had tried to call at ten and

Traci had noticed Mrs. McIlhaney's car wasn't in the driveway when she and her parents had returned home from a tent revival. The preacher had been real long-winded, and it had been well after midnight before the final "Hallelujah!" had died down and everyone felt sufficiently saved for the night.

Chapter 10

6   CONTINUED:

> COOTER
>
> I thank you kindly, but I reckon I'll pass on the pie. I came to see if my fiancée wanted to take a stroll and enjoy the cool night air.

CLOSE-UP as Loretta stares at the floor. CAMERA WIDENS as Zachery crosses to her and pulls her to her feet.

> ZACHERY
> (jovially)
>
> 'Course she does, Cooter. It's time you two got to know each other better. Why, you'll be hitched afore you know it. Martha would have been so proud, may she rest in peace.

> COOTER
>
> Amen. May she rest in peace.

(CONTINUED)

Hal Desmond twisted the gold chain around his neck and scowled at his watch, then switched to a conspiratorial smile. "Arly, honey," he said, "I realize you're doing your job, and I'm sure you're damn good at it. The thing is, the day is almost gone and I'm up to my ass in revisions. Carlotta thinks she does the writing, but she's an amateur and I've been in the industry for thirty years."

We'd done name, rank, and serial number, and ascertained he'd formed Glittertown Productions, Inc., only a year ago. Before that, he'd been involved in "numerous projects, hard to say, deals that soared, deals that soured, but hey—that's the business, you gotta love it."

"One of your team was murdered," I said politely. "My job is to determine who did it. Yes, I'm doing my job."

"I have to tell you, when you tilt your head like that, there's something there. I can't quite put my finger on it, but it's there. You're Capricorn, aren't you? Hiding fiery passion behind those dark, appraising eyes?"

Plover had been summoned to the barracks. As irritated as I was with him, I rather wished he were straddling the chair and harrumphing under his breath. "No, I'm not a Capricorn, and all I'm hiding is an urge to transport you to the sheriff's department to continue this," I said, less politely. "We might be there until midnight."

"Yo, take it easy. No harm intended." Hal lit a cigarette and tried to find a comfortable position in the chair. There wasn't one, naturally, and eventually he conceded and gave me another smile, this one intending to be apologetic (but too toothy for my taste). "I can't deny it's in my blood. I'm possessed by it. I see a sunrise—I see opening credits. I see a beautiful woman—I see a leading lady. Even my wet dreams are in Technicolor. The other day I was telling Brando that—"

"Mr. Desmond," I said, "could we please continue with your statement concerning the events of the past three days? I have other people to interview and calls to make. From what I've heard thus far, everything was proceeding as scheduled. All of the company except for you and St. James arrived in the van in the middle of the afternoon. Why did the two of you come on a later flight?"

"Couldn't shake loose. Had a lunch lined up that was too important to pass up, even though the guy's a swish. Anderson had to do a little last-minute shopping. I picked him up and we tore out to LAX with ten minutes to spare. Carlotta made sure there was a rental car waiting for us at the airport in whatever that town was, and a map and thermos of martinis on the front seat. She's not a sexual fantasy, but I gotta admit she's professional."

"What about the others? I've heard several times how professional Meredith and Miss Kaye were."

"We're all professionals, even those two little hayseed lovers. Fuzzy requires a baby-sitter, but as long as he stays off the juice during work hours, he does a good job . . . for nonunion. We're one big happy family at Glittertown Productions, Inc., and that's why we can make tight little movies that earn a solid profit."

"How much does a movie like *Tanya Makes the Team* earn?" I asked. I admit it had nothing to do with the investigation, but I, along with most of the popcorn eaters of the world, was intrigued by Hollywood and its hypnotic aura of fame and fortune.

"It should have pulled in two or three million," Hal said proudly. "We did that baby on less than two hundred thou, which isn't even peanuts in the industry—it's the shells that were scattered in the sawdust after the circus split. The trick is to lock up the distribution early in the game. We're talking the foreign rights, the video, the cable deal, even the novelization, although we haven't had much luck there. I'm on the track of a little outfit in Peoria or someplace that wants to do a line of comic books."

"Like the *Classic Comics?*"

He dropped his cigarette on the floor and ground it out with his heel. "Like that, yeah. Listen, doll, I've got so much work to do that I'll be up all night, so let me run through it. Anderson and I arrived here before dark. We stashed our stuff, met the others in the barroom, had a few laughs with the locals, and went to bed. The next morning Carlotta, Fuzzy, and I made the grand tour of most of the sites. After lunch, jet lag caught up with me and I took a nap while Carlotta finished up on her own and pulled everybody together to distribute the schedule. We ate, then I went back to my room to meditate so I'd be vibrating with intensity this morning when we started rolling. I channel all my energy so it's like a friggin' laser beam. You ever meditate?"

"I don't even mediate," I said absently, making a few notes, including one about a few laughs with the locals. One local in particular came to mind . . . one with a badge and an adolescent mentality.

"Meditation's hot these days. You should give it a try. Tell you what—you come by my room later tonight, and I'll share my expertise with you. We'll get really, really comfortable and loose, then—"

"Neither Meredith nor Miss Kaye did anything out of the ordinary? They didn't mention seeing someone they knew, or having plans to go somewhere?"

"Naw, but I was preoccupied with the production. I don't much mingle with the others; it stifles me. I prefer to isolate myself, and if I want companionship, I take a quick look around and find someone who's fresh and exciting." He winked at me, in case I'd been out to (make that "doing") lunch and missed his hint.

"I don't think so, but I'll keep it in mind, Mr. Desmond. What can you tell me about the murder of Anderson St. James's wife? I gather it took place while you all were on location?"

He lit another cigarette and exhaled at length. His eyes were as mine were reputed to be: dark and appraising. "That's right, we were making *Satan's Sisters* in some podunk in Nevada. You ever caught that?" I shook my head. "Try it sometime; it puts me in tears every time I watch it. Anyway, we were close enough to Vegas that I didn't have to pay hardship wages. You been to Vegas? Now, there's a place you'd enjoy, Arly, and lemme tell you, I'm always welcome at Caesar's. Limo, suite, champagne, fruit, a front table for the shows—the whole number. How about it one of these days, you and me?"

I held in a shudder as I imagined sharing a suite with him, champagne and fruit be damned. A few weeks ago I'd been grousing about my floundering social life. Since then, I'd been invited to make sparks with a fire fighter, call a handsome actor by a diminutive, and go to Vegas with a social disease. Plover was huffing around, to be sure, but he hadn't trudged into the sunset. If I wasn't careful, my dance card would be full.

"I've been to Vegas," I said. "Let's return to the subject of the St. James murder, shall we?"

"I can get tickets to Wayne Newton just like that," he said, snapping his fingers. When I stared, he resumed toying with the gold chain and flicking ashes on my floor. "Right, right. Can't waste time until this mess is resolved, but don't hesitate to give me a call if you change your mind. Like I said, we're shooting in this podunk, and it's going like satin. Gwenneth's screwing up her lines and missing her marks, but what else is new, and nobody's worried because we're well under budget and the light at the end of the tunnel's as green as a hundred-dollar bill. We do the final wrap, get so soused that I'm thinking Carlotta looks like Monroe— maybe better—and call it a night. The next morning Fuzzy, the Merediths, and Gwenneth decide to continue the party in Vegas. I give Frederick and Anderson a ride back to L.A. in my Mercedes, and we have a helluva time, laughing and drinking and discussing some of the seriously bizarre scenes involving holy water. Talk about your symbolism—''

"And then?" I said, wondering why the mention of holy water was evoking such a smirk. A large population gave it mystical significance, but I'd never heard any hint of its ability to intoxicate or induce hallucinations.

"I dropped Anderson off, and was backing over his hibiscus when he came running out of the house. Looked like a—I don't know—one of your stars of *The Night of the Living Dead*. I'm talking the original in black and white, not the remakes. He was yelling about the ambulance and the police, that kinda thing. Frederick took a fast look inside while I tried to calm down my blubbery buddy. Before I could say Metro-Goldwyn-Mayer, we had police and medics all over the place.''

"There was never any suggestion that Anderson was involved?"

"From what I heard, she'd been dead since the middle of the night." He gave the chain a yank. "Like Kitty, I guess. Damn, she was class, real class. We're gonna miss her. Carlotta's trying to do the revisions as we speak. The footage we did this morning will work, even if Meredith's in Mexico by now. We were planning to dub his voice in later, anyway."

"Wait a minute," I said, determined to remain focused despite these abrupt tangential flights. "There's no way Anderson could have had anything to do with his wife's murder, right?"

"Lodging in Podunkville was tight, worse than here. We all had to share rooms, and I swore to the police that he was snoring across from me all night. It was a kind of a tragedy, because there was this little blond waitress in the coffee shop who thought she had talent and was more than willing to prove it. Problem was, she had this truck-driver boyfriend who might have shown up at her place, and—"

"I think this will do for the moment, Mr. Desmond," I said hastily. "When you get back to the motel, would you ask"—I consulted the list—"Fuzzy Indigo to come to the PD?"

"I'll do anything for you, darling. Look, here's my card, and I'm going to put my private number on the back so you won't have to go through the service. Night or day, you give me a buzz and I'll send you a first-class ticket to Vegas. There'll be a limo at the airport and anything you want—and I mean it—in the suite. You name it, Hal Desmond can get it."

He dropped a card on my desk, leered for a minute, and left before I could produce an appropriately couched remark that might have alluded (but very delicately, I'm sure) to castration and a dull knife.

Having negotiated a settlement with Estelle, Ruby Bee knocked on the door of #4 and waited impatiently. This was the room assigned to Fuzzy and Frederick, whom she'd swapped for Anderson St. James down at the other end, in #6. Estelle had been real misty about it, but Ruby Bee hadn't done it to be generous; she'd figured she had a better shot overhearing something from the peculiar one and/or the smart-mouthed one.

"Whattya want?" shouted the latter.

"I brought a tray of sandwiches. The deputy says you all can't leave your rooms just yet, and I thought you might like something to tide you over until I can fix a proper supper."

The door opened, and she went on in without waiting for an invitation, in that she doubted she'd get one. The beds were unmade, and there were beer cans and dirty glasses everywhere. "I'll set this on the dresser," she said, trying not to let on how disgruntled she was by the mess. "Is your friend in the bathroom?"

Frederick studied her for a minute, and when he spoke, his drawl sounded familiar in an eerie way. "No, he wandered off earlier, and although it's possible he's in some other bathroom, you kin rest assured that he's not in this one. But thank you kindly for the tray, ma'am. My innards was beginnin' to grumble something fierce."

Ordering herself to overlook his insolent manner, Ruby Bee managed to find a place for the tray. "Would you like me to tidy up just a bit?"

"Suit yourself. I thought it was kinda homey, myself." He took a sandwich and lay down on the bed, watching her as she began to fill a wastebasket with beer cans and other assorted debris. "Any sign of the media invasion yet?"

"No, the police are doing their best to keep it real quiet."

"Is it true the head cop is your daughter?"

"Her name's Ariel Hanks, and she's been the chief of police ever since she moved back here from a real fancy apartment in Manhattan, which is downtown in Noow Yark City.''

"No kidding," he murmured. "She any good at solving murders?"

Ruby Bee stopped dumping ashtrays and frowned at him. "She's solved a whole passel of murders since she got home. Why, only last year a woman was poisoned by one of those cream-filled sponge cakes, and Arly—" She stopped as the telephone rang.

"Hold that thought," Frederick said as he picked up the receiver. "Marland here." After a moment, he covered the mouthpiece with his hand and said, "Just leave the mess and run along. One of these days we'll do a drink and you can finish this fascinating story."

Ruby Bee took the wastebasket and headed for the door. As she stepped outside the room and pulled the door closed, she heard Frederick say, "Listen, darling, I'm not going to blab about last night, so stop sniveling."

She was thinking about it as Hal Desmond crossed the parking lot and went into his room. Estelle had won him, although she didn't notice how readily Ruby Bee had passed when his name arose. Now he was back in his room, and would have plenty of time to peel off his clothes before Estelle showed up with a tray. The imagined scene put a tiny grin on Ruby Bee's face, and she had to scold herself to stop gawking and get on back to the barroom.

She was glad she did. Dahlia was in the middle of the dance floor, surrounded by a variety of locals, all of whom were looking either pleased as Punch or sorely perplexed.

"Ruby Bee!" Dahlia thundered. "Guess what I just heard!"

"Don't split a gusset," Ruby Bee said over the gabble

of voices and the jukebox. She nudged her way through the crowd. "What did you hear?"

"They're gonna keep making the movie, and I'm still in it! You don't mind if I hunt up Kevin to tell him, do you?"

"You go right ahead. Did you hear any more about your part?"

"The assistant lady's gonna tell me what to say when we get up there and start filming. She said it'd be right easy for me to remember. In the meantime, I'm supposed to practice looking excited." Dahlia screwed up her face, but the unspoken consensus was that she looked more constipated than anything else.

Ruby Bee went on into the kitchen, where Estelle was poking black-eyed susans in juice glasses.

"I thought it might cheer them up," she said. "Make 'em more talkative."

"I'm sure it will," was all Ruby Bee said. She might have mentioned Hal Desmond's fondness for being buck-naked, or her suspicion about the plot of *Wild Cherry Wine,* or even the disappearance of Fuzzy, but there were a lot of other things she could have mentioned, too, and she let it go.

I wasted a great deal of the local taxpayers' money, along with the proceeds of speeding tickets and fines for the endless and often diverting string of misdemeanors committed on Saturday nights. I did this courtesy of Ma Bell and the insidious technological advancement called "hold," as in "I'll put you on . . . and see if Detective Cannelli is back from the meeting," and five minutes later, "his partner says he's here somewhere, lemme put you back on . . . and run down to the locker room."

After a hundred dollars or so, the detective came on the line. I explained the present situation, which elicited a whistle, and asked about the status of the St. James case. I was told it was open but covered with blue-green mold and stored at the very back of the filing cabinet.

"There was never any question about the husband?" I asked, scrunching up my forehead in the precise way that Ruby Bee keeps saying will leave permanent wrinkles on my forehead and no chance of a ring on my finger.

"Oddly enough, I remember this one," Cannelli said. "Murder's the *crime du jour* these days, but the more popular M.O.'s an assault weapon from a moving car. Which isn't to say we don't get knifings—very popular in alleys behind bars."

"The St. James case?"

"Sorry, honey. We looked at the husband, of course, along with the wackos in cardboard boxes and the recent graduates of the psycho wards. The word was that Mr. and Mrs. St. James were on the verge of a divorce, and not a friendly one, due to both property and accusations of infidelity. He admitted he'd moved out of the house, but said he went by to suggest a civilized discussion over champagne. Seems like he was making a movie in another state or something. In any case, he had an alibi for the time we considered significant."

"Thanks," I said. "I know you're busy, but is there a chance you can dig up some background on all these people? I'm out of my league. I'm not even in the minors."

He didn't sound particularly enthusiastic, but he did say he'd make a few calls and get back to me when he could. I read the list and then thanked him at length, thus adding to the long-distance bill but ensuring cooperation, and hung up just as Plover came into the PD.

He dropped a folder on my desk and went into the back room, mumbling something about coffee. The folder was dog-eared and stained, its contents sparse. Billy Dick MacNamara had made marginal grades in Farberville, had been considered uncooperative by most of his teachers since kindergarten, but had never had a major problem with the principal, nor had he had a brush with the juvenile authorities.

"I wonder if he ever reported a fire in Farberville," I said loudly enough to be heard by Roy Stivers, should he have been rocking outside the antiques store.

"He could have done so anonymously."

"I realize that. If someone does say his name, do they put it in the report?"

"You'll have to ask your chum in Emmet."

"You're a pain in the butt," I said, but not so Roy could hear it, or even Plover. I decided to ignore his pettiness (and get my revenge later, when I had time to polish it). "I called L.A. and talked to Detective Cannelli."

"He a bachelor?"

I gripped the pencil so tightly that my knuckles looked as if they were dusted with frost, but I kept my voice level. "I didn't ask, but I hope so. I'm shacking up with him in Vegas for a long, passionate weekend as soon as this is cleared up. Once he stopped making kissy noises, he said that they investigated St. James's alibi and cleared him."

Plover came to the door, a mug in his hand. "What about the other members of the company?"

"They had finished the film that day, partied, and were sharing rooms in some little town in Nevada. I presume they all had the same alibis—roommates. It's not our case, so I suggest we occupy ourselves with the present problem."

"This coffee must be a week old," Plover said as he sat on the corner of my desk. "I checked on the prints at the scene. They matched the ones on the personal effects of the victim and her husband, except for a few ancient ones that are apt to be Ruby Bee's. The murderer must have worn gloves."

"I'm not amazed." I glanced at my watch. "Desmond was supposed to send Fuzzy Indigo here. He should have arrived half an hour ago. I guess I'll call his room." I reached for the telephone, but as I did, it jangled. "Arly Hanks," I said into the receiver, which smelled faintly of onions.

"I know that," Ruby Bee said. "Don't you think your own mother ought to recognize your voice?"

I switched the receiver to the other ear so I'd be sandwiched between the two most irritating people I knew. "I'm in the middle of an investigation, Ruby Bee. What is it?"

"Well, excuse me. I didn't realize you were as busy as an ant at a Sunday school picnic. I happened to have some information to pass along, but I'll just wait until you have time to listen to me."

"I'm listening."

"I thought you might be interested to know that that Fuzzy fellow disappeared a while back."

I gulped. "What?"

"I took a tray out to number four in case they were getting hungry. Mr. Famous Frederick said Fuzzy had gone off earlier and hadn't come back."

From the way Plover was frowning at me, I must have looked more than a little perturbed. I let out a breath and said, "Let me get this straight, Ruby Bee. You took a tray to one of the motel rooms? What about the state trooper who's stationed there to prevent anyone from disturbing the movie people?"

"Oh, he's just fine. It's mighty hot out there, so I
took him a piece of pie and a glass of iced tea. He was
real grateful." Her tone indicated who wasn't.

"And Frederick Marland told you that Fuzzy wasn't
in the room?"

"In a manner of speaking, he did. I got to run now.
I'd tell you to come down for supper, but it's more
crowded than last year's ice cream social at the Methodist church."

She hung up before I could respond, which was just
as well. I sat back and looked at Plover, who was trying
not to grin. "That was a news bulletin from the Pinker-
ton Agency. Detective Petunia reported that Fuzzy left
his room and hasn't returned. The trooper on duty is
enjoying the snack said detective was gracious enough
to take out to him."

"Shall we mosey down there and have a word with
him?"

"Yes, I think a mosey might be in order." I stood up
and headed for the door.

22 INT.—LUCINDA'S TRAILER—NIGHT
    Billy Joe comes into the trailer, his cap in his
    hands. CAMERA WIDENS to include Lucinda in a
    rocking chair.

                    LUCINDA
        Is you okay, Billy Joe?

                   BILLY JOE
        Sure am. Why wouldn't I be?

                    LUCINDA
        Ain't you heard? Cooter says he's gonna
        kill you iff'n he so much as lays eyes on
        you. He's carryin' a shotgun. You better
        not set foot in town.

BILLY JOE

But what about Loretta? We got to make plans to escape.

He sinks to the floor in front of her and puts his head in her lap. She begins to ruffle his hair.

LUCINDA

I'd take a message to her, but Cooter knows I'm your first cousin and he'd be mighty suspicious.
(beat)
What if I was to take a message to Preacher Pipkin? Then when Loretta goes to the church, he kin slip it to her.

BILLY JOE

Kin we trust him?

LUCINDA

I don't reckon you got a choice, Billy Joe . . . unless you aim to let Cooter have his way with Loretta.

BILLY JOE

(brokenly)

I jest don't know what to do, Cousin. I feel so cold and lonely.

LUCINDA

You poor baby. You come with me to my bed and I'll make you nice and warm like we used to do in the hayloft all the time.

CAMERA FOLLOWS them as they head for the bedroom. Billy Joe remains tortured by his thoughts, but Lucinda has an excited look on her face as she unbuttons her blouse.

CUT TO:

Brother Verber was on his knees, not in the Voice of the Almighty Lord Assembly Hall, where he might be interrupted, but in the privacy of his living room. He was in the midst of an almost testy conversation with His Superior about the lack of divine protection during a stressful time when he (lower case) had been investigating Satan's handiwork and He (upper) hadn't so much as lifted a Finger. It wasn't at all like those Hollywood people had said. Brother Verber had never peeped in a window in his life, except when he was doing so for the good of his flock.

"It was most humiliating," he said, his eyes uplifted and, despite the potential for retribution, his voice tinged with accusation. He considered a few other remarks, then realized he might better spend his time trying to think what to do.

To heap injury on top of insult—and there was a heap of insult—some woman claiming to be the director's assistant had called a while back and told him that he was going to be in the movie or else. Else, she'd explained, was telling folks in town exactly who'd been immortalized in a window with his eyes popping and his tongue hanging out of his mouth like a hound in heat. She'd gone on to mention how easily they could allow everyone to screen it for himself or herself.

Herself included dearly beloved Sister Barbara. After the unpleasantness the previous year, he'd been obliged to listen humbly for hours about his lapse from grace, and had been reduced to whimpering on his knees in front of her and swearing he would never again entertain the slightest lust in his heart or so much as glance at what he himself considered illuminating study material to aid him in his relentless war against Satan.

He flopped back on the sofa and fanned himself with a catalog. "What kind of a name is Preacher Pipkin!" he muttered to himself, having given up pleading with the Lord. "I should have told her I was a man of the cloth and entitled to a name befitting my—"

The telephone rang. Gaping at it as if it were a rattlesnake, he finally reached out his hand and picked up the receiver. "Praise the Lord," he said in a shaky voice.

"I would like an explanation," Mrs. Jim Bob said briskly.

Even though the blood was draining from his face, Brother Verber fumbled frantically in his mind and came up with an approach. "Yes, praise the Lord, Sister Barbara. Let us lift up thine eyes and offer a prayer of thanksgiving."

"Have you been in the sacramental wine again?"

He avoided looking at the glass on the coffee table. 'No, I have such wonderful news that it qualifies as a miracle."

"So was water being changed to wine. I am calling about where you were earlier in the day. I happen to know—"

"Praise the Lord!" he persisted, fanning himself to keep from passing out. "Now those little orphans can have warm food and new shoes. It's all I can do not to break into a hymn right here so you can share the miracle with me."

"Lottie and Eula are coming by to discuss certain factions in the Missionary Society who are disruptive. I need to put on the kettle and set out some cookies. Stop dithering about orphans and explain this miracle business so I can see to my duties as a hostess."

He swallowed nervously. "I have been asked if I would be willing to participate in this movie that's being made here in Maggody. I believe its title is *Wild Cherry Wine.*" Her snort warned him that he needed to get on with it. "I won't be paid much, but I can consider this a windfall for those little orphans, because every last penny will go right to them."

"Why do they want you to be in the movie?" she asked, not sounding as impressed by his generosity as he'd hoped.

"So I can donate all the money to the orphans. I am on my knees this minute, Sister Barbara, and my heart is overflowing with the bountiful joy that comes of being able to help orphans, even the ones of a different-colored persuasion."

Mrs. Jim Bob worked on it for a minute, but concluded it wasn't worth the effort. A minor white lie seemed in order; that kind didn't count, especially when done in order to salvage the Missionary Society election and get the kettle on. "I think I hear Lottie and Eula on the porch, so I must run."

"Praise the Lord," Brother Verber intoned. Once he'd hung up, he repeated the phrase two or three more times, with increasing sincerity. He went so far as to lift his glass in salute before gulping down its contents and heading for the kitchenette to refill it.

Chapter 11

After I'd berated the trooper, who had flakes of crust on his chin and a decidedly penitent expression on his face, Plover and I went to #4. I managed to knock without putting my knuckles through the door. Frederick Marland opened it, a sandwich in his hand, and said, "My turn for the rubber hoses and cattle prod?"

"It will be shortly," I said. "I've heard a report that Fuzzy Indigo left this room earlier this afternoon and hasn't returned. Is this true?"

He held up his hands. "Whoa there, Chief Ariel. Don't rearrange my boyish features; they make me lots of lovely money. Why don't you and your friend step inside to avail yourselves of the amenities of the Flamingo Motel? Would you like a drink? How about an egg salad sandwich? Mighty good, lemme tell you."

Plover plowed into the room, almost running me down. "Mr. Marland," he said coldly, "a violent crime was committed in the next room, and a woman was killed. If she was not a close friend, at the least she was an associate with whom you've worked for a year. We're taking this very seriously. I suggest you do so, too."

"Sorry, I'm like really sorry about that. I admired Kitty and Meredith. They were old enough to be my parents, so we didn't see much of each other when we weren't on location. But I didn't mean to sound so flip; it's a defense, I suppose. A way of coping." He pulled up the bedspread to cover the rumpled sheets and gestured at it. "I'm afraid the seating's limited."

Plover sat down on the chair, but I leaned against the wall by the door, my arms crossed, and said, "When did Fuzzy leave?"

"I'm not sure about the exact time. We came and talked for a few minutes about—what we'd heard."

"And what were your opinions?" I asked.

He sat down on the corner of the bed and rubbed his temples. "I was upset, and to be real blunt, scared shitless. I thought we ought to pack up and get out of Dodge while we could. Fuzzy ranted incoherently about pigs and perverts, and managed to trip over the bed twice. The second time he got the sheet wrapped around him and started screeching that he was being attacked by a loaf of bread. I don't know how he manages to stay drunk all the time. He must have some sort of I.V. hooked up to a bottomless bottle in his pocket."

"I noticed his condition in the barroom," I admitted. "Then what happened?"

"I was still in makeup, so I took a shower and changed clothes. When I came out of the bathroom, he was gone."

"And you have no idea why he left or where he might be? He didn't say anything at all?"

"No, but I'd suspect it has something to do with his fondness for alcohol. While we were playing poker yesterday, he finished off the last drop in the room. If his bottomless bottle finally went dry, he might have gone stumbling along the highway in search of a liquor store."

Plover stood up and came to the door. "I'll send someone to the pool hall. Is there anyplace else?"

I thought for a minute, then shook my head. "Not until the edge of Farberville. He wasn't with the group last night, either." I frowned at Frederick. "Do you know where he went last night and when he returned?"

"He didn't say anything to me, and I didn't ask. He's a live wire, good ol' Fuzzy. He reminds me of those Vietnam vets who go crazy and climb a tower to snipe at anything and anybody that moves. He hardly ever says a word, but he's very aware of what's going on—when he's sober. When he's not, he wouldn't notice being flattened by a cement truck."

"Is he capable of the sort of violence that took place in the next room?"

"I wouldn't think so, but I don't know him that well. I see him during production. I don't even know where he lives. I think his wife finally gave up and left him not too long ago."

"I'll be back," Plover said, then left to rally a second search party.

"And you have no idea about last night?" I said, trying to think of a place Fuzzy could have gone on foot. I gave Frederick a sharp look. "What time did you say he returned?"

"I didn't say. I told you we didn't discuss it."

I sat down in the chair Plover had vacated and whipped out my notebook and a pencil that looked as if it had been attacked by tiny beavers. "What's your real name, Mr. Marland?"

He stalled in much the same way Wanda Sue Thackett had, but eventually we determined that his birth certificate was graced with Freddie Marland, originally from San Diego, age twenty-five, currently residing in an apartment in Burbank. He'd enjoyed a brief stint on a soap opera, followed by a less stimulating stint in a pizza parlor before he'd been (he sketched quotation marks with his fingers) "discovered" by Hal.

As I read what I'd scribbled, a fragment of conversation came back to me. "Did you suggest this area for the location of the film?"

"Cannes, I would have suggested. Paris, Rome, Acapulco, all sorts of places. But Maggody, Arkansas?"

"Carlotta said someone in the group had suggested it," I said. I made a note to ask her, then crossed my legs and gazed at him. "Okay, where were you last night?"

"I ate at the barroom, then came back here and worked on my lines. We are making a film, you know."

"Then why don't you know what time Fuzzy returned?"

"Because I don't keep track of him." He took a bite of the sandwich and chewed it slowly, all the while covertly watching me to see if I was buying. I made it clear I wasn't. He swallowed, then put the remainder of the sandwich down and said, "I was with one of the local girls, and I don't want to get her in trouble, okay? She drove me into some town so I could buy some decent suntan lotion. We grabbed a bite, and then she brought me back here."

"Who're we talking about?"

"I promised her that I wouldn't tell anyone about our jaunt. She doesn't want her parents to know about it, or her boyfriend, for that matter."

"May I use the telephone?" I asked for form's sake. He nodded, and I dialed the number of Ruby Bee's Bar & Grill. When the proprietress answered, I said, "Which local girl took Frederick Marland for a drive last night, where'd they go, and what time did they return?"

"Is this some kind of spy service?" he said angrily as I listened to the response and hung up.

"This is a very small town," I said. "Darla Jean Mc-Ilhaney picked you up at seven-thirty in her mother's car, drove you to Farberville, and the two of you had not returned by one in the morning. The only weakness in the grapevine is after midnight, since folks tend to go to bed early in order to rise with the chickens and get started on the biscuits."

His mouth opened and closed several times. "All that just by one telephone call?" he said at last.

"I have excellent sources. You do realize I'll have to talk to Darla Jean, don't you? If you tell me what happened, I can try to avoid embarrassing her more than necessary."

He laughed. "You're one mean cop. I heard how you solved the cream-filled sponge cake murder, so I guess grilling a high-school girl won't be much of a challenge." He realized I was not sharing his amusement. "Okay, she picked me up and drove me into town. After I'd bought the lotion, we went to a bar and had a few drinks. Talked about this and that, drank some more, and somehow it was really late. She drove back here as fast she dared, dropped me off, and made me swear not to tell anyone."

"Which bar?" I asked innocently, very aware that bars in Farberville were careful to avoid serving minors. Because of the college there, showing one's driver's license was ritualistic. Darla Jean looked her age.

"How would I know? It was a bar, that's all. Little tables, loud music, watered-down drinks, dark as the inside of a cow." He stood up and began to pace, although the room was small and he couldn't do more than a few steps without risking an encounter with a wall. One, two, three—oops; one, two, three—oops.

"No problem. I can ask Darla Jean. She must know the name of the bar where the two of you stopped."

"All right, maybe we went somewhere for some privacy. Ever since the soap, I get propositioned in the supermarket at home. Girls send me X-rated videos of themselves. They knock on my door and try to invite themselves in for a little romp. This Darla Jean's no different. She made it clear she was . . . interested. She's a pretty little thing, and I was bored. No big deal."

I tried not to grimace as I gazed at him. "And where did you find this privacy?"

"A dark road, downwind from a chicken house." He was trying to sound nonchalant, but his hand trembled as he picked up the sandwich, studied it, and dropped it on the bedspread. "This doesn't have to be put on the grapevine, does it? The girl and I had a little fun, that's all. No one was harmed, and there's no reason why she should catch hell from her parents and her boyfriend."

There probably were several very good reasons why she should, but I wasn't in the mood to cause Darla Jean any grief. "I'll have a quiet word with her," I said, "just to confirm the story. I suggest you keep away from the local girls in the future, Mr. Marland. They may be impressed with your stature as a movie star, but I'm not. If this gets out, you may find vigilantes knocking on the door, and that would seriously interrupt the shooting schedule, wouldn't it?"

I stomped out of the room, and stopped in the parking lot to cool off. I wanted to find Darla Jean and give her a long, harsh lecture about her lack of judgment, but I decided to wait until I was calm enough to do so without shaking her so violently the barrettes flew out of her hair.

I closed my eyes and tried to think about my next move. The sound of voices interrupted my thoughts, which weren't going anyplace, anyway, and I spotted Estelle at the edge of the parking lot, griping at the trooper. He was defending himself as best he could, but I took pity on him and went over to rescue him.

"Well, thank goodness," Estelle said as I approached. "This boy's being about as ornery as a treed coon. You just go ahead and tell him that I can take this tray to Mr. Desmond in number two. It's a mite heavy, and I have no intention of standing here wearing myself out on account of—"

"Stop," I said. I gave her a second to settle her lips into a bloodless line of indignation, then said, "This officer is under orders not to allow anyone to go to any of the motel rooms."

"Are you aiming to starve them into confessing?" Estelle countered. "I watch enough lawyer shows on television to know that confessions have to be made voluntarily. If you so much as slap your suspect, the judge can—"

The noise that came from my throat was primitive, perhaps primeval, but it was effective. I finally got my teeth unclenched far enough to say, "Take the tray to Desmond. Just don't pester him or ask him any questions—okay?"

"Okay, Miss Mussolini," Estelle said, then marched off before I applied an egg salad sandwich to her face.

I followed her across the gravel, but continued on to #3 to ask Carlotta if she had any ideas about the latest defection from the production company. I knocked on the door; Estelle did the same at #2. Carlotta opened the door, but as I started to speak, I heard a shriek. I jerked my head around in time to see Estelle shove the tray at someone inside the room and scuttle away more quickly than a sand crab. Self-righteous mutters drifted after her as she went past the trooper and around the corner of Ruby Bee's.

Carlotta darted around me and was at #2 before I could stir myself. She opened the door a few inches and said, "Hal, Arly's here. Why don't you come to my room in a minute?"

"Is everything all right?" I asked.

She closed the door and joined me. "I'm afraid Hal was getting ready to take a shower, and he must have startled Estelle. Is there something you need to ask me?"

I followed her into the room, which was littered with enough paper to constitute several novels and a volume or two of an encyclopedia. The beds had been pushed back to make room for a card table that was nearly invisible under a small computer, monitor, printer, stacks of paper, notebooks, and copies of what I assumed was the script. More papers were thumbtacked to the wall.

"Kind of a mess," she said as she moved some of the clutter off the bed. "Revisions generate a lot of paper. Martha Biggins is now resting in peace, but I don't know what we can do about Zachery. He's pivotal."

"Who?" I said, wondering if they were bringing in more actors. The thought was not pleasant; I had quite enough Hollywood natives as it was.

Carlotta chuckled. "Sorry. Those are characters in the film, and by now they're more real to me than the actors who portray them. I realize that sounds strange. Anyone who works in the industry has to be slightly strange in order to survive."

"Speaking of strange, do you know where Fuzzy is?" I asked optimistically.

"Damn fine question," Hal said from behind me. He wore a lush white robe, the front agape to allow a display of white chest hair and damp flesh. "I told him I wanted to review today's footage. We still have to figure out how to shoot around Buddy until he surfaces, and we don't have all day, you know."

Carlotta grabbed her clipboard and started for the door. "Right, Hal. I'll go see if he's ready yet."

"Wait a minute," I said, feeling as if I were in a movie and merely watching myself in the midst of the action on the screen. "Fuzzy's disappeared. I came here to ask you if you knew where he was."

"Disappeared?" Hal echoed. "Whatta ya mean with this *disappeared* shit? He's the cameraman, fer chrissake! It's one thing to put Martha Biggins in her grave, and, if we have to, tuck Zachery beside her, but who the hell's gonna shoot the scenes?" The robe rose to expose bony knees as he shook both fists at the ceiling. "I've had enough of this, Arly. You just go find him and bring him back *tout de suite*. I personally will keep him locked in his room until we get this baby wrapped."

Carlotta was less explosive, but she sounded disturbed as she said, "He just . . . disappeared, like Buddy did?"

"All I know," I said, "is that early this afternoon he left the room that he's sharing with Frederick Marland and has not returned. The trooper at the edge of the parking lot swears Fuzzy didn't go past him, so my guess is that he cut around the corner of the building, climbed over the fence, and went on his merry way across the pasture."

Hal glowered first at Carlotta and then at me. "I can't deal with this. I feel my blood pressure zooming straight up like one of those—I don't know—one of those missiles. I suppose tomorrow Anderson will have gone poof, and nobody can find Gwenneth, and Carlotta's gonna be hitchhiking to hell, and—"

"Shut up!" I snapped. "I think we need to round everybody up right now and count noses. You two stay right here; don't even take a step." A sudden thought washed over me like a pitcher of iced tea. "Where is Gwenneth D'Amourre? Isn't she sharing this room?"

"She's . . . ah, she's in my room," Hal said. "I was coaching her on some of the more intricate scenes. Every time she bobbles a line, it costs time, and time costs money, and money's the bottom line."

"I'll go get her," Carlotta said in a strained voice, and hurried out of the room before I could reiterate my order not to take a step.

She was already in the next room as I went to the opposite building, told Frederick to go to Carlotta's room, and then went more slowly toward #6, which I knew contained Anderson St. James. All afternoon I'd been delaying my interview with him, and I still felt uneasy about facing him. It might have been because I had information about his wife's murder and it seemed like an intrusion of his privacy. Then again, it might have been because I felt like an inarticulate idiot when he regarded me with those chocolaty eyes.

Reminding myself that we were in the middle of a murder case that was escalating a mile a minute, I tapped on the door.

He opened it and gave me a pleased smile. "I was wondering when you'd remember me. Do we have to go to the torture room, or can we stay here? I promise to behave as long as it's official business, but after that, you never know what might come over me."

I promptly blushed. "It's official business for now," I said, furious with myself and therefore worsening the situation. "We've got a new problem, and I want everyone to come to Carlotta's room to discuss it."

He was no longer smiling as he stepped outside the room and closed the door. "Have you found Meredith?" he asked as we walked across the lot.

I shook my head. "Not yet, but we're still looking."

"Any leads on the maniac who murdered Kitty?"

I shook my head again and led the way into #3. Carlotta had cleared the beds and single chair, and was
stacking papers in the corner. Hal lay on one of the
beds, the robe now displaying not only bony knees but
also flabby white calves. Frederick Marland sat on the
chair. As Anderson sat down on the second bed, Gwenneth came out of the bathroom, tugging on the strap of
a halter.

I ignored her little wave and waited until she sat
down next to Anderson. "I still have questions to ask
some of you, but at the moment we have a new problem." I then told them about Fuzzy's vanishing act,
which elicited snorts from Hal, a sigh from Carlotta, a
tiny squeak of disapproval from Gwenneth, a frown
from Anderson, and a flicker of anger from Frederick.

It did not, however, elicit any suggestions as to where
Fuzzy was or where he'd been the previous evening.

"This place is creepy," Gwenneth contributed. "It's
like a black hole that sucks people in. I think we ought
to split before something happens to the rest of us."

"We're making a picture, not visiting in-laws!" Hal
said, rousing himself long enough to jab his finger at
her. "You're gonna stay here and emote your little heart
out until we're done, or face a breach-of-contract suit.
You're no bankable star, and don't forget it."

Gwenneth burst into tears and dashed into the bathroom, which was fine with me. I waited until the door
slammed, then said, "Can any of you think of someone
who might have a grudge against Glittertown? Someone who felt he or she deserved a role, or was fired?"

Hal flopped back on the bed and closed his eyes,
perhaps to meditate. Anderson and Frederick both
seemed to find the faded floral pattern of the carpet
worthy of their attention.

"Anyone at all?" I asked Carlotta.

"I wish I could rattle off a name or two, but I can't,"

she said bleakly. "There's some competition, of course, but nothing of epic proportion. We auditioned a few people who weren't suitable. One of the bit players in *Tanya* felt he was underpaid; his contract indicated otherwise, and his lawyer was informed of it. At one point Fuzzy had an assistant, but the kid was offered a better job and took it."

Gwenneth came out of the bathroom, a tissue in her hand, and brightly said, "What about the pirate?"

"Pirate?" I repeated. "As in Captain Hook?"

"As in distribution," she said as she sat down and took out the dreaded nail file.

Carlotta looked as if she were considering mayhem, but instead sighed and said, "Illegal copies were made of two of our three films, including the last one. Some of our markets, such as specialty video stores and independent cable companies, are willing to buy cheap and claim they had no way of knowing they weren't dealing with an authorized distributor. It's cost us maybe several hundred grand so far."

I was struggling to understand. "So there's someone out there who's sabotaging the company?"

"Or someone in here," Gwenneth said. "We've hashed it over and over, and there's no way an outsider could have gotten an unauthorized copy. One of us has made quite a profit."

"Oh," I said wisely, having absolutely no idea what to do with this information. After a moment of silence in which my confusion reverberated in my ears, I told them to stay in their respective rooms with the doors locked, and to call me if anyone thought of anything. As I left, the only sound in #3 was the arrhythmic drone of Hal's snores and the scratch of the nail file.

The gas station was prehistoric. There were no pumps for self-service, nor was there a miniaturized grocery store inside with overpriced snack food, "male" magazines, and a microwave oven. At one side of the building, tires were piled like deflated black doughnuts. The rest rooms were in the back, although only the most desperate traveler would ask for the key.

He braked and swung into the station. A man, as greasy and surly as he'd ever seen, came out to the truck. "Whatta ya want, cowboy?"

"Fill it up and check the oil." He got out of the truck and went into the office to take the rest-room key off a hook. He ascertained that the man was occupied, then assessed the possible exits. Three doors: the one he'd used, which could be padlocked from the outside; a second, that led to a windowless storeroom; and a third, that led to the single bay. The last could not be locked, but that presented no problem.

"Two-dollar eighty," the man said from the doorway. "Forget using the john, you cheap sumbitch. How many times do I have to tell you to wait until you need more than a coupla gallons in that rust bucket of yours, huh?"

He put the key back on the hook, handed over the money, and went back to his truck. There was plenty of time to work out the details. It would be a night of magic, he was sure. Not only of dragons, but of orange fireballs, coarse black smoke, and screams.

He was soon to become a wizard. No one dared to insult a wizard.

✧✧✧

"It's what they called a closed set, Kevvie," Dahlia said as she popped the last cookie in her mouth and dreamily masticated. "It means they don't want a bunch of folks hanging around gawking. Carlotta says it slows them down something terrible, what with someone sneezing during a real important moment, or blurting out a remark." She swallowed, brushed off the sparkles of sugar on her cavernous tent dress, and struggled to her feet. "We're gonna do it in the morning. Now I aim to practice, so you kin just run along and find somebody else to bother."

Kevin was aching inside worse than when he had the flu. He wasn't real clear which fellow was gonna smooch with his beloved, but he'd had a gander at all of them and they were all handsome, and probably rich enough to steal her heart with fancy candy and dozens of roses. Before he knew it, she'd be waving good-bye from the backseat of a limousine, and he'd be left standing in the ditch, choking on the dust.

"I said you kin run along," Dahlia repeated, interrupting this vision of gloom and despair. "I got to practice."

"Why can't I watch?"

"I don't want you to disturb my concentration. Carlotta said to stand in front of a mirror, not in front of some jealous fellow who doesn't understand about actresses and how they do things because they're in a movie."

A plan crept into Kevin's mind. It did so slowly, as most everything did, but it kept inching along and growing bigger and bigger until it was throbbing like a boil. It was risky. It was more dangerous than stealing a watermelon from Perkins's patch behind his house. But he was tormented by his vision, and he was, in his own eyes, a knight in shiny armor with a maiden in dire need of defendin'.

"What's the matter with you?" the maiden snapped. "You look bumfuzzled like you got knocked up the side of the head with a two-by-four."

He had his pa's car. Time was running short. Iff'n he ever hoped to marry his betrothed and live in a cozy mobile home, have a hot supper waiting for him when he came home from work, treat his dumpling to supper at Ruby Bee's when they could afford it, be a proud papa, and live happily ever after in such sublime bliss, he had to act. Iff'n he failed, he'd be left reading about her in *People* magazine and watching her on the screen at the picture show.

"I was thinking," he said slowly, "that you might like a hot fudge sundae before you commence practicing. It won't take but a little bit, and I promise I'll bring you right home so you can work in front of the mirror." When she hesitated, he added, "I'm so proud of you that you can have extra whipped cream and my cherry."

"And you'll bring me home without any sass about lightning bugs and Boone Creek?" she asked, puckering her lips and regarding him suspiciously.

"Cross my heart and hope to die."

"Well, I don't see any harm in that." She went into the house and visited the bathroom long enough to make a face at the mirror. This time she did look somewhat excited, although it might have been at the prospect of extra whipped cream.

Had she but known what lurked in Kevin's mind, she would have made a face uglier than death's grandmaw.

By the time Plover came into the PD, it was dark outside. He stopped by the door and said, "Any news?"

"No bodies have been found, dead or alive. The movie people are having dinner in Carlotta's room, and I think we ought to put on a second guard when they scatter for bed."

"I'll do my best. Not much from the lab, by the way. The weapon was a knife with a six-inch blade and a nick on one edge. If we find it, we can hope for a positive ID. The . . . word on the mirror was written by a gloved hand. The body's been sent to the state lab for an official autopsy."

"I won't hold my breath until they determine the cause of death," I murmured.

"What about your firebug?"

"Les Vernon left a message that Willard Yarrow does okay in school and is neither liked nor disliked. The counselor talked to him several times about getting carried away with this role-playing game to the exclusion of school-related activities, but that's all." I tipped back in the chair and stared at the water stains on the ceiling. "I'm not going to spend a lot of time trying to nail Billy Dick. I'm a helluva lot more worried about the production company. Hal made a joke about everybody disappearing, and I was in a cold sweat until I rounded them up. Where can Meredith and Fuzzy be? Even if one of them killed Kitty Kaye, he can't just evaporate. Somehow both of them simply walked into the sunset—and in Fuzzy's case, the sunset took place in the middle of the day."

"We're checking every place along the highway," Plover said, "and I suppose we can search the ridge tomorrow."

"I'll be sure and ask Harve for helicopters and dogs. Maybe he'll lead one of the posses."

"In a tutu," Plover said with a chuckle. It was the first time I'd heard it in a long time, and we smiled at each other. "You have plans for tonight?" he asked.

"I'm afraid I do," I said. I did not elaborate, and he tossed out something about calling in the morning as he went to his car. This left me in a fine position to savor a can of soup and a novel in my apartment, and that's where I was headed when I remembered I hadn't asked Carlotta who suggested Maggody. The magnetism of soup and novel was strong, but I went back into the PD and dialed her number.

"Yes?" Gwenneth answered. In the background I could hear Hal and Carlotta arguing, but I asked to speak to her and she sounded composed when she came on the line.

I asked my question and poised my pencil over my notebook. After a while I put it down and said, "You did say one of the crew was from around here, didn't you?"

"I'm trying to remember. It was on the set of *Prickly Passion,* during a lull, and I think it was Buddy. He put on this really absurd accent and started hunkering around and acting like a yokel. Hal caught the tail end of the act, decided it would do well as a concept, and then Buddy said he grew up in some minute town in the Ozarks that would be perfect."

"But he wasn't from Maggody," I said, puzzled.

"No, it was some dreary little place that was down to a handful of people and a few houses. We required something a tad livelier than"—she paused and then sighed—"something like Pineville or Peenville. It's not even a wide place in the road anymore. I was through it before I realized I'd been in it, and I kept right on going."

I thanked her, locked the PD, and went to my apartment to hunt through my collection of road maps. In the southwest corner of Missouri I located a dot named Pineyville. No more than an hour's drive, I decided with more enthusiasm than the discovery merited. Even if this was Meredith's hometown, he had no way to get there—or a reason to go there, unless he'd murdered his wife and needed to hide.

But it was the first link between the area and the Hollywood people. Maybe I'd learn that Pineyville was indeed a black hole that had sucked in Meredith and Fuzzy and was now awaiting its next inhalee.

Chapter 12

WILD CHERRY WINE (REVISED 5/24)

26   INT. CHURCH—DAY—CLOSE ANGLE—PIPKIN
PREACHER PIPKIN is sitting in a pew. CAMERA FOL-
LOWS Loretta as she comes in furtively and sits
in the pew behind him. Pipkin does not acknowledge her.

              LORETTA
You got to help me, preacher man.

              PIPKIN
The Good Books sez you got to honor
your father and dear, departed mother.
Ain't nothing I can do to dissuade your pa
from makin' you marry Cooter.

              LORETTA
All I want you to do is give me sanctuary
until Billy Joe can fetch me. Just let me
hide in the choir room for the night. Lucinda's helping Billy Joe find a car so we
can leave.

PIPKIN

Who knows you're here?

LORETTA

No one. Billy Joe thinks I'm waitin' at home, but I heard Pa talking to Cooter about rushing up the ceremony. You got to let me stay. . . .

(beat)

And you got to get a message to Billy Joe telling him where I am.

A calculating expression comes over Pipkin's face. He rubs his palms together.

PIPKIN

And what's in it for me, Loretta? I ain't gonna risk havin' Cooter after me for nuthin'. If I let you hide in the choir room, you got to make it worth my while.

LORETTA

I ain't got no money.

PIPKIN

I ain't talkin' about money. I reckon I'm talkin' about that cot in the choir room. Is you comin'?

CAMERA CLOSEUP of Loretta's face as she realizes what he's talking about. Desperation is replaced by resignation as CAMERA WIDENS and she rises.

LORETTA

And you a man of the cloth . . .

PIPKIN

That's why I keep a sheet on that little cot. Close enough.

CUT TO:

I was burrowing in my bed and doing my best to wrap the sheets around myself tightly enough to interfere with my circulation. The ringing of the telephone was almost welcome, although it took me a minute to untangle myself and flop across the far side of the bed to grab the receiver. As I mumbled hello, I glanced at the alarm clock. It was a few minutes shy of midnight.

"Arly, this is Wade, Wade Elkins. We've got trouble."

"What's wrong?"

"A fire at the gas station in Hasty. I have to get back there; I just wanted to let you know. Sheriff's on his way."

He hung up before I could ask any questions, but from his panicky tone I realized whatever was happening was damn serious. I pulled on the nearest clothes, ran a comb through my hair and pulled it into a tight ponytail, and ran down the outside stairs and across the road to my car. My gun was inside the PD. I couldn't think of a reason why I'd need it, but I went inside and strapped it on, because, I regret to admit, I could think of reasons why I'd like to use it. I hurried back to the car, hopped in, and turned the key.

Silence.

"Damn it!" I said as I turned the key more tightly and willed the car to start. I might as well have willed it to produce rotors on its roof so I could hover over Hasty. I'd been telling the town council for over a year that I needed a dependable vehicle, and for over a year I'd been met with whines about the budget and promises, never meant to be taken seriously, that allowed us to end the meetings in a spirit of levity.

I couldn't call Wade back. Maggody was dark; not one window was lit, nor did so much as a chicken truck breach the blankness of the road. I ran down the pavement, through the Ruby Bee's Bar & Grill parking lot, and headed for #1. And crashed into a warm body that grabbed me by the arms and barked, à la drill sergeant, "Where do you think you're going?"

For a wild moment, I wondered if I was in the clutches of the maniac who'd murdered Kitty Kaye. I was struggling to free myself when I remembered the guard whose presence I personally, stridently, and at length had demanded. "It's Arly Hanks," I said between gasps. "Chief of Police Hanks."

My arms were released, and the man stepped back to appraise me in the gloomy darkness. "Sorry, Chief, you about scared the skin off me. Why in thunderation are you dashing around like this?"

"I need a car. Mine won't start. I'm going to borrow my mother's, and she lives in that first unit."

"Can't see anything wrong with that," he began, but I missed the rest of it as I hurried to Ruby Bee's door and pounded on it loudly enough to rouse everyone within a mile or so, including those in fancy pastel boxes out behind the Methodist church and six feet under.

It took Ruby Bee a good while to answer the door, and when she did, she wore a robe and slippers. Her face was slathered with cream, and the fat pink rollers on her head were hidden under a plastic shower cap. "Arly?" she said querulously. "Land sakes, what time is it?"

"I don't have time to field questions. I need the key to your car."

"It seems awful late for you to be galloping off like this. You might have taken more time with your hair and face. That T-shirt's all stretched out of shape, and those pants are just plain baggy. Maybe you ought to go home and put on something—"

"The key, Ruby Bee. It's official police business, and it's an emergency."

"Well, I never," she grumbled as she went to her purse and took out her key chain. "I'd like to think there'll be some gas left when you bring it back. Estelle and I are planning to run over to—"

I snatched the keys out of her hand, pulled the door shut, and got into her car. The trooper saluted me as I drove past him, but I was too frazzled to return the professional courtesy. I turned left and headed for the county road to Hasty, replaying Wade's terse message in my mind. The only gas station in Hasty was across the street from Willard Yarrow's house. A peculiar co-incidence, if that's all it was. Gasoline was certainly flammable (or inflammable, if you prefer), so a fire was not unthinkable. Still, we had Billy Dick's playmate and a fire in close proximity.

As this mental debate raged on, I realized I was driving more and more slowly, until I was virtually crawling between the rows of dark buildings and the sporadic streetlights, some of which worked. There was no reason why I needed to rush to the fire; I was trained for nothing more useful than crowd control, and Harve and his men would be there by now.

I reached a decision before the car came to a complete halt. Billy Dick MacNamara might be sound asleep in his bed, dreaming of sugarplums, with his mother there to swear he hadn't left the house since supper. Or he might not be.

As I drove up his driveway, I noted that the house was dark. A truck was parked in the yard, however, and as I pulled in next to it, my (Ruby Bee's) headlights flashed on two figures sitting on the top step of the porch. I cut off the lights, took a deep breath, and got out of the car.

"I want to talk to you," I said as I approached them.

"Fine night, ain't it?" Billy Dick said. "We're j-just sitting here admiring the moon." Beside him, Willard was motionless; for all I knew, he could have been unconscious and propped up next to him like a cardboard silhouette.

"How long have you been admiring the moon?"

"Couldn't say. You know, when the moon rose a while back, it was real big and this fierce, hot orange color. It looked like a demonic jack-o'-lantern, but only till it cleared the trees. Now it's real pretty."

I stepped in front of his companion. "How long have you been here, Willard?"

"Since dark, I reckon," he said uncertainly.

"Have you found your way out of the dungeon?" I asked him.

Billy Dick leaned forward and in a whisper said, "Xardak the Wizard was real sure he could sneak by the dragon, but he made a bad decision and the next thing he knew, he was nothing but a crispy critter."

They both began to giggle. The noise was foul, almost pornographic, and I had to order myself not to get back in the car and leave them to their games and dark fantasies. Instead, I went to the truck and put my hand on the hood.

"The engine's hot," I said. "If you've been sitting here for hours, who was driving it in the past few minutes?"

"It's always hot," said Billy Dick. "Sometimes it gets so hot that I'm afraid it'll burst into flames. Is that what happened to your car, Chief Hanks? Did it burst into flames, with clouds of black smoke pouring up from it to fill the sky until you couldn't hardly breathe? Or did it explode like someone had put a stick of dynamite under the hood?''

"Why do you think something happened to my car?" I asked evenly, not allowing myself to admit how much he was unnerving me. Had he done something to my car? Was he implying he would? I didn't care for either.

"I just noticed you weren't driving your official police car with the blue light," he said. I couldn't see his face well, but I could hear his smirk perfectly. "I guess you need the lights when you're in a hurry."

"I'm in no hurry," I said. "You're claiming you've been here since dark and the truck overheated while parked in this spot, right?"

Billy Dick took a drink from a can as he elaborately scratched his head. "Maybe it's some kind of spontaneous combustion, where something gets hotter and hotter until it goes up in flames. Don't stand too close to it, Chief Hanks. It might get too hot for you to handle. You might get burned."

"And be careful with your own car," Willard said. "This spontaneous-combustion stuff could be contagious."

I realized I was gripping my gun, and I uncurled my fingers. Ignoring what we all knew were threats, I said, "Then neither one of you was in Hasty tonight? You don't know anything about a fire at the gas station?"

"How could we?" Billy Dick abruptly grabbed Willard's arm and yanked him up. "Hey, I think we should go over there and take a look, don't you? Those gas tanks might put on a real pyrotechnical display."

"Sure, Billy Dick," the younger boy said. He was trying to display the same level of bravado, but I sensed he was frightened. "Maybe it's burning my house down, too. Boy, that'd piss Pa off."

"But Willard, isn't there some guy who works there

at night? You think he might have been in the station when the fire started?"

"Gee, Billy Dick, I don't know, but I hope not. If the doors got jammed, he may be up shit creek."

"Or on his way to hell," Billy Dick countered cheerfully. "See you later, Chief Hanks." As I stared at them, they walked past me, got in the truck, slammed doors, and drove away.

I waited until the taillights disappeared, then sat on the fender of my (Ruby Bee's) car and mulled over what they'd said, what they'd implied, and what I could do with it. Not a blasted thing, I concluded. If I tried to nail them on the basis of the hot engine, they'd remember that they went to the Dee-Lishus for drinks or took a drive in the country, and I'd be hard pressed to prove otherwise. The rest of it could be written off as paranoia on my part.

I was very glad I didn't work at a gas station in Hasty, I told myself as it began to sprinkle. I stayed where I was until rain was beating down on me like frozen bullets and I could barely make out the dark house and vacated porch step.

"Kevin Fitzgerald Buchanon, you're as good as dead! I hope you know that," Dahlia said, her face beet red with anger. In the splotchy moonlight he could see her fists, which were size of softballs and clearly poised for contact. "You're more useless than a dog without a flea," she continued, moving past the car door. "If I get my hands around that scrawny neck of yours, you're gonna regret the day you was born. I'll bet your ma did right there in the delivery room!"

Kevin sidled around the car, keeping it between them and prepared to do so all night, or until his honey bunny calmed down, which wasn't looking like it would happen real soon. An owl screeched somewhere in the woods; the noise startled him, but not enough to make him look away from the avowed murderess with the burning eyes and ominous fists.

"Now, sweetums," he begged, easing around the trunk as she advanced, "I told you how I did what I had to do. I couldn't let those people woo you into going to Hollywood. I love you too much for that." He smiled hopefully at her, but he kept moving, nevertheless.

"You love me so much that you kidnap me by bringing me up here, driving so fast I'm feared to jump out, and then rip that wire out of the car so we're stuck?" She took a step. "It's as plain as the nose on my face that you're nothin' but a jealous, low-down, lyin' sumbitch, and a sight meaner than a two-headed snake. If I don't get to be in the movie, I aim to rearrange your face so your kinfolk won't recognize you!" She took another step, but so did he, and she figured she wouldn't have much success lungin' across the hood. Lungin' was not one of her fortes. "You find that wire this very minute and fix this car, and I mean it."

"I threw it as hard as I could out yonder in the bushes," Kevin said, whimpering. "There ain't no way I can find it in the dark."

"If you find it in the morning, can you put it back where it goes and get me to town?"

Kevin crossed his fingers, in that car repairin' was not one of his fortes. "Of course I can, my beloved. I'm truly sorry I did what I did, and I promise I'll never do anything like this again. My brain just kinda snapped, and all of a sudden I was feeling like I'd drunk a quart of field whiskey and didn't know what I was doing. Kin you forgive me?" He considered getting down on his knees, but he couldn't risk giving her an advantage.

Dahlia stopped puffing and stared at him. "The only way I'll forgive you is if I'm in the movie tomorrow. If I'm not, you can kiss your ugly face good-bye forever."

"You will be," he said earnestly.

She put her hands on her hips and turned around to study the only shelter within twenty miles—twenty miles of narrow, rutted road, rotten logs, fearsome dark shadows, bears, and who knows what other starving, slobbering, sharp-fanged animals. A raindrop hit her nose, and pretty soon another splattered on her chin. The one that hit her forehead dribbled down her cheek like a tear.

"Come on, Kevin," she muttered, "there ain't no point in standing out here in the rain. You may not have the sense to come out of it, but I reckon I do. Fetch the flashlight and the food and the blankets. It's most likely filthy in there, but it'll be tolerable for one night."

The flashlight and the food and the blankets, Kevin repeated to himself in an increasingly frantic voice, having implemented his first kidnapping with a minimum of planning. Robin Buchanon's cabin had been deserted for a lot longer than a year, and it hadn't been a Holiday Inn honeymoon suite to begin with. Now it was likely to house rats, spiders, roaches, snakes—all the things his love goddess didn't much fancy.

"You wait there on the porch while I get everything," he called. He got back in his pa's car and opened the glove compartment. There was a flashlight and a chocolate bar. Dahlia usually carried a few provisions in her purse, but she hadn't brought it with her. She was anticipating a picnic supper, sleeping bags, and some form of protection.

He could lock himself in the car, he supposed, where he'd be safe until it was light enough for her to find a rock and smash the windshield. He told himself knights in shiny armor didn't do that sort of thing, tempting as it might be, and took his two treasures to the porch.

"I'll fetch the rest after you're inside where it's safe and dry," he lied gallantly. He pushed open the door and gestured for her to proceed him. He even went so far as to shine the light for her so she could avoid the animal life.

"O my Gawd!" she said with a scream, retreating so rapidly that she stumbled into him and the two continued off the porch, arms and legs flailing like windmill blades in a hurricane, and right on into the muddy yard. "Kevvie, there's a dead man in there!"

He was having some difficulty breathing, in that she was sprawled on top of him, but he did the chivalrous thing and said, "Are you sure, my love object?"

"His eyes was wide open and there's a knife sticking out of his throat," she managed to say, before she fainted.

Kevin dearly hoped the rain would revive her before too long.

I arrived in Hasty half an hour later. Unlike the previous fires, this one was not under control. Cars and pickup trucks blocked the road, and the spectators were out, although most of them were dressed in bathrobes or raincoats and no one carried coolers and lawn chairs. With the darkness, the rain, and the smoke, it was difficult to recognize anyone; if Billy Dick and Willard were present, they were not in sight.

I abandoned the car in a driveway and hurried among vehicles and clumps of people. A sheriff's deputy allowed me through the line. Wade and his volunteers were huddled a good block away from the fire, which was burning furiously despite the rain. Sparks swarmed upward like a plague of lightning bugs. The air was bitter with the stench of burning rubber and gasoline. The road was littered with debris from periodic explosions.

As I caught Wade's arm, a muffled boom sent balls of fire into the sky. All of us instinctively retreated a few steps. "What happened?" I demanded.

"Someone heard a bomb go off, looked out the window, and called us," he said. "We arrived three-quarters of an hour ago, but there isn't anything we can do, and I'm not risking anyone's life for a damn gas station. Rain'll see to it sooner or later."

"Could there be someone inside?"

"The guy that works there made it out a window. He has a nasty burn on one leg, and we sent him to the hospital. I don't know how many storage tanks there were, but they must have been full. We've been watching fireworks since we got here."

Harve found us. His black plastic raincoat clung like glittery lizard skin, and a battered canvas hat decorated with fishing flies did little to keep the rain off his stony face. "I'm getting mighty tired of our firebugs," he said. He started to take out a cigar butt, then realized he wouldn't have much success in the steady rain. "If we ever catch them, they're gonna be real sorry."

I told him and Wade about my earlier interview. "They were playing with me," I added. "Ever seen a cat with a baby rabbit?"

Another boom sent us skittering to the shelter of a doorway, where Harve felt he could risk lighting a cigar. "How ya doing with the other case?" he asked as he struck a match.

"We've had a minor setback. However, I may have stumbled onto a connection that might mean something," I said, sighing. I was going to pull him aside to explain further, but he seemed more interested in the fire, and I finally went to my (Ruby Bee's) car and drove back to Maggody.

Darla Jean McIlhaney stared at the shadows on her bedroom ceiling. Frederick Marland had called earlier in the evening with the bad news: Arly knew. The good news, he'd assured her, was that Arly didn't know everything. Once Darla Jean'd stopped crying, he'd told her what to say, and had stayed on the telephone to coach her with the lines until she felt comfortable with them. Sorta comfortable, anyway. She was never comfortable telling lies, not even when she knew she'd get grounded if she told the truth.

This particular truth could get her grounded until she was old enough to settle into a rocking chair alongside Adele Wockerman at the county nursing home. Telling Arly that she and Frederick had parked on a dark road and fooled around wouldn't make her parents break into applause, but the truth was downright gawdawful and she was planning to admit only to some kissin' and neckin' and a lot of chattering about famous Hollywood stars.

The worst of it was that the gossip was out there, somehow. Otherwise, how could Arly have found out so easily? She rolled over and looked at the clock. It was too late to call Heather or Traci to find out if anyone was talking about having seen the car at the motel. But she couldn't sleep and she couldn't stop sniveling, and finally she dialed the number of Frederick's room.

"Yeah?" he answered in a thick, irritated voice.

"It's me," she whispered. "I can't do anything but toss and turn since you told me about Arly coming to talk to me. What if she knows about the motel?"

"We went over this for an hour. There's no way she can find out about it. If she knew, she'd have asked me for details. You don't want me to relate details, do you?"

Darla Jean grabbed her pillow and clung to it as if it were a life preserver and her bedroom a shark-infested pool. "No, and you promised you'd never say nothing. I still don't understand why it matters where you were if that lady actress had an accident. I mean, why does—"

"Standard police procedure," he interrupted. "I need to sleep, darling. Carlotta's handling the camera in the morning, and we're shooting as many scenes as we can. In that I'm playing a sixteen-year-old, I don't need bloodshot eyes with bags under them. I told you what to say to Arly. If you can't lie, tell her whatever you wish. Good night."

He hung up, but her call had disturbed him and left him wide awake. A drink was in order, he decided, and he got out of bed to find the small flask he kept in the bottom of his suitcase. Sharing a room with Fuzzy had taught him the wisdom of hiding anything he himself had hopes of drinking. As he filled a glass, he glanced out the window and noticed that directly across the lot, a light was on in Carlotta's room.

Interesting. Were she and Gwenneth staying awake to guard the door, or was Carlotta pecking out revisions while Gwenneth amused Hal in the next room? In a way, he felt sorry for his blond costar. Hal had something on her, something from her past, and he alluded to it often enough to keep her under his control. Frederick had heard rumors that she'd been offered roles by other companies. Not major companies, of course. Her talents were limited, and her capacity to express anything more complex than enthusiasm was unremarkable.

Despite his irritation with her, he realized he felt fraternal affection for her. They'd run away from bad family situations to Hollywood, and arrived with the shared curse of imperfect teeth, blotchy skin, pathetically punk hair and clothing, and arrogance. They were both young and inexperienced in the murky, power-perverted ways of the industry. Since their "discoveries," Hal's thumb had held both of them down as if they were insects. Frederick had already decided *Wild Cherry Wine* would be his last film with Glittertown, but he wasn't sure Gwenneth could break away as painlessly as he could.

Then again, he thought as he finished off the drink and returned to bed, every now and then her baby-blue eyes turned gray and her voice hardened like that of a motorcycle gang mama. Maybe Sister Gwenneth was capable of all sorts of things.

So, at nearly one in the morning, an incredibly late hour for this much activity in a back corner of Stump County, some folks were awake and others not.

The majority of the citizens of Hasty were, because it was hard to sleep through bombastic explosions, cars, sirens, horns, shouting, and general bustle, the likes of which had never been seen before in town.

In contrast, most of the citizens of Maggody were asleep, with a scant handful of exceptions. Billy Dick's mother was dishing up eggs and grits at the truck stop; her back was aching something terrible, but her shift didn't end until six. She refilled an endless line of coffee cups and tried to smile.

The chief of police was in her bed, but she was glaring at a cast-iron character she'd found in a drawer. It was no more than three inches high, cheap and crudely made. The seams were rough, the features indistinct, the base slightly crooked. But anyone with half a mind could see it was a wizard in a pointed cap and a long cloak. He had a beard, a crooked nose, and a sharp chin, but where his eyes should have been, there were unfathomable holes.

Ruby Bee sat in her living room and wondered where her car was and if there'd be enough gas left in it to go to the flea market in Piccard.

Carlotta was talking on the telephone, although the only person (locally, that is) who knew this was the trooper, who'd seen her light go on and dashed down for a peek in the window to make sure she wasn't in the throes of being murdered. He was kinda disappointed.

Hal, Gwenneth, and Anderson were all beset with insomnia, for a variety of reasons.

But others were asleep, like Mrs. Jim Bob, whose dream was chaste, and Jim Bob, whose wasn't. Brother Verber's dream was chaotic, to put it charitably. Raz snored on his lumpy bed, and Marjorie snored on the floor nearby; (any speculation about the content of either's dream must be of your own doing.) Estelle was in the midst of a steamy dream starring Vidal Sassoon. Since she didn't know what he looked like—and it was *her* dream, after all—he closely resembled Buddy Meredith.

The bit players, like Eula, Elsie, Lottie, Kevin's parents, and Dahlia's granny, not to overlook the younger set, such as Heather, Traci, and Dwayne (Darla Jean's boyfriend), were asleep. As were Perkins and his eldest, Roy Stivers, the hippies who owned the Emporium, the two or three drunks sprawled in the mud outside the pool hall, and others of no interest whatsoever to the "sequential development of the plot." There may be a little white lie in there somewhere, but not a vital one.

Moving beyond the city limits of Maggody, Kevin and Dahlia had opted to sleep in the car until morning, since it wouldn't be seemly to cohabit with a corpse. Still in his chivalrous mood, Kevin had volunteered to take the front seat so his beloved would have more room in the back. He hadn't really had much choice, but he made the gesture early in the game and felt real proud of hisself.

Sergeant John Plover's teeth were grinding as he slept; it made no difference, since he slept in solitude. Eventually Wade Elkins and his fire fighters made it home. Harve Dorfer's deputies did, too, but he went to his office and slept on the couch.

Toward dawn the rain stopped, and by then every last soul was asleep. Serenely or fitfully, with smiles or with grimaces, under ironed sheets or under nothing but chilly air, all were asleep.

Chapter 13

26 INT. CHURCH—DAY—LONG SHOT

PREACHER PIPKIN and HARRY DORK walk down the aisle of the church. They stop and shake hands.

> DORK
>
> I appreciate you takin' the time to talk to me, Preacher Pipkin. I'm feelin' better, and I reckon I better get back to the farm.

> PIPKIN
>
> Glad to help, Harry. Now you just keep your distance from that pretty little heifer and pay more attention to your wife.

Dork exits, and CAMERA FOLLOWS Pipkin as he sits down in a pew and wipes his face with a handkerchief. CAMERA WIDENS to cover Loretta as she comes in furtively and sits in the pew behind him. Pipkin does not acknowledge her.

(CONTINUED):

Everybody and everything looked dingy as I went into Ruby Bee's and crawled onto a stool. "Coffee," I said, ignoring said everybody, which consisted of the proprietress behind the bar, Estelle on her usual roost, and over in the booths a smattering of truck drivers, supermarket employees, and the trooper I'd bawled out the night before. He slid down in his seat, but I lacked the wherewithall to ascertain that he was officially off duty. I barely had a wherewithout.

"Nice of you to bring back my car," Ruby Bee said as she set down a cup of coffee.

I took a sip. "I didn't bring back your car."

"You can't just take people's property like in a Communist country," Estelle said from the end of the bar. "What's more, you owe your mother an explanation for waking her up like that and causing her to sit up half the night sick with worry, Miss Don't Give a Hoot."

My mother the martyr nodded vigorously. "There weren't no way on God's green earth I could get back to sleep till nearly dawn, and then I had to get up to start my pies. If there's not enough gas for Estelle and me to go to—"

"Stop," I said with a growl. "I didn't get much sleep, myself. I am not commandeering your car; I am borrowing it because I need to run up to Missouri. It has to do with the investigation, but I am not—repeat, not—going to explain the purpose of the trip. Take Estelle's station wagon wherever it is you're going." I took all the change from my pocket and let it clatter on the counter. "Gas money, ladies."

I stalked out of the bar, fuming so hard I nearly ran into Carlotta and Harve.

"Oh, here you are," she said. "I know this sounds

callous, but we've got to keep shooting in order to come in anywhere near budget. Sheriff Dorfer has agreed to handle security at the sites, and we'll keep the sets closed . . . if you don't object.''

"Can't see that it'll hurt,'' Harve said uncomfortably.

I took a closer look at him. "Why are you in civilian clothes, Sheriff Dorfer? Considering the craziness going on, it doesn't seem like the best time to take the day off to go fishing.''

It was the very first time I'd seen him blush, and it was not a pretty picture. His nose and ears were scarlet, and blotches were creeping up his neck like eruptive hives. He ducked his head and hunted around in his pocket until he found a cigar stub, stuck it between his lips, and mumbled something as he struck a match. Shakily struck a match, that is.

"I didn't quite catch that,'' I said, amusement replacing the deep aggravation that only Ruby Bee and Estelle could arouse in me (and did so on a daily, if not hourly, basis).

He mumbled something again, but Carlotta put her hand on his arm and said, "Since the sheriff's going to be there, we offered him a small role as a local farmer seeking spiritual guidance. It won't propel him to stardom, but he thought it might be entertaining for his friends and family to see him on the screen one of these days.''

"Gonna be in the movies, huh?'' I said. "Wow, Harve, I'm impressed. Can I have your autograph?''

"This lady called me at the office and asked if they could keep working on their movie. I couldn't see any reason for them to sit in their rooms, so I said it was all right with me. This way we can keep them in a group and under guard.''

Carlotta shot me a dry smile, but she sounded appropriately humble as she said, "We are so grateful to you people. This murder is a terrible thing; we're all devastated with shock and grief, and we want nothing more than for you to catch Kitty's killer. Hal's popping pills like they were peanuts, and Gwenneth's convinced her death is imminent. None of us got much sleep last night. Is there any news about Meredith and Fuzzy?"

I shook my head. "I talked to Plover earlier this morning. His men are working their way along the road in both directions, and we may have to start beating Cotter's Ridge and the banks of Boone Creek if we don't have any luck. It doesn't make any sense for either of them to have gone into the woods, but none of this makes any sense."

"Surely they'll turn up," she said without conviction. "Meredith's a great guy, and even Fuzzy has his endearing moments. But, as the sheriff mentioned, it won't do any good for us to sit and worry."

"I don't care," I said. "It's just as well for you to be together and protected, if only by an aspiring student of the art of cinematography. I'll be gone for a few hours, but I may need to find you all when I return. Where will you be shooting?"

She consulted her clipboard. "The entire schedule's been modified until we know if Meredith's coming back. We're slotted for two scenes at that oddly shaped church at the south end of town. I don't anticipate any problems there, unless our amateurs are overcome with camera fright. An hour there, maybe twice that, and then we'll shoot as many as we can at"—she scanned the page—"Jim Bob Buchanon's house. Two exteriors and three interiors. I should think we'll be there until dark."

"Wait a minute—you're doing two scenes at the Voice of the Almighty?" I said, mystified. "What does Brother Verber have to say about this?"

"He also has a small role," Carlotta murmured.

"He does?" I said, more mystified.

Her expression was impossible to read, and her voice was as bland as spring water. "He fit into the picture perfectly, and was delighted to offer his church as a site. I did a few revisions, and *voilà!*"

Throughout this exchange, Harve was scuffling his foot in the gravel like a child in the principal's office, although it's doubtful a child would be allowed to puff on a cigar butt in such an august setting. "Well, I'd better get my men organized down at the Assembly Hall. Where'd you say you was going, Arly?"

"I didn't. Have fun, Harve, and don't forget to emote."

"What's that mean?"

"Carlotta will tell you all about it," I said. I frowned at her. "Do you have another photograph of Meredith?"

"I have some standard portfolio shots in the room. Why do you need one?"

"I don't know if I need one or not, but I'd appreciate it if you'd loan me one for the day."

Carlotta returned with an eight-by-eleven glossy print of a smiling man with pleasant but unremarkable features. I went back to the PD, checked the map once more, and drove north toward Pineyville, Missouri, intending to use the time wisely to organize my thoughts about the murder. Discipline did not prevail. So Harve and Verber were in the movie, along with Mrs. Jim Bob and Dahlia. By the time I returned, the entire population might be signed up. Hell, I might end up not only with a full dance card but also with a new career.

I began to whistle "Hooray for Hollywood" as I passed the sign that denoted the city limits of Maggody . . .

"You must take me this morning," Mrs. Jim Bob said into the receiver. "The movie people are shooting here today, and that's certainly more important than going to a flea market on the other side of the county."

"No, it ain't," said Estelle. "Ruby Bee and I have been aiming to get over there for more than a month, and I arranged my appointments so we could go this morning. I might change my plans for one of my regulars, but I don't seem to recall you darkening my doorstep since Eve ate the apple. Why don't you call that high-falutin place you patronize in Farberville?"

Mrs. Jim Bob figured it wouldn't be politic to admit she already had and that they were booked solid for the morning. She had a sneaky suspicion they would have accommodated her if she tipped more generously, but she didn't go into it. "Now, Estelle," she wheedled, "there's no reason to get your nose all bent out of shape. I was planning to start using you even before the Hollywood people showed up. I was telling Jim Bob just the other night how much more convenient it would be for me to patronize Estelle's Hair Fantasies instead of driving all the way to—"

In that she was talking to a dial tone, she gave up and replaced the receiver. "You know," she said loudly to Perkins's eldest, who was out in the hallway waxing the floor, "not only is Estelle snooty, she has a lack of charity in her heart. One might wonder if she's not jealous because no one offered her a role in the movie. Now, I'll grant you that I prefer to have my hair done in Farberville, but that's no reason for her to act this way in what is clearly an emergency."

Perkins's eldest adjusted the headset and turned up the volume of the transistor radio in her pocket. She was growing fond of rap music and becoming a devotee of the lyrics.

"I don't suppose you've ever fixed anyone's hair?" Mrs. Jim Bob called from the other room. The inaudible response was not a challenge to interpret. "Considering how you wear your hair, I'd be the first to agree with you that you lack expertise in that area. From the looks of it, I'd be surprised to hear you wash it once a month. Cleanliness is next to godliness, as those of us who attend church know."

Jim Bob came into the kitchen. He'd been given a list of chores over coffee, even though he'd tried to weasel out of them by claiming he had to be down at the store to receive deliveries. But the trash was in the cans; the cans hosed; the grass mowed (out in front, anyway); the shrubs trimmed (on the side visible from the window); his closet neat (he doubted they were doing closet scenes, but she was adamant); his papers stashed in desk drawers; and his wife, for some inexplicable reason, was again sitting in the living room having a grand conversation with the walls.

If the truth be known, he was planning to take off from work because he was as excited as his wife. Carlotta had said that Gwenneth, the Marland guy, and the saint-somebody guy would be on the set all afternoon. Gwenneth D'Amourre, Jim Bob thought, sucking on his teeth. If her honkers were half so luscious as they'd been in *Tanya Makes the Team,* he figured he'd be in heaven. Not in Brother Verber's and Mrs. Jim Bob's version, which was chock full of harps and angels and that kinda crap. His heaven had honkers.

Saliva trickled down his chin as he went out the back door and drove down to the supermarket, but he didn't notice. The assistant manager did, though, and gleefully told everyone in the break room that Jim Bob was nearing the time when he could hide his own Easter eggs.

"I wanna be a bad street dude," Perkins's eldest said along with the voice blasting into both ears. Her ample rump swishing with the beat, she moved down the hall. "I tell you, Mama, I gonna be rude."

"Did you say 'rude'?" Mrs. Jim Bob said from her post in the next room. "I'm glad you agree that no matter how hard I strive to maintain a Christian attitude, there's no getting around it. That Estelle Oppers is just plain rude!"

Kevin struggled to wake up as his head bounced against the upholstery of the front seat. His ears were being gripped so tightly he almost yelped, but before he could do much of anything, his head bounced again, this time hard enough to rattle his brains.

"Git up, I said," Dahlia muttered as she leaned over the back of the seat, hanging onto his ears like they were pitcher handles, and determined to shake him awake if it killed him. "Git up afore I rip your fool ears off your head and feed 'em to the bears."

"I'm awake, my darling, so you kin let go now." Once he was free, he sat up and rubbed his eyes while he tried to recollect where they were and why. It came back to him like a splash of ice water. "What do you reckon we ought to do?" he asked humbly.

" 'We'? There ain't no 'we,' Kevin Fitzgerald Buchanon. What you're going to do is get out of this car and commence to crawl around in the bushes until you find that wire. Then you're gonna put it back where it came from and drive me to town. While I'm making the movie, you kin go tell Arly about that dead body in the cabin."

"That sounds like a real good plan. What is it you're gonna do whilst I hunt for the wire, my sponge cake?"

"Sit right here with the doors locked," she answered tartly. "Sometimes I wonder why I agreed to be bespoken to you, 'cause you're more addled than a preacher in paradise. There's a dead body not but a stone's throw from us, and that means there's likely to be a murderer lurking around for his next victim. That's why I'm staying in the car and you're hunting the wire."

"Of course, my dumpling," Kevin said, although there was something about her logic that didn't fit well. He looked at the snarly woods. He'd been on the hysterical side when he threw the wire, what with Dahlia screaming at him and the Hollywood nightmare possessing him, and he disremembered the precise direction he'd chosen.

He caught her reflection in the rearview mirror, and it was enough to propel him out of the car and into a mud puddle. "You lock the doors real tight," he said solicitously, "and I'll just get the wire and put it back real fast."

The wire didn't weigh much, and he figured it couldn't have gone too far. What he hadn't gotten around to mentioning to his Venus was that he'd also thrown the key ring at the same time—not intentionally, of course, but because it was in the same hand.

The woods were clogged with scraggly pines, vines thick enough to choke a bull, clumps of hungry thorns, and the rotting remains of tree trunks. Heavy clouds threatened to produce another deluge. Birds shrieked at him, and a squirrel sputtered as it assessed him through rabid black eyes. There was a path of sorts, not much to speak of but better than fighting the briars and mushy leaves hiding snakes, so Kevin gave Dahlia a halfhearted salute and forged into the wilderness. By the time she rolled down the window to ask where in tarnation the picnic basket was, he had disappeared from view.

Pineyville, Missouri, made Maggody look like a seething metropolis. There were a dozen or so houses, a few trailers, and a small store sporting a variety of rusty tin signs that hawked products from much earlier in the century. There was no church, post office, or redbrick building with a cooperative police officer to whom I could direct my questions.

I went into the store. The man behind the counter wore overalls and a cap and appeared to be no more than thirty, although he'd had time to grow a beer belly and to develop a seasoned sneer. I tapped my badge and said, "I'm Chief of Police Hanks from Arkansas. I'd like to ask you a few questions."

"About what?" He turned around and began to straighten cans on the shelf.

"About this man." I put the photograph of Meredith on the counter and waited until curiosity turned him back around. While he studied the photograph, I said, "I have reason to believe he grew up in Pineyville. He's about fifty now, so he would have lived here before your time."

"What did he do?" the man asked idly. "Kill somebody?"

That indeed was the question. "Nothing that I know of. He was in Maggody and left a couple of days back. There's been a death in the family. I need to find him so I can let him know about it. One possibility is that he has family here and came back to visit."

"I ain't seen him." He dropped the photograph and returned his attention to the dusty cans. "Ain't ever seen him," he added, "and never will."

I went back outside and gazed glumly at the houses along the highway. Some were only slightly unkempt;

others were patched together with mismatched sheets of plywood. Old appliances and cars on concrete blocks dotted the neglected yards. I selected one of the tidier houses, crossed the road, and knocked on the door.

The woman who answered was elderly, as were her limp housecoat and slippers. Her hands were contorted with arthritis. Under a few whisps of thin white hair, her face was as shriveled as the doll heads made from dried apples, but she sounded alert as she snapped, "Are you one of those missionaries? I dun told you folks that I belong to my own church, and I ain't of a mind to listen to a bunch of tomfoolery."

I explained who I was and repeated the story I'd told the man in the store. She opened the screen door far enough to snatch the photograph from my hand, then told me to wait where I was. The door slammed. Pineyville was less cordial than Maggody, I thought as I watched a truck pull into the lot across from me. The driver spat in the dust as he went inside the store. Definitely not a place for tourists—or anyone else, for that matter.

I'd been waiting for ten minutes when the woman returned, opened the screen door far enough to thrust the photograph through the slit, and said, "What'd you say his name is?"

"Meredith. Buddy Meredith," I said carefully.

"Well, it ain't. I asked my sister Maybella and she agreed. Maybella has some doddly spells when she thinks she's back in pigtails and pinafores, but she and I both recognized this here man's face, even if he weren't half as old when he left town a good twenty-five years ago. He was lucky to get away with his backside intact."

"What is his name?"

"There's no need for you to shout at me, missy. Maybella may be deaf, but I ain't, or not yet, anyway. I still got my hearing and my teeth." She gave me a flash of the latter, which were the best money could buy from a mail-order catalog. "His name's Buddy Oliphant. Maybella seems to think he came from the Oliphants over in Macrumb, but I say his foreparents was in Hiana before they died out."

I wrote down the name and stared at it. "He grew up here, though, rather than in Macrumb or Hiana?"

"I didn't say that," she said challengingly. "Don't go putting words in my mouth like those slick-talking missionaries with their fancy clothes and bicycles."

I tried a new tack. "But you and your sister recognized Buddy Oliphant."

"We did, and he weren't calling himself Meredith. Back then Oliphant was good enough for him, and it was good enough for little Becky Hopperly, too. I swear, that gal didn't have the brains God gave a goose, but she was a fine-looking thing with big blue eyes and bright yellow hair."

I was making notes and getting more confused. Becky Hopperly, big blue eyes, yellow hair. Oliphant was good enough for her, if we ever found out who she was. "Was Becky his girlfriend?" I asked.

The woman cackled. "And a lot more. Buddy was working for her pa, who had the biggest farm in the county. Buddy was supposed to sleep in the barn with the other fellows, but it turned out he preferred Becky's bed. Her pa caught on after a spell and got his brothers together. Those Hopperly boys were always meaner than dockroot. They told Buddy he didn't have no choice but to do the honorable thing, iff'n he wanted to keep his manhood between his legs rather than in a jar." She hesitated, her face puckered with pleasure as she remembered what must have been a juicy scandal. "Why don't you come inside and set yourself down?"

I followed her into a dark, dreary room crowded with

furniture that wouldn't have interested Roy Stivers. It reeked of camphor and dust and decay; the windows had probably been nailed down for decades. My hostess told me to sit on the sofa, then went to check on Maybella, who purportedly had a tendency to meander in the attic. I concentrated on breathing through my mouth.

She returned and settled down beside me, still clearly excited by the opportunity to relate the melodramatic story to a new audience. "Maybella's doing poorly just now, so I left her upstairs, going through a trunk. Now, where was I?"

"The Hopperly boys ordered Buddy to marry Becky," I said, doing my best to suppress my frustration at the leisurely pace. I had no idea if this was leading anywhere of relevance, but I had to listen to it. If I tried to shake it out of her, her teeth might end up on the far side of the room. "Did he marry her?"

"Don't rush me. I ain't swatting flies in the outhouse," she said crossly. "After the Hopperly boys told Buddy how the cow ate the cabbage, so to speak, he sez that's fine with him on account of he loves Becky and is planning to marry her as soon as he saves up some money for the ring. Old man Hopperly allows that Buddy better start puttin' in some overtime. That was that for the time bein', with him and Becky allowed to spoon on the veranda, where her Pa could watch them, and Buddy workin' all day at the farm and then doin' odd jobs for folks when he could get 'em."

"And did they get married?" I asked, feigning patience.

"There you go again, rushing me. If you don't have time to listen, then you can run along and I'll get back to hulling peas for supper."

I lowered my eyes. "No, ma'am, I'd like to hear what happened."

"Then mind your manners. Well, afore too long it turns out that Becky's in the family way, and her pa sure ain't gonna wait until Buddy has enough money, not with everybody in town commenting slyly on her waistline and asking about wedding plans. Old man Hopperly gives Buddy some money and tells him to take the truck to Hiana to buy the ring and the marriage license." She glanced sharply at me, in case I was plotting to rush her along. I sat stoically. "So Becky borrows a dress from her cousin Charlotte, who was a might pudgy, and invites everybody to the wedding, to be the very next day. Maybella and I argued half the night about which of us was gonna' wear Mama's pearls. She finally won on account of her being three years older. Looks it, too."

"So they got married?" I said, despite my efforts to keep quiet.

"Do you mind? So the preacher's at the house, along with most everybody in town, and there's flowers on the table and cookies and punch all set out in the kitchen. Becky's looking real sweet in Charlotte's dress, even though it was snow white and it was as plain as the nose on your face that Becky wasn't a virgin, not with a bun in the warmer. At first we're all chattering and having a fine time, but after a while we're glancing at the clock on the mantel. The preacher keeps smiling and telling Becky not to worry her little head. Long about dark, even he couldn't tell any more lies. The Hopperly boys went to Hiana that very night. They didn't find hide nor hair of Buddy Oliphant. What they did find was the truck at the bus station. Turned out the boy lost his nerve and took the first bus that came along."

"And that was the last anybody saw him?"

"Not hardly," she said with a snort. "He is the Wite & Brite man, after all. Maybella recognized him the first time he was on the television. She said, 'Look, Augusta, if that ain't Buddy Oliphant, then I ain't sitting here eating watermelon and spittin' seeds. He's still got teeth like a picket fence.' "

"But he's never been back in Pineyville?" I asked out of desperation.

"He's liable to be too scared to ever show his face, even though the Hopperlys died out to a man. The bank foreclosed on the farm, but they never could sell it to anybody, and after a while it was nothing but a mess of rotting wood and weeds."

My theory about the Hopperly boys' revenge evaporated. "What about Becky? Is she still living here?"

"Land sakes, no. Not more than a day or two after Buddy ran out on her, she was sent to stay with her aunt in St. Louis. We never laid eyes on that poor girl again."

"Do you and Maybella remember the aunt's name?" I asked, desperation lapsing into total despondency. The odds on finding someone who'd lived in St. Louis that long ago were not good; they were almost non-existent. If any of this meant anything. If the girl had nursed a grudge for all this time, and if she found out that Meredith was in Maggody, and if she decided to murder his wife . . .

"I don't think I ever heard tell the aunt's name," the woman, now identified as Augusta, replied slowly. "I did hear that Becky died, if that helps. Lordy, that must have been fifteen years back, maybe more, because Maybella had had her stroke and I had to shout at her so she could hear me."

"Is she buried here?"

Augusta scratched her scaly pink scalp. "I seem to recollect she is, but you can look for yourself in the cemetery beyond what used to be the Baptist church.

Take the dirt road next to the store and look for a washed-out sign."

I did some brilliant calculations that added up to twenty-five or so, as in years. "What about her child? Did he or she come back here after Becky died?"

"According to Hopperly, she miscarried a month after she went to St. Louis, but he still didn't want anything to do with her. He was real proud of telling everybody how he never sent her any money or went to her funeral when she died. We could see he was upset, though, when the body came back in a plain pine box. He took to drinking and raving something awful about how Becky had been a slut all her life and that her sinful ways had finally caught up with her and killed her. His tractor tumped on him a few years later. Maybella was of a mind that he did it on purpose."

Clucking and head-shaking were expected of me, so I obliged while I scanned my notes. The pathetic story would make a fine movie, I supposed, but it wasn't giving me any clues about Kitty Kaye's murder or Meredith's disappearance. There was no reason why he would have returned to Pineyville, and several reasons why he wouldn't have—not even on a bet. It would hardly provide a sanctuary. Any remaining almost in-laws would not have welcomed him back.

"What's the matter? Cat got your tongue?" Augusta snickered. "A while back, you couldn't stop yammering. Now you're sitting there like a wart on a pickle."

It was a fair analogy. I thanked her for her time, refused a cup of tea, and went out to my (Ruby Bee's) car. I found the cemetery and walked among the headstones, most of them cracked and coated with moss. A tall gray monument with Freudian overtones stood in the middle of the Hopperly family plot. I pulled back weeds from a few of them, but I couldn't determine which Hopperly boy had been Becky's father, in that they'd been busily dying two decades earlier.

I was about to give up when I stubbed my toe on a small, flat marker. I knelt beside it and brushed off the dirt. Becky Hopperly had been twenty-six years old when she died. During her short lifetime, she'd lost a lover, a baby, and a father. As I rose, I found myself wondering if she'd still had big blue eyes and bright yellow hair when she died.

Chapter 14

"I appreciate you takin' the time to talk to me, Preacher Pipkin. I'm feelin' better, and I reckon I better get back to the office," Harve said. He squinted into the light. "Was that better?"

"Cut, damn it!" Hal slammed down the script on a pew, threw his hands into the air, and stomped up the aisle of the Assembly Hall. "Someone save me from amateurs! What was I in a past life—a maggot? Is this godforsaken town some sort of cosmic joke?" He made some other comments (real sizzlers, too), but they wouldn't get past a humorless copy editor.

Gwenneth and Frederick, sitting next to each other on a pew, exchanged frustrated sighs. They were in costume and makeup, and it was hot inside the metal structure. Anderson St. James was equally uncomfortable in a suit and bow tie, but he glanced up for only a second before returning to a novel he'd had the foresight to bring.

Carlotta switched off the camera and picked up her script to see if there was any possible way to delete the Dork character without letting him know he was by far the worst actor she'd ever encountered. "Let's run over this one more time, Sheriff Dorfer," she said with a forced smile. "All you do is say your line, shake hands with the preacher, and go on out the door. Don't say another word, don't look at the camera, and remember—you're getting back to the farm, not the office. Okay?"

The only other person allowed on the set was Brother Verber. He was in his Sunday best, but the effect was ruined by the heavy sweat stains under his arms, around his neck, and even beginning to show through on his back. The script trembled in his hand. If Sister Barbara ever caught wind of what he was supposed to say right there in front of the camera, she would come down on him worse than a darn truckload of concrete. The reference to the pretty little heifer wouldn't fool a half-wit (although Harve Dorfer was so befuddled he had no idea what anybody was saying, much less what was meant by it). The reference to the choir room wouldn't fool a reject from the Buchanon clan with a charter membership in Dumb Anonymous.

Licking his lips, Brother Verber watched Harve stammer out the line several times. When Carlotta was satisfied, she curled a finger at him, and he hesitantly found the chalk mark she'd drawn on the floor. He gave her an imploring look. "Listen, little lady, don't you think it'd be better if I just warned Harve here to behave in a Christian—"

"No!" Hal bellowed as he came back down the aisle, snatched the script from Carlotta, and began to jab his finger at it with the fury of a jackhammer. "What's in the script is there for purposes of sequential development of the plot. It is vital to establish the scene in which the girl—what's her name? Loretta, yeah, that's it—Loretta battles the forces of corruption to maintain her innocence. We're into religious symbolism, fer chrissake. I don't need some pissant preacher to write my scripts!''

Carlotta took Brother Verber's handkerchief from his back pocket, blotted his face, and dusted his nose with a brush to counteract the sheen. "They're merely words," she said soothingly. "When taken in the total context, they evoke a complex imagery that Hal's striving to achieve. Try to visualize the allusion and let yourself flow with it. Do you have your lines?"

"I have the script with my lines written in it," Brother Verber said, desperately trying not to visualize anything at all because he was terrified out of his skin that something might start flowing.

"No, what I meant was, do you know your lines? Do we need to run through them again?"

"O my Gawd," Gwenneth said, rolling her eyes. "We've run through this—what? Ten times, twenty? My mascara's melting, you know, and so is the rest of me. The entire scene's not two minutes long, and we've been here two hours."

"Come on, Hal," Frederick added. "Gwenneth's shorts are so tight she can barely breathe. You may want pink cheeks, but do you want blue toes?"

"Oooh," Gwenneth said with a squeal. Her blond curls disappeared as she bent over to examine her toes.

Hal pointed his finger at Brother Verber. "Do the first line," he commanded.

Brother Verber blinked. "Do what to it?"

"Don't *do* anything to it. *Say* it."

It struck Brother Verber that fighting Satan was a darn sight easier than figuring out what these Hollywood folks were talking about. He manufactured a smile of sorts. "Glad to help, Harry. Now you just keep your distance from that pretty little heifer and pay more attention to your wife," he recited in a monotone.

Gwenneth reappeared. "Let's just get it the hell over

with." She rose and brushed past the preacher, giving him a good look at her halter and its contents. "This is mega-maddening."

"Positions," said Hal. He waited until Harve and Brother Verber found their marks, and Gwenneth was poised outside the door. He nodded at Carlotta, then said, albeit [without much hope], "Action."

"I sure do appreciate you takin' the time to talk to me, Preacher Pumpkin. I'm feelin' better, and I reckon I better get back to the . . . uh, the farm," Harve said. This time he made real sure he didn't squint into the light. "Was that better?"

"You know what's occurred to me?" Ruby Bee said as she put down a chipped cup and picked up a saucer with pretty lavender flowers.

Estelle glanced at the saucer and shook her head. "Cracked," she whispered. "Not worth a dime, much less fifty cents. These prices are enough to gag a goat."

As they continued to move alongside the table, frowning at various objets d'art, Ruby Bee said, "I was thinking about that Fuzzy fellow and how come he upped and disappeared."

"And?" said Estelle, distracted momentarily by a promising candy dish made of bubbly green carnival glass.

"Now, every time we saw him, he was drinking or already drunk," Ruby Bee said out of the corner of her mouth. There were other browsers, and she'd sworn not to breathe a word about the murder so's not to alert the media. You never could tell when one might be prowling around—and in disguise. "What's curious is that he was potted when the deputy brought them back to the bar to tell 'em the bad news. I saw him stagger to his room, and he was weaving worse than a bowleg-ged centipede.''

"You just said he was all the time drinking.''

"But yesterday morning they were making the movie at Raz Buchanon's shack, so he must have been drink-ing there. If I remember rightly, Fuzzy was talking to Raz the evening before, too. They were in a booth all by theirselves for at least an hour, just as cozy as that pair of salt and pepper shakers.''

Estelle decided the candy dish was overpriced and continued on to a stack of old magazines. "Does this have something to do with the price of tea in China?''

"Would you stop gawking at this table of junk and listen to me?''

"If you aim to continue speaking to me like that, you might find yourself hitchhiking home.''

Ruby Bee decided to be generous and overlook the remark. "This is important. What if Raz let Fuzzy try some of that rotgut moonshine everybody knows he's making on Cotter's Ridge?''

"Most likely he'd be dead. That stuff's supposed to be nasty enough to strip the hide off an alligator.''

"What I'm getting at is that if Raz let something slip about where the still is, Fuzzy might have taken off to find it. When I saw him, he looked drunk enough to go off on some hare-brained mission to find Raz's stockpile.''

"Then why hasn't he come back?''

"Because he found it, that's why.''

Estelle put down a gingham sunbonnet, took Ruby Bee's elbow, and hustled her out of the tent and across the parking lot to her station wagon. Once she'd made sure no one was following them, she said, "So you think that the Fuzzy fellow is on a toot up on Cotter's Ridge? He found Raz's stash of field whiskey and is stay-ing drunker than a boiled owl?''

"I don't see why not," Ruby Bee said as she freed her elbow and made a show of rubbing it and wincing. "I'm not sure what we ought to do about it, though. Arly's awfully busy with the murder, and I'd hate to send her all the way up past Robin's cabin if it turned out to be nothing but a wild-goose chase."

"You think maybe we should . . . help her?" Estelle murmured, wiggling her eyebrows like her forehead itched.

"That way, if we're wrong, we can just go on about our business without Arly throwing a fit because she thinks we're interfering in"—Ruby Bee paused dramatically—"her official police investigation. But first I think we ought to have a word with Raz. If we do it right, he won't even know what we're asking him."

"It can't hurt." Estelle got in the station wagon. Ruby Bee wasn't convinced, but she got in, too.

When I got back to Maggody, I cruised past the Voice of the Almighty Lord Assembly Hall. Several official vehicles and the Glittertown van were parked by the highway, and two deputies were standing by the door. Carlotta was running behind schedule, I noted with a grin.

Everything seemed under control, however, so I went to the PD. The telephone started ringing the minute I stepped inside, as if my mere presence were the stimulus for somebody somewhere to decide it was time to pester me. I answered it without enthusiasm.

"Oh, Arly, thank goodness, I've been trying to find you all morning," Eilene Buchanon said in a whoosh. "It's Kevin."

"What's Kevin?"

"He's disappeared. He left right after supper and he

didn't come home last night, and now it's nigh onto lunchtime. I've racked my brain, but I can't think where he could be.''

"Calm down, Eilene," I said as I sat down behind my desk. "Maybe he's at Dahlia's house. They're still engaged, aren't they?"

"I drove over there first thing this morning. He's not there, and neither is she. What's more, he's got his pa's car, and it goes without saying that his pa's fit to be tied. Maybe Kevin and Dahlia were in a horrible wreck, and now he's unconscious in a hospital or even worse."

I didn't point out that he was unconscious most of the time. "If he was in a wreck, you'd have been notified. He and Dahlia must have gone on a jaunt somewhere. They'll turn up soon, but I'll pass along the plate number and a description of the car to the sheriff's department and the state police."

I wrote down the information, made some more reassuring noises, and hung up. The telephone rang.

"Arly, good," Plover said, forgoing any minor pleasantries. "Merganser did a preliminary at that gas station in Hasty. The front door has an exterior padlock, and it was locked. Merganser had a helluva time poking around what was left, but he's fairly sure the point of origin was in the bay—not out by the pumps. That indicates arson."

"And attempted murder," I contributed flatly.

"And attempted murder." He told me he'd be there shortly and hung up. The telephone rang.

"Arly, this is Elsie McMay. Do you happen to know where Estelle is? She promised to do my hair at eleven, and it's nearly noon now."

I was almost afraid to ask. "Did you try Ruby Bee's?"

"Yes, and no one answers. I knew they were going to a flea market in Piccard, but Estelle said they'd be back by eleven so Ruby Bee could open for lunch. It's not like Estelle to miss an appointment.''

I told her I'd keep an eye out for them and hung up. I glowered at the telephone for a minute, daring it to ring with more ominous news. Then, still watching it out of the corner of my eye, I made a list of lost souls:

1.   Buddy Meredith, missing thirty-six hours; not in Pineyville, Missouri
2.   Fuzzy Indigo, missing twenty-four hours
3—4.   Kevin Buchanon and Dahlia O'Neill, missing eighteen hours
5—6.   Ruby Bee Hanks and Estelle Oppers, missing at least an hour; not earth-shattering, but interesting

Numbers three through six could take their own sweet time surfacing, but I had to figure out where numbers one and two were. I mentally tried to reconstruct the evening preceding the murder. The company had met to determine the shooting schedule and then retired to Ruby Bee's Bar & Grill for dinner. Afterward Fuzzy had gone off, presumably under his own steam. At ten o'clock Meredith and Kitty Kaye had gone to their room, and during the next two hours, she'd been stabbed in the neck and he'd vanished, either voluntarily or not. Gwenneth went to her room at eleven; Carlotta went for a walk. Frederick Marland had been in Farberville with a girl. Anderson had been alone in his room.

Just one big happy family, these Hollywood people. Making low-budget films and oodles of money. No one with any known motive to disrupt the production and therefore their respective incomes.

I opened my notebook and read through the statements I'd taken. Thus far no one had much of an alibi. I realized I hadn't gotten around to confirming Frederick Marland's story. I was flipping through the directory when (take a guess) the telephone rang.

"Chief Hanks? This is Detective Cannelli in L.A. I have a few tidbits for you, but nothing exciting. Ready?"

I grabbed a pencil. "I'll take anything."

"I ran the names through Equity and our computer links. Gwenneth D'Amourre, née Wanda Sue Thackett, is from Cedar Rapids, and there's an outstanding warrant for her arrest on a hit-and-run. Frederick Marland, né Freddie, is clean, at least with the feds. Katherine Kaye, née Katherine Kaye Winkleman, had a few traffic violations. Meredith's real name is Buddy Oliphant. Harold Desmond has been booked twice for possession of a controlled substance, but kept both of them out of court. Carlotta Lowenstein's clear, as is Anderson St. James, born James Allen Anderson. Francis Indigo, a.k.a. Fuzzy, has a sheet from here to San Diego and back. DWI's, public drunkenness, disturbing the peace, failure to comply, resisting, all that sort of thing."

"Wait," I said, scribbling as fast as I could. "Is there a chance any of them could have some sort of involvement with a ring that distributes pirated tapes?"

"You'll have to ask them," Detective Cannelli said, then wished me a good day and hung up.

My mood had not improved when Les Vernon came into the PD. "I missed you this morning," he said, "but I heard about the fireworks at the gas station in Hasty. Anything you want me to do about those damn firebugs, short of shooting them?"

"Pick them both up and take them to separate detention rooms at the sheriff's department," I said. "Give me a call when you get there. I'm going to question each of them until one breaks. I don't care how long it takes." He started out the door, but I made the mistake of looking at my list. "Hold on, Les. It seems we've misplaced some more people. Not anyone important, but I guess we ought to alert the patrol cars." He snickered when I read the list, then departed before I could come up with any more assignments.

I left a note for Plover and drove to Darla Jean McIlhaney's house. Millicent was startled to see me, but admitted Darla Jean was upstairs in her room, no doubt, gossiping on the telephone with her friends, because that was all they seemed to do these days, and why on earth did I need to speak to Darla Jean? I did not enlighten her as I went up the stairs. Darla Jean's voice was drifting through the door as I knocked; I heard her laugh as she told someone she'd call back.

As she opened the door, any lingering trace of laughter vanished. "Arly?" she said with a croak. "What do you want?"

"I want to talk to you, and I suggest we do it in your room with the door closed."

"Sure, yeah, like come on in." She stepped aside, and once I was in, closed the door and locked it. "Sit on the bed if you want, or over by the window, or wherever you want."

"You sit on the bed," I said, taken aback by her ashen face and watery, terrified eyes. "I'll stand. I need to hear what happened when you drove Frederick Marland to Farberville."

"Nothing, nothing at all." She tried to give me a defiant look, but the tears spilled out of her eyes and she began to snivel. "I didn't do nothing. We went to that drugstore on Thurber Street, and then we drove around, and then he said did I want something to drink and I said—well, I said okay, but then he said not Cokes, and—I couldn't—he said let's go—he wanted to, but I didn't—and then . . ."

I sat down beside her and put my arm around her shoulder. "Calm down, Darla Jean. No one's accusing you of doing anything terrible. Thoughtless, perhaps, but not all that terrible.''

"But it *was* terrible," she said, twitching as she held in sobs. "He said it would be fun, but—"

"What would be fun?" I asked gently. "Necking on a dark road?"

"The motel," she said with a moan.

Startled, I clasped her shoulder more tightly and said, "What motel? Did you two come back to the Flamingo Motel?"

She stopped moaning and gave me a blank look. "Why would we do that?"

"There was . . . a problem there that night."

"Oh, yeah, I heard that one of the actress ladies fell and broke her neck or something."

"That's right," I murmured. "Which motel are you talking about, Darla Jean?"

"That one on the corner of Thurber Street and the highway," she said. The tears started flowing again. "After he got his fancy suntan lotion, he told me to drive to a liquor store, and when he came out, he had a bottle of whiskey. He wanted to go to a motel. He said we were just going to drink and watch a racy movie."

"And you bought that?"

Her nose was flowing as freely as her tears. Still shivering, she wiped her face on the corner of her bedspread and tried to smile. "Frederick Marland's a real famous movie star, Arly, and the best-looking guy I've ever seen. I guess I thought it'd be really neat if I could tell Heather and Traci that we'd had a few drinks and messed around. I wasn't about to . . . you know, go all the way or anything. It sounded so sophisticated and romantic."

"Did it turn out to be romantic?" I asked drily.

"It turned out to be the awfulest night of my life.

The first couple of times, he mixed whiskey with Coke for me, but then he started splashing it straight from the bottle to the glass and telling me to drink it without ice or anything. There was some movie on, something about naked nuns, but before I knew what was happening, we were on the bed."

"Did he take precautions?"

"I don't know," she said miserably. "I told him over and over that I wasn't like slutty Robin Buchanon, that I didn't live in some shack on the ridge and act like an animal. He thought that was real funny and asked me all kinds of things about Robin and what she was rumored to do. Then he started doing things I didn't like, and after a while I pretended I wasn't even there. Sometimes he'd let me rest for a few minutes, but then he'd shake me awake and start up again with stuff that hurt. It's all real murky. I remember I threw up once. He was mad about that, but then he made me drink more whiskey, even though the first bottle made me sick." She hid her face in her hands, fell back on the bed, and curled into the fetal position, her knees almost touching her hands. "Don't tell my parents, please . . ."

"I'm not going to tell your parents, Darla Jean, but I strongly encourage you to do it. What time did you get home?"

"It was after midnight. I was too drunk to drive, and I threw up again on the way home. The next morning I felt so bad I wished I was dead and buried."

Despite the temptation, I didn't spout off the standard platitudes about letting that be a lesson, et cetera. Instead, I sat beside her and rubbed her back until she relaxed a bit, then assured her I'd be there to help her if it turned out the lack of precautions resulted in any unwanted problems. Her parents were the type to react in much the same way the Hopperly boys had twenty-five years ago. In this case, however, the miscreant would be two thousand miles away and Darla Jean would be all alone in the eye of the hurricane.

Millicent was waiting at the bottom of the stairs, a grimly inquisitive look on her face, but I brushed past her and went out to my (Ruby Bee's) car. A pungent smell caught my attention, and after a brief search I found a burned book of matches under the driver's seat. The smell was fading, but the matchheads were warm.

I looked around, admittedly rather wildly, but there was no one in the McIlhaneys' yard or any traffic on the road. I resisted the urge to crumple the matchbook in my hand and hurl it out the window. The paper cover was charred; fingerprints were out of the question. Still, I told myself as I set it on the dashboard and put the key in the ignition, it was evidence of a sort. It was also a message.

I started to turn the key, then jerked my hand away as if I'd grasped a red-hot coal. One of the damn firebugs had been in the car, which hadn't been locked. He'd left the matchbook. Had he left anything else— under the hood? Cursing, I rubbed my face and tried to rally a little courage, or at least bravado, in myself. Was I going to allow myself to be intimidated by a pair of pimply teenagers with a sick fondness for fire?

Damn straight. I went back to the house and told Millicent I had car trouble and would come back later. I waved off her offer of a ride, glanced at Darla Jean's window as I crossed the yard, and took off down the road, swinging my arms so violently I could imagine one flying out of its socket. My heels crunched on the gravel.

By the time I reached the highway, I was calmer. Clearly Les Vernon had not yet picked up Billy Dick and Willard, but he surely would before too long. They no longer faced misdemeanor charges. Their little hobby of removing eyesores from the landscape had escalated into attempted murder. It was likely that they would be tried as adults.

As I walked toward the PD, I tried to determine what had provoked this sort of seriously antisocial behavior in them. Billy Dick's father had been an alcoholic, but his mother seemed to be struggling to provide for the two of them. The house was adequate, as was the Yarrows' house in Hasty, and in both cases, there were vehicles in the driveway and television antennas on the roof. No soul-twisting poverty, no indication of physical abuse or neglect.

Darla Jean McIlhaney was in hysterics because she'd done something of which she knew her parents disapproved. Becky Hopperly had, too, and had suffered for it. But most of the local teenagers did so, and they survived. A few ended up at the state juvenile facility, but the majority eventually graduated from high school and either married or disappeared into the outside world.

I considered my adolescence. My father (and this was the first time in years I'd allowed this to trespass into my thoughts) had walked out on Ruby Bee, and apparently kept on walking until he reached the edge of the earth and took the critical step. In a way, he'd walked out on me, although I'd been *in utero* and therefore unavailable for good-byes.

My childhood had been peculiar. Not all children dine in a bar and reside in their own motel rooms. Peculiar, but not dehabilitating. I'd had enough sense to leave for college the day after high-school graduation. Which isn't to say I hadn't fumbled. There'd been mistakes resulting in vile hangovers, speeding tickets, ill-judged liaisons, and bad grades, and a particularly noteworthy one resulting in divorce.

So why, when most of us blundered along the road, did Billy Dick and Willard head down a dark alley?

A calculating expression came over Brother Verber's face, and this time he remembered to rub his palms together. He took a deep breath and said, "And what all's in it for me, Loretta? I ain't gonna risk havin' Cooter after me for nuthin'. If I let you hide in the choir room, you got to somehow do something to make it worth my while."

From the pew behind him, Gwenneth said, sniffling, "I ain't got no money."

She spoke so sweetly that he wanted to pat her on the shoulder (or thereabouts), but Brother Verber was getting into the swing of things, and he made himself sound as cold as a well-digger's ass. "I ain't talking about money, honey child. I reckon I'm talking about that cot in the choir room. Is you comin'?"

"And you a man of the cloth . . ."

He almost leered, but he'd tried that earlier and the director had lectured him like he'd snuck a toad into Sunday school. "That's why I keep a sheet on that little cot. Close enough." He stood up, as did Gwenneth behind him, and he was keenly aware of her flowery perfume as she followed him down the aisle.

"Cut," Hal said. He and Carlotta conferred quietly. Then he glanced at his watch and said, "It's past lunchtime, but we've only got one scene left, so let's put on our happy faces and get it done."

Brother Verber watched Carlotta and Anderson unplug lights and carry them past the pulpit and through the doorway beyond it. "Excuse me," he humbly said to Hal, "but now that I'm done, I think I'll go over to the rectory for just a moment to make sure none of my flock has been trying to reach me."

"You're in the next scene." Hal beckoned to Gwenneth and Frederick, and the three of them went through the doorway that led to a small storage room.

His copy of the script ended with CUT TO: just below his "close enough" line. Scratching his chin, he followed the others, and found the chairs pushed back and the room flooded with white light. While Anderson struggled with an Army surplus cot, Carlotta left and returned with the camera. Frederick positioned the lights in the middle of the room. Gwenneth flipped through her script, which was a sight thicker than his and scribbled up with marks.

"No, over here!" Hal barked at one of them; Brother Verber wasn't sure which. The cot was moved several times, as were the lights. Anderson went to a corner and began to brush powder on his forehead. Gwenneth took out a compact and applied lipstick.

"Excuse me," Brother Verber said to the room in general, "but I don't seem to have a copy of this next scene."

"I must have left it in my motel room," Carlotta said. "But you did splendidly, and all you have is one simple line. Why don't I just tell you what it is and not burden you with a script?" Brother Verber nodded. "Your line is: 'Cooter! What are you doing here?' Think you can handle it?"

"Cooter, what are you doin' here?" he echoed obediently. "Who's Cooter?"

Anderson signaled with a finger and smiled. Carlotta hustled Brother Verber over to a corner, studied her clipboard, and said, "Cooter and Loretta have already blocked the scene. I'll draw a nice 'X' on the floor for you, next to the cot where she'll be. When the action starts, you're standing there, looking down at her. Mustn't touch, though. The door opens, Cooter comes in, and you say . . . ?" She smiled encouragingly.

"Cooter, what are you doin' in here?" Brother Verber said, thinking how easily he had learned how to go about making a movie. It was kinda fun not knowing what was going to happen next. "Is that all?"

"Cooter has some lines. He shoves you aside, and after that, you're off-camera. From then on, be as quiet as a mouse and watch."

Brother Verber nodded, but he was distracted by the sight of Loretta peeling off her halter and exposing what he referred to as the devil's handiwork. His jaw was on his chest, and his eyeballs zoomed halfway across the room. "Is—is the young lady—is she supposed to— where do I . . . ?" he said, stuttering.

"It's all very symbolic," Carlotta said. "Now, strip down to your boxer shorts and we'll see if we can get a wrap on the first take."

"Say what?"

"Do you mind?" Gwenneth said, rolling her shoulders and letting her head fall back. She flipped her hair over her face, then shook it back into place. "I'm absolutely starving. Let's do it so we can eat."

Symbolic my foot, Brother Verber told himself. It was so unreal that it verged on an out-of-body experience. Why, he could be floating near the ceiling, watching himself and the others as they buzzed around. Most likely he'd be floating right above the cot.

No one paid any attention as he sat down on a folding chair and took off his shoes and socks. He put his jacket and shirt on the chair, then held on to the back of it while he tottered on one foot to pull off one pants leg, then on the other foot to do the same.

He felt naked. The lights captured each bead of sweat, each bulge of fat, each dimple of cellulite, each dirt-lined crease. More than anything he wanted to snatch up his clothes and cover himself, but as he hesitated, Gwenneth positioned herself on the cot and stretched out her arms to him.

"Come find your mark, Preacher Pipkin," she cooed. "And please don't screw up your itty-bitty line."

His feet carried him across the room, where the view sent jolts of electricity throughout him like he'd poked a fork in an outlet. Someone said "Action!" but he barely heard it. Gwenneth gave him a resentful look, but her ripe lips and half-closed eyes said something entirely different.

"I—er, I—is this . . . ?" he managed to say, unaware he was engaging in what the Hollywood folks called ad-libbing.

The door opened. Out of the corner of his eye, Brother Verber saw Anderson stride into the room, his face that of a gargoyle and his fist held up menacingly.

A line. He was supposed to say a line. He thought he heard the girl hiss something, but it might as well have been in a foreign language.

"What do you think you're doing?" this intruder roared. He took another step and swung his arm.

Brother Verber's nose exploded in pain. He touched it, and then goggled at the red smears on his fingertips. "Now, why'd you go and do a thing like that?" he asked wonderingly.

"That's what I'd like to know," came a voice from the doorway. Not Cooter's, by a long shot. Not any of the cast members, not Hal's, not Carlotta's. Not even Harve Dorfer, who'd been sent outside to recuperate.

Even though he was wearing boxer shorts, Brother Verber's hands flew down in the classic gesture of modesty.

Mrs. Jim Bob tapped her foot in a staccato rhythm that spoke of doom. "Well?"

"Cut!" Hal threw the script into the air. It fluttered down noisily in the ensuing silence.

He had hoped for a sacrifice, but it hadn't happened. The man had been burned—badly, from all reports—but had survived. He needed a sacrifice if he was to become a wizard. He hadn't known it at first. The fires had been enough. The fires made him feel strong, potent, superior.

Now the dragon demanded more than dry wood, or even gasoline tanks and tires. The dragon demanded flesh to devour. His put his fingertips on his temples and waited. When it came to him, he smiled. The dragon wanted a woman.

Chapter 15

"Les can't seem to track your firebugs down," the dispatcher told me on the telephone. "He called and said to tell you he'd been to both houses. The MacNamara boy's ma had no idea where he was, and nobody was home at the other boy's house. Les is heading back to Hasty one more time."

"When you hear from him, tell him at least one of them was in Maggody less than an hour ago," I said. "We've got to find them before they go totally out of control."

"Amen to that," she said, then hung up.

Plover still hadn't shown up, but I couldn't wait for him any longer. People were popping underground like a bunch of prairie dogs. I called the state police barracks and requested that someone examine my car and Ruby Bee's for explosives, tucked in my shirttail, and walked down the highway to the Assembly Hall.

The deputies watched me as I came up the walk, but I merely nodded and went inside. What I saw was not my envisionment of a movie set. Carlotta and Hal sat in a back pew. She had the clipboard on her knee and a pencil in her hand and was saying, "No, this'll work and we can salvage the first half minute. The camera swings around Cooter's back and comes in from his left for a close-up of Loretta's reaction. He yanks her up and drags her out the door, snarling, and then a freeze frame of the empty cot and cut to Billy Joe and the earth mother. The audience won't have time to wonder if Pipkin bled to death or what."

Hal chuckled nastily. "Then we keep the bloody-nose bit? Gawd, that was classic. I haven't heard anyone stutter like that since I ran over the maid's cat in the driveway."

Neither of them looked up as I continued down the aisle. Brother Verber was on his knees in front of the first pew, clad in boxer shorts and a sloppily buttoned shirt. His head hung down and his hands were clasped so tightly his fingers were bloodless. Mrs. Jim Bob stood over him like an executioner (*sans* ax), and as I went past, said, "And in the house of the Lord! Nakedness and fornication! Bare breasts!"

I found this intriguing, but to my regret his response was not audible. I crossed the platform and went into the storage room, where things seemed more normal. Gwenneth sat on a cot, filing her nails. Frederick Marland leaned against the wall, watching her, and Anderson glanced up from a book and smiled.

"The cavalry arrives," he murmured.

"What's going on?" I asked him. "Why's Brother Verber out there in his underwear?"

"Oh, just one of those artistic scenes," Anderson said. When he approached me, I could see a veneer of greasepaint on his face and a day's growth of stubble on his cheeks and chin. His hair was combed back in an oily pompador, and his ill-fitting suit and crooked bow tie did nothing to enhance his appearance.

"Who are you supposed to be?" I asked. "The PeeWee Herman of the Ozarks?"

"The evil, scheming villain, my pretty." He squeezed my shoulder and leered. "If my hopes are dashed—and they will be in six or seven scenes—I'll throw myself on your tender mercies, and perhaps your bed."

Frederick and Gwenneth were observing his theatrics, although without much interest. I plucked his hand from my shoulder and led him by the wrist to the dimmest corner of the room. "What's this movie about?"

"Film, not movie," he said, edging forward until he had me blocked off (not that I was in any great hurry to escape). "The film's about love, dear Arly. Spring flowers, fragile dreams, young lust."

"And half-naked preachers?"

"Very symbolic, that."

"Symbolic of Thanksgiving, maybe," Gwenneth said. "One look at him and all I could think of was a self-basting turkey."

I lowered my voice and upped my intensity. "What's this film about, Anderson?"

"Gwenneth and Frederick, better known as Loretta and Billy Joe, have the hots for each other, but her father, Zachery, insists that she must marry yours truly, a thoroughly despicable fellow named Cooter who's in need of a shampoo and a competent tailor. There are a few diversions, but ultimately the two dewy-faced youngsters escape and consummate their love."

"How do Verber, Dahlia, and the others fit in?"

"Background. Peripheral characters dedicated to either helping the lovers or thwarting them, depending on how many lines they can remember. Hal feels that they give the film texture and a sense of locale, and, conveniently, they're eager to work for pocket change and promises."

I tried to ignore the heat of his body and the faint odor of after-shave mingled with makeup as I thought about the film's plot. "Does the girl have to get married? Is she pregnant?"

"Good heavens, no. It's a veritable tribute to Gwenneth's talent, in that she's supposedly a virgin throughout. A ripe virgin, certainly, and in the mood to alleviate the condition, but determined to save herself for Frederick over there."

"But her cruel father is forcing her to marry your character?" I said, frowning so hard I could barely see through my eyebrows. "She's upset about it?"

"He slaps her around, if that's what you mean. Oh, and there's a scene in which he takes a tad too much pleasure in her butterfly, but she hightails it to safety."

"And Kitty Kaye was the mother?"

His smile disappeared. "That's right. She's the one who makes the original deal with Cooter. Carlotta doctored the script to exclude the role." He started to run his hand through his hair, then stopped before he gave a literal translation of the phrase "greasing one's palm." "Have you found out anything about what happened to her?"

"I don't know," I admitted. "I thought I might have, but I'm more confused now than I was this morning. Meredith's the only one who can answer some of my questions, and he's not available."

Other witnesses were, however. Metaphorical gloves laced tightly, I came out of the corner and told Anderson and Frederick to wait in the main room of the Assembly Hall. Gwenneth appeared to be fascinated by her fingernails, but she was watching me as I pulled over a chair and sat down near the cot.

"Want to discuss Cedar Rapids, Iowa, and an outstanding warrant for a hit-and-run?" I asked pleasantly.

She held out her hand to admire her work. "No, I don't believe I do. Do the girls around here have man-

icures, or do they chew off the rough spots and spit
out the pieces?''

"How'd you end up in Hollywood?''

She resumed filing her nails. "I bounced around fos-
ter homes until the accident. I decided I'd better split
for L.A. and stardom. Stardom wasn't quite ready for
me, so I turned some tricks, did some supersleazy flicks,
and waited tables.'' She looked at me through slate-gray
eyes, and her voice seemed as scratchy as the sound
emanating from the file. "That accident happened a
long time ago. Nobody's cares about it, and nobody's
gonna stop me now.'' She stood up, dropped the file
on the cot, and sauntered to the door. "Are we here to
have a prayer meeting or to shoot some footage?'' she
called in a sugary voice.

"We're ready to resume,'' Carlotta said as she came
into the room. "Arly, I didn't know you were here.''

"I'm here,'' I said, "and I need some answers.''

"Try out to be a *Jeopardy* contestant,'' Hal said as he
took Gwenneth's arm, led her across the room, and
settled her on the cot. "We've got this thing pulled
together, and we're going to shoot it. Anderson, this is
right after the punch. Carlotta, over Cooter's right
shoulder, and then quickly to his left. Frederick, get the
lights.'' He looked stonily at me. "This is a closed set,
Chief. If we want spectators, we'll issue engraved in-
vitations.''

Clearly I was dismissed, but before I could mention
that a murder investigation had precedence over a
movie scene, he continued. "Okay, Anderson, glance
over the lines. You're furious. Gwenneth, doll, Cooter
just burst into the room and smacked the preacher.
You're terrified, so do a whimper and cringe thing.''
Without looking up from the clipboard, he pointed a
thumb at me. "Carlotta, my beloved, she's still here.
Clear the set. Let's have continuity in terms of undress,

Gwenneth. Where's Frederick? I told him to get the lights. Can't you people do anything without wasting time? We've got a film to make, fer chrissake!''

Somehow or other, I found myself in the empty Assembly Hall, the storeroom door closed firmly behind me. Brother Verber and Mrs. Jim Bob had departed. As I went slowly up the aisle, I heard Hal Desmond shout, ''Action!''

Ruby Bee knocked on Raz's door. ''Yoo-hoo,'' she called in a real nice voice, ''it's Ruby Bee and Estelle, Raz.''

''I kin see that for myself,'' he said from behind a bush at the corner of the shack.

''You liked to scared me half to death!'' Estelle snapped. She remembered the purpose of the visit and forced herself to wave at him. ''How are ya doin', Raz? We came to ask you a little question.''

He stepped into view, a shotgun in his hand. ''What be it? I got critters to deal with out in the barn. Some of those rats is bigger'n polecats, and twicest as mean.'' He flashed his tan teeth at them and hooked his thumb under the strap of his baggy overalls. ''Biggest durn rats in the county,'' he added with a proud grin. ''Wanna have a look-see?''

Ruby Bee clutched her heart. ''No, thank you kindly, but Estelle and I have other things we have to do. We came here because we were hoping you could help us.'' She gave him a conspiratorial smile but stopped short of a wink. ''What with Arly being so busy, we're looking to find that cameraman named Fuzzy. By happenchance, I noticed that you and he had a nice talk in the bar. I was wondering what he said to you.''

''Said all kinda things,'' Raz said. He spat, wiped his

mouth on his crusty cuff, and narrowed his eyes. "Disappeared, did he? When did he take off, and which way'd he go?"

"That's what we were hoping you could tell us," Ruby Bee said. "It's possible he cut across the pasture behind the motel and came this way. Did you see him?"

"Nope, but I found some mighty peculiar footprints out behind the barn. I reckon somebody was snooping around out there. Made afore the rain last night, too, since they're filled with water." Raz scratched his neck with the barrel of the shotgun, and later Ruby Bee swore she could see he was doing his best to think. "He came over one night to have a little snort with me and Marjorie. Don't know why he'd be down by the creek, though."

"Could he have been looking in the barn for something?" Estelle asked. "Like jars of whiskey, for instance?"

"Ain't nuthin' in the barn except the rats and hairy spiders. Mebbe you'd like to make sure of it yourself?"

"No, I don't believe I would." Estelle started backing across the yard. "Not today, anyway. I'm wearing my good shoes." She went through the gate and stood behind it. "Some other time, maybe."

Ruby Bee sniffed at the quantity of cowardice on display. "Now, Raz, try to remember if you said one little ol' word about where your still is. Most everybody in town has a pretty good idea, but these Hollywood people wouldn't know where to begin."

"I dun told you I ain't running a still," he said, shaking his head so hard crumbs flew from his whiskers. "And I ain't running it up past Robin Buchanon's cabin, neither, and if I was, I wouldn't spout off about it to that goofy feller from Hollywood." He held up the shotgun and began to jerk it like a pom-pom. "And if he's up there messing with it, he's gonna have a back-side of buckshot for his trouble.''

"Ruby Bee," Estelle called, her good eye intent on the shotgun, "I do believe we ought to run along now. I'm sure Raz would like to go shoot rats or something.''

"He's gonna be a sight sorrier than a goddamn reve-nuer," Raz continued, his rage rising faster than Boone Creek in the spring. "He ain't gonna sit down till the cows come home!''

"Coming, Estelle," Ruby Bee trilled. She backed out of the yard, grabbed Estelle's hand, and they hurried across the road. They could still hear Raz's sputtery threats as they got in the station wagon, rolled up the windows, and locked the doors. Neither spoke until they were down the road a piece and out of range.

"I believe we learned something of interest," Estelle said.

Ruby Bee stared out the window. "I believe we might have stirred up some trouble, that's what I believe. I'd feel dadburned awful if Raz goes up the ridge and shoots Fuzzy. I don't know what we can do about it, though.''

"We got no choice but to warn him," Estelle said as she turned right at the highway and headed for the nar-row road that led into the scruffy jungle of Cotter's Ridge.

While Plover made coffee in the back room, I told him the sad little story I'd learned from Augusta.

"Sounds rather typical of the times," he said as he came to the doorway. In the back room, the coffee maker groaned and gurgled as if it were bleeding to death.

"Maybe I'm crazy to force parallels between Becky

Hopperly's story and the script of *Wild Cherry Wine,*
but there's something there." I bore down on the pencil so fiercely that the point snapped. "Oliphant hopped
a bus to Hollywood. He changed his name, married a
famous actress, built a solid career, and from all reports,
was leading a happy life. Until he came back to the
Ozarks, anyway."

"And murdered his wife, with whom he was reputed
to be madly in love?"

Shrugging, I took a pocket knife from the drawer and
began to whittle a new point on the pencil. "What if
one of the Hollywood people is a long-lost Hopperly?
He would have a good, old-fashioned, redneck motive:
revenge."

"Because of the abandonment," Plover said help-
fully.

"Becky's father sent her away in disgrace and refused
to send money. Unwed mothers were not in vogue
then, and I doubt she had any employable skills. She
died when she was still young. If Buddy had married
her, they might be running the family farm, baby-sitting
for grandchildren, and rocking away the evenings on
the porch."

"All right, I think you're stretching, but let's go with
one of them being a relative, or even someone who
cared about Becky and was enraged by her death. That
doesn't narrow down the field, you know."

"I need to ask them about their backgrounds and then
try to verify the stories. On television shows, the detective drives across town, parks right in front of the
house or apartment building, and encounters babbla-
tive people with lots of lovely information. I don't
know where to start, and if I did, I'd have to do it by
long distance and account for the bill at the next Town
Council meeting."

"Life's tough," Plover said, then stopped as the telephone rang. "A television producer from Hollywood, perhaps?"

"More likely Ruby Bee from a jail somewhere," I said. I picked up the receiver and muttered my name.

"Arly?" Carlotta said shrilly. "You'd better get over here—and fast."

"Are you still at the Assembly Hall?"

"No, we came back to the motel for a break. Please get over here. There's been another—I don't know." She began to sob, and I could make out only a few words. One of them was "dead."

I banged down the receiver and told Plover what she'd said. We drove to the motel in his car. Ruby Bee's parking lot was empty, but the van and rental car were parked in front of the row of motel units on the left. As we stopped, Carlotta came out of #3.

"Hal, in there," she said, gesturing weakly. "I was taking him some food."

"Wait in your room," I said, then took a breath and followed Plover into #2. Hal Desmond's body lay on the bed, nude except for a plastic bag over his head. Below his flaccid jaw, the bag was secured with a necktie. The plastic adhered to the contours of his face and head like a shiny, transparent skin. The flesh beneath it had a bluish tinge.

Plover felt Hal's neck for a pulse, then shook his head. "Call the barracks, Arly. Use a phone in another room."

I made the call from Carlotta's room. She came out of the bathroom, her arms wrapped around herself, and slumped against the wall.

"Where's Gwenneth?" I asked her.

She slid down the wall until she was hunched on the floor. "This is too bizarre," she said with a moan. "Kitty, and now Hal. Is there some maniac killing us one by one? I can't deal with this. I just can't deal with this."

She certainly sounded as if she couldn't. I left her on the floor and went across the lot to Frederick's room. I pounded on the door, and after a moment, discovered it was unlocked and went into the room. The bathroom door was closed. I could hear the shower running.

I opened that door and through the steam, shouted, "Frederick!? It's Arly Hanks! Come to Carlotta's room immediately!"

"I'm taking a shower!" he yelled back, in case I was less than astute.

"Just do it!" I said, then left his room and hurried to Anderson's. He came to the door, a script in his hand, and gave me a puzzled look. I repeated the order, ignored his questions, and went back across the lot as Plover stepped out of #2 and closed the door behind him.

"What?" I said, too frantic to formulate anything more complex.

"Beats me," he said. "He was asphyxiated by the bag, obviously, but it's hard to say offhand if it was an accident, suicide, or murder."

"What?" I repeated cleverly.

"There's enough cocaine in there to keep the entire county high for a week. There was paraphernalia on the bedside table, so it's probable he did a few lines in the last hour. He could have put the bag on his head for kicks, or someone could have done it for him and held him down. The medical examiner will take a closer look, but I saw some bruising on the upper arms, as if someone knelt on him . . . until he stopped kicking."

"What's going on?" Anderson demanded as he joined us.

"That's what I'd like to know," I said. I left Plover to explain and went back to Carlotta's room. She was still on the floor, but she was no longer moaning. "Tell me what happened."

She took off her glasses and let her head fall back against the wall. "About an hour ago, we finished at the church. The entire schedule's a shambles, so we came back here to grab a bite to eat and figure out what to do. The bar and grill was closed. Everybody went to their rooms, and I sent the trooper out for hamburgers. When he came back, I unloaded the sack, sorted out the orders, and took Hal's to him. That's when I—"

"Is it true?" Anderson said as he came in the room.

Frederick followed him, his hair damp and mussed and his T-shirt clinging to his back. "That cop says Hal's dead. What the hell is going on? Where's Gwenneth?"

"That's what I'd like to know," I said.

Carlotta sighed. "When we first got back, Hal told Gwenneth to come to his room. He used her often, with the excuse that it helped him to release cerebral tension and maintain a creative flow. It had to do more with his ego, I think. He knew he was old and unattractive—deadly sins in the industry, unless you're very powerful, in which case people are afraid to cross you, and you know it."

"So he snapped his fingers at her when he wanted sex?" I asked evenly. I looked at Anderson and Frederick. "Did all of you know about this?" They both nodded. "And the coke? Did you know about the impressive quantity of coke in his room?"

"He said it heightened his awareness of reality," Carlotta said in a numb voice. "I guess this time he didn't like what he saw."

"He's put a bag over his head before?" I asked. My knees wobbled and I sat down quickly on the bed. I felt as if we'd all begun to converse in a foreign language, one I'd never studied. "You've actually seen him do this?"

"When he approached orgasm," she said, looking at her feet. "Some autoerotic thing about the lack of oxygen intensifying the experience. He always pulled it off at the last second."

"You know this from firsthand observation?"

"My job description's more inclusive than you might expect. It takes more than talent and initiative to get hired right out of school."

Outside, car doors slammed and voices barked at each other. Plover was giving orders, tersely but loudly. A police band radio crackled. The door of the next unit banged open and closed. The sounds of footsteps and muffled voices came through the wall.

"So where's Gwenneth now?" Frederick asked, interrupting the uneasy silence inside the room.

"That's a very good question," I said. "Where have you been for the past hour?"

"We stopped outside the van and told Carlotta what we wanted to eat. I went to the room, turned the air conditioner on high, and lay down on the bed for a while. Then I took a shower."

"And you?" I asked Anderson.

"I took a nap, and was working on my lines when you knocked on the door."

I turned to Carlotta, who said, "After I gave the order to the deputy, I stayed in here to do revisions. We'd decided not to use the mayor's house. The wife was a bit upset when she weaseled her way onto the set this morning, and I had a feeling we wouldn't be welcome. I was trying to see if we could shoot the Cooter interiors here without it coming off as a motel."

"You didn't see Gwenneth after she went to Hal's room?"

"No, and I was concentrating too hard"—she grimaced—"to hear anything through the wall. The printer was running, and I tend to mutter under my breath when I'm doing dialogue. I was in a fog when the trooper came back with the food, but I pulled myself

together and noticed we were short a couple of sandwiches and a drink. I sent him back, sorted out what
we did have, and went next door." She swallowed several times. "It was just an accident, wasn't it? He did
too much coke, and passed out or something?"

"I wish I knew." I told them to stay where they were,
then went out to the narrow walk in front of #2. The
door was open, and inside the room the troopers from
the barracks were dusting for prints, photographing the
body and adjoining areas, measuring, scraping samples
of white powder into bags, and all the while making
vulgar jokes about the corpse on the bed.

I sat on Plover's fender and waited until he came outside. He had a worn manila envelope in his hand. He
allowed the contents to slide onto the hood of the car,
then tapped the edges to arrange them so that we could
see each clearly.

"A clipping about a hit-and-run," he said, bending
over to read the print. "Six years ago, child on bicycle,
witnesses who saw a dark blue or black subcompact,
one bushy-tailed enough to write down the license plate
number."

"And another clipping about the murder of a house-
wife who chanced upon a burglar in a Beverly Hills
mansion," I said. I scanned the article, which was dry
and unembellished. "The police declined to comment
on possible suspects or any similarity to other crimes,"
I read aloud. I did not read the final line, which had
been underlined in ink: "The husband, well-known actor Anderson St. James, was on location in Nevada at
the time of his wife's death."

Plover nudged a photograph toward me. "What's significant enough about this to merit inclusion in the collection?"

It was a small black-and-white photograph. The two
people seated at a table were blurry, and one was par-

tially obscured by a branch. Both appeared oblivious to the camera. "The one on the right is Carlotta Lowenstein," I said, squinting, "and she's holding something. The other person's male—dark hair, skinny mustache, jewelry. I don't think they're in a restaurant. It looks more like a patio."

"Let's have a closer look." Plover went into the room and came back with a magnifying glass. He held it over the photograph, then handed it to me and said, "The doorway behind them looks as if it leads into a living room. She's holding a box, I think."

I took my turn, then straightened up. "A videocassette, I think. Yo, ho, ho."

"And a bottle of rum?" Plover said blankly.

"Or blood."

Chapter 16

It was still daylight on Cotter's Ridge, although a lot of folks swear, to this day, that the sun never shines there very brightly. Dark, grumbling clouds had settled more firmly on the ridge; the air was heavy with impending rain. The gloom had silenced the birds, sent the squirrels to their nests, even squelched the drone of mosquitoes and hornets.

The explosion was sharp, loud, and unexpected by a variety of people, most of whom were converging, unbeknownst to each other, on a decaying shack at the end of a road better described as a washed-out creekbed.

Kevin Buchanon dove nosefirst into a hollow of sodden leaves and briars, and burrowed like a mole. He had never been out of the state, much less across the ocean to an exotic place like Vietnam, but he'd seen a lot of war movies and he couldn't stop himself from picturing small, dark-skinned foreigners sneaking along the ridge.

With a shriek, Dahlia O'Neil forced her bulk to the floor of the car (no small feat) and put her arms over her head. Then, when it occurred to her that the car was in plain sight of the madman, she squirmed and grunted until she was sitting up, got out of the car, gaped at the cabin containing a corpse, and thudded down a path to a sanctuary that had served her well in the past. Once she was seated with the door hooked, she peered through a knothole but she didn't see a soul.

Ruby Bee and Estelle ducked behind a rock. They stayed there for quite a long time, agreeing that it had sounded like a gunshot and debating what to do. It was a hissy conversation at best, and Ruby Bee finally stood up, brushed off her knees, and announced that she wasn't scared of an ol' geezer like Raz Buchanon. She took off up the road, and after tossing a few tart remarks at her back, Estelle followed. Billy Dick Mac-Namara and Willard Yarrow froze at the sound, but when it was not repeated, they exchanged nervous looks and sat down on a damp, mossy log. A few minutes later, Trudi caught up with them. Panting, she sat down at the end of the log, as far away from them as she could manage.

"What was that?" she asked.

"Squirrel hunter, most likely," said Billy Dick.

Trudi wrapped her arms around herself and tried not to shiver. "I must have been crazy to come up here with you two pathetic nerds."

Willard glanced slyly at her. "But if we steal Raz Buchanon's moonshine, we can make all kinds of money selling it to everybody for five bucks a quart."

"We should be able to carry six jars apiece," Billy Dick added. "You can buy yourself a skimpy little halter like that blond movie star wears."

"Keep your filthy eyes off me," Trudi said. "Let's just

get this over with, okay? This is dumber than that stupid make-believe game you two play all the time." She gave Billy Dick a particularly venemous look. "I'll bet you get real excited when you pretend you're a fairy, doncha? Do you put on your ma's petticoat and prance around in front of a mirror?"

"Yeah, and he looks real pretty," Willard said with a giggle.

Billy Dick stood up and offered her his hand. She allowed him to pull her to his feet, but the clamminess of his hand, along with the flush of excitement on his face and the glazed flatness of his eyes, made her uneasy and she jerked her hand away.

They resumed their hike along the logging trail.

Raz responded to the sound with a cackle. There weren't nobody that was gonna steal his moonshine. He told Marjorie they was going to stay close as stink on a skunk till the feller was long gone, but she looked so glum that he took out a jar and unscrewed the lid, took a swig, and obligingly held it under her snout.

"Hal was blackmailing you," I said flatly. I held up a Baggie that contained the photograph. "Would you like to examine the evidence?"

"I've already seen it," Carlotta said. "He hired some private investigator, who climbed a tree to get the shot when I handed over the pirated tape."

"Who's the man?" Plover asked.

"An underling at Cinerotica. It's a distribution company for . . . specialty films. He had access to the equipment to make copies and the list of outlets. We split the profits." She made a face and shrugged. "I needed the money to start my own production company. Working for Hal was lucrative, but less than aesthetically satisfying."

A stern young state trooper came into the motel room, nodded deferentially at me, and said to Plover, "We searched all the rooms and the immediate area for the girl, but we didn't find her. There's more, sir, but I don't know if . . . I should report in front of a witness." At Plover's suggestion, they went into the bathroom and closed the door.

"So he knew you were cheating the other members of the company," I said, returning to business despite a gut-wrenching urge to tiptoe to the door in order to eavesdrop.

"He took fifty percent of my share. He didn't object to the arrangement, in that he made more money this way than he would have if we'd gone through usual distribution and prorated the net with the others. It didn't appear on the books, and I doubt he reported the income to the IRS."

"But something happened and he threatened to expose you?" I asked.

"No. This production is more difficult than others, but we were at budget and I would imagine Hal was expecting to receive the illicit money for it in a few months."

"Did Kitty or Meredith find out about it?"

"If they did, they didn't tell me," she said. "It doesn't have anything to do with what happened here."

She sounded sincere, but I was beginning to realize these people sounded however they damn well pleased. I scowled at my notes until Plover and the trooper returned, then sent Carlotta away with the latter to give a statement at the barracks, and waited for the former to enlighten me. He opted to sit down and smile. It went no deeper than his teeth. The dimple was absent.

"What's the latest?" I said, trying not to sound irritated.

"Cocaine . . . it falleth like the gentle rain . . . everywhere," he murmured. "Among other places, it falleth in Anderson St. James's room. Shall we ask him about it?"

I wasn't overwhelmed with astonishment, but I was disappointed, as much in myself as in Anderson. However, there was no need to convey this to Sergeant Smug, so I nodded and followed him across the lot to #6.

Anderson let us in, then sank down on the bed, rested his elbows on his knees, and stared at his limp hands. I crossed my arms and stood by the door, motionless and emotionless. Plover finally got the message and said, "Mr. St. James, you are under arrest for possession of an illegal substance, specifically cocaine." He reeled off the *Miranda,* asked him if he understood his rights, and nodded when Anderson declined to call an attorney.

"So I do a little coke," he said dully. "It's as common as Evian in the industry. I didn't kill Hal, and I didn't kill Kitty. I have no idea what's happened to Meredith, Gwenneth, and Fuzzy. One of them must have gone off the edge and decided to decimate Glittertown. Frankly, I'd feel a lot safer in a jail cell than in this local version of Bates Motel, so feel free to take me into custody as soon as possible."

"We're occupied at the moment," Plover said, "but I'll put a man outside the door."

"Whatever." Anderson looked at me. "Would it be possible to have a moment with Chief Hanks?"

"Fine with me," I said without inflection.

Plover shot me a tight look as he left the room. I waited until the door clicked, then I exploded. "What is it with you people? Drugs and sex and treachery— and what else? Are you secretly making a snuff movie? Transporting children across a state line to make porno flicks?"

"The veneer has slipped," he said wryly. "You have discovered the deities of the silver screen are but mortals with feet of fertilizer. It's not easy to be a deity, you know. It's hard work."

"Forget the crap!" I dug my fingernails into my palms and reminded myself that I was a police officer—and one tough cookie. "Was Hal blackmailing you, too? Is that why you were willing to make low-budget films for such a sleazy little company?"

"The reason's a bit more mundane, I'm afraid. Incredibly handsome faces stroll down every sidewalk and crowd the waiting rooms at cattle calls. I'm a decent actor, but not Burton or Olivier, and I have to pay the rent like everyone else."

"Let Carlotta write the dialogue," I said, frowning at the backside of the door. "The night of your wife's murder . . . Hal and you supposedly shared a room, but he might have preferred Gwenneth's company. Were you left out in the cold, and so angry at your wife that you decided to pay her a late-night visit?"

"As usual, Hal wanted Gwenneth. Carlotta and Fuzzy decided they would continue the celebration in her room, privately, so I ended up with Frederick. I drank way too much and passed out. The next morning at my house, when we were waiting for the police, we decided it wouldn't look quite right in the official report to admit to musical beds, so we all claimed to have spent the night celibately and in our original rooms."

"Then why did Hal save a clipping and underline a reference to your alibi?"

"Frederick told him I'd said a lot of wild things about my wife and even threatened to drive to L.A. and kill her. I don't remember saying those things, but it's possible. I moved out of the house the night she told me she'd had an abortion that morning, lunch with her friends, and a quickie with my agent in the hot tub before cocktails."

I ignored his plea for sympathy. "That doesn't explain why Hal thought he had something on you. The rantings of a drunk don't constitute evidence, and Frederick could give you an alibi, couldn't he?"

"I suppose so. Hal told me that he had proof that someone had taken his car during the night. He had the oil changed while we were on location, and the guy at the garage wrote down the mileage on a sticker inside the door. It didn't jibe with what it should have been, unless the car had been driven a good ways."

I leaned forward. "Did you drive back to L.A., Anderson?"

"I don't remember." He raised his head to stare at his reflection in the mirror. In a voice that parodied himself, he said, "Let us examine the well-known actor Anderson St. James. Alas, the ravages of age, drugs, and booze are visible. Wrinkles are beginning to show, around the mouth in particular. The voice doesn't glide like it used to, and before too long the body will slowly and insidiously sag. There goes Anderson St. James, shuffling down the street to beg for a bit on a commercial or an extra in a crowd scene. Remember him? No? Wasn't he in *Tanya Makes the Team?*"

"That's all you are?" I asked.

"That's all that's left of me." When he smiled at me, I could see the fine lines around his mouth, the puffiness under his eyes, the softness of his jawline and neck. "Maybe I ought to retire to a little town somewhere and learn to spit and fish."

"Spitting's not all that much fun," I said, then left before I tripped on my own weaknesses and fell into the chasm of his self-pity. Plover was in the doorway of Hal's room, conversing with someone inside. I went to Frederick's room and knocked.

"Any leads on Gwenneth?" he asked as he let me in. "Have you got cops looking for her? Is there anything I can do to help?"

"I thought she irritated you."

"Of course she does," he said. He sat down for a second, then stood up and began to pace. "But she's kind of like a kid sister, you know?"

"Not really," I said truthfully. "How'd you feel about the way Hal Desmond treated her?"

"I thought he was a black-belt slime. Gwenneth told me he had information about something she'd done back home and that he would turn it over to the police if she didn't indulge his appetite. She acted as if she didn't really care, but he was a gross old man, nothing but a fat white satyr."

"I understand she was in his room the night Anderson's wife was murdered," I said, "and Anderson was with you."

"Gawd, that was a long time ago." Frederick went to the window and pulled back the curtain, then let it fall back into place. "Anderson shared a room with Hal. Fuzzy, the wunderkind of the camera, was with me."

"That's what you all told the police, but it wasn't true. Anderson's already admitted that everyone switched rooms."

He flopped down on the bed and directed his words to the ceiling. "We all got plastered in Hal's room, then scattered when Daddy Dearest decided he wanted to do some coke with Gwenneth. Anderson and I finished off a bottle in my room, and he was really carrying on about his wife and what a slut she was. Made my innocent little ears burn. The next morning he swore he didn't remember any of it, including when I had to wrestle him to the floor to keep him from continuing his rampage outside the room.''

"But he did stay in the room all night?''

"I was drinking pretty heavily, too. I got him on the bed, took off his shoes, made it to the other bed, and passed out faster than a snake goin' through a hollow log. The next morning my tongue was coated with fungus and my head was echoing with cathedral bells. Anderson wasn't all that chipper, either, but we survived.''

A charming picture. I put it aside and said, "Where were you born?''

"I told you, San Diego.'' He lifted his head to look at me. "You can check with my folks, if you can find them. My old man's in the Navy, and he might be stationed anywhere from the Pentagon to the Persian Gulf. Then again, if he retired, they might be living in a lighthouse in Maine or a houseboat in the Okefenokee Swamp.''

"You don't know?'' I asked, wishing just one of my suspects came from a Beaver Cleaver home that was still inhabited by June and Ward—who could be called on the telephone. If there were any families left that fit the description.

"I split when I was eighteen. The old man wanted me to follow in his soggy footsteps, and I wanted to see the world without wearing a funny hat.''

I told Frederick someone would take him to the barracks, then went outside and watched the ambulance pull slowly out of the parking lot. No need for sirens and lights after the fact.

This was reality—sunshine, men going about their duties, car doors slamming across the road at the supermarket, a wasp assessing the eave as a building site. The movie was fantasy—a shallow, happily-ever-after plot about young love. The people in the movie existed in a netherworld between the dichotomies. Becky Hopperly had been real; Loretta never would be.

And Buddy Meredith was most likely dead, I realized as I stood there.

After a long while of snuffling wet leaves and holding his breath, Kevin decided gooks were not patrolling the ridge. He stood up, brushed himself off as best he could, wiped his face with a muddy hand, and hurried back down the path to make sure his beloved was safe.

The car was empty. He wanted to call for her, but he was afraid to make so much as a peep. Instead, he hesitantly made his way across the yard and porch of the shack, opened the door, and whispered, "Dahlia? Are you in here?"

Being careful not to look at the corpse in the middle of the room, he edged inside and repeated the question. There was no place large enough to conceal her, but there was another door that led to a bedroom.

"Aw, shit!" said a voice from outside the shack.

Kevin stumbled across the room, let himself into the bedroom, and closed the door just as the front door opened. He flopped on the floor and wiggled under the rotting remains of a corncob-filled mattress on a wooden frame.

"Well, what do we have here?" the voice continued,

sounding more bemused than maniacal. "You don't look so good, buddy boy. That must smart. I think you ought to do something about that knife, don't you?"

Kevin watched a spider creep within inches of his nose, but he was too terrified to move. The door opened. Shoes encrusted with mud approached the primitive bed. A face appeared below the edge of the frame, and a toxic wind engulfed him as the man said, "This is really weird."

Before Kevin could plead for mercy, or much of anything, footsteps clattered across the porch. The voices were loud and on the shrill side.

"Oh, my goodness," said one. "He's—he's dead."

"Don't faint on me now, Ruby Bee. There ain't no way I can carry you back to the station wagon."

"You're the one who's whiter than a baby's hindside. We'd better get out of here and go for help."

"Ain't nobody goin' nowhere," snarled a third voice, this one male. "Hands up, all of you."

"Tell this clown to put down the gun," said a fourth, also male.

"We weren't doing anything," said a fifth, female. "It's not against the law to walk in the woods."

"We're just kids," said the sixth, male but with a pubescent squeak.

The face that was hovering beneath the bed vanished. As Kevin squirmed out from under the bed, he heard a babble of voices interspersed with threats, demands, protests, and some right colorful curses. He thought about staying put where he was in hopes they'd all go away, but he finally went into the front room to see who all was there and what in tarnation was going on—and if his betrothed was among them.

"Fingerprints all over the room, naturally," Plover said. We'd availed ourselves of the key to the bar and grill and were sitting in a booth, untouched coffee cooling on the tabletop between us. I'd switched on a light above the bar, but the overall dimness seemed more suitable to my mood.

"But they were in the room for that meeting, so it doesn't mean anything. Any of them could have killed Kitty Kaye, for that matter." I toyed with the cup, sloshing the coffee until it splashed on my hand. "Any of them except Frederick Marland, who was in a motel room in Farberville with one of the local girls. He's damn lucky she's above the age of consent; I'd like nothing more than to bust him for statutory rape."

"Contributing to the delinquency?"

"I suppose so, but I doubt Darla Jean wants to testify in a case that's liable to attract the national media. It may take some time for her to heal, but she will." I put my finger in the coffee and on the Formica drew the antithesis of a happy face. I wasn't sure if it was Darla Jean's or my own. "No one has an alibi for the time of Hal's death, and if it was an accident or suicide, then I'm Meredith in drag and you're having a B-grade nightmare. Carlotta, Frederick, and Anderson were in their rooms, and Gwenneth was known to have been in Hal's room. The vigilant trooper, who might have been able to tell us about suspicious movements in the parking lot, was at the Dairee Dee-Lishus picking up cheeseburgers. I don't know if we should be concerned with past crimes, present crimes, or even future crimes."

"Past as in the unsolved murder of Anderson St. James's wife?" Plover said, although with an admirable absence of malice. I'd told him what I discovered about

the members of the Glittertown family. I hadn't elabo-
rated on my personal reaction, but he was being nicer
than usual, for which I had to give him his due. His
lack of expression was easier to handle than sympathy—or pity.

"Even if he did drive to L.A. that night, he still doesn't
have a motive for the murders here," I said.

Harve came into the bar, located us in the shadows,
and came to the table. "We can't find hide nor hair of
Gwenneth D'Amourre, or any of the missing persons,"
he said. Sighing, he slid into my side of the booth.
"Arly's gonna be chief of a ghost town the way things
are going. We've got nine missing at last count. They
must have chartered a damn bus."

Plover gave me a perplexed look. "Nine?"

"I forgot to mention some of it," I said, "because it's
unlikely to be relevant. You'll agree when you hear the
names." I rattled them off, and for those who've lost
track, we were searching for (with varying amounts of
dedication): Buddy Meredith; Fuzzy Indigo; Kevin
Buchanon; Dahlia O'Neil; Billy Dick MacNamara; Willard Yarrow; Ruby Bee Hanks; Estelle Oppers; and the
latest addition to the list, Gwenneth D'Amourre.

"Wow," Plover murmured.

"We can't hide this from the media much longer,"
Harve said. "I already had a call from some television
station. Somebody must have noticed the activity out
back and alerted 'em. I said we'd hold a press confer-
ence in the morning."

"We're not going to look good," I said as I sank into
the plastic upholstery. "I guess there's no reason why
we should look good. A production company comes to
Maggody, and before anyone yells 'Action!' one's been
brutally murdered and another's disappeared. Now
we've got another corpse and lost two more of them

and a handful of locals to boot. If I were a reporter, I'd be salivating at the possibility of a Pulitzer . . . for absurdity.''

"Sheriff Dorfer!" said a deputy as he banged open the door. "I reckon you ought to see this!"

"See what?" Harve said with a growl.

"It's kinda like a parade." The deputy ducked back through the door.

"Vans from the television stations," I said hollowly. "Buses filled with reporters, and a limo with lunatics from the tabloids.''

"I suppose we'd better have ourselves a look." Harve slid out of the booth, and Plover and I followed him outside.

Estelle's station wagon was creeping down the middle of the road. She was at the wheel, her face slathered with fury. Ruby Bee, jammed in the middle of the front seat, looked no happier. On the far side, Trudi Yarrow looked downright murderous, as did Billy Dick in the backseat. In that he was scrunched between Kevin and Dahlia (who spread across half the available space), his expression was understandable.

Other things were not. I shaded my eyes and let out a whistle when I saw Marjorie in the back of the wagon, her snout pressed against Dahlia's neck. Willard Yarrow was plastered against the tailgate.

Only a few feet behind the bumper, Raz Buchanon was in his truck, leaning out the window with a shotgun in his left hand. Fuzzy Indigo sat beside him. He was the only one of the participants who seemed cheerful.

"Now you jest pull over right there!" Raz shouted, aiming the shotgun at the station wagon.

Estelle pulled into the parking lot and cut off the engine. Nobody so much as twitched. Raz parked behind her, slid out of his truck, and waved at us. "Got you

another dead 'un here in my truck," he said genially.
"I don't know what all these folks have to do with
it, but they was all sneaking around up on Cotter's
Ridge. One of 'em was hiding in the outhouse, if you
can imagine. I rounded them up and brung 'em down."

"Oh," said one of us, or perhaps all of us.

Chapter 17

Harve finally shook himself into action and ordered the deputy to escort Raz's dubious crew into the bar and grill, separate them as he saw fit, and keep them from assaulting each other until we could try to sort out the latest development, which was a real doozy. A trooper was dispatched to retrieve the remaining members of Glittertown—Carlotta from the state police barracks, and Anderson and Frederick from their respective rooms. Of the original eight, we were down to four, with three murdered and one currently missing. It was beginning to look as if Maggody was not the perfect location for the filming of *Wild Cherry Wine.*

Plover went to his car to set the homicide team in motion for the third time. I stayed by the truck. Even though we'd covered the body with a canvas tarp, it was difficult not to hear the flies that had already converged on Buddy Meredith's remains, and equally difficult not to react to the miasma that made it clear he'd been dead for several days.

After an interminable delay, the coroner arrived from Farberville, took a quick look, and sonorously pronounced Meredith deceased. He was willing to speculate that death was the result of the knife that protruded from the corpse's throat. I went around the corner, threw up on a spike of weeds, and returned in time to hear the coroner peevishly add that it was clear to anyone with more than formaldehyde for brains that the corpse had been dead for a long time—and in a warm place.

The team arrived. Plover issued orders, then took my arm and guided me into the barroom. We had quite a crowd (including a soporific sow) scattered around the room. I consulted with Harve and Plover, then took center stage and started with the firebug and his apprentice.

"Why were you on Cotter's Ridge?" I asked.

Billy Dick gazed defiantly at me. "We fixed some sandwiches and went for a picnic. I thought we might all go skinny-dippin' at that spring."

Willard's giggle held the same foul edge I'd heard the night of the gas station fire. "It was Trudi's idea," he simpered in the voice of a playground tattletale. "She wanted to tease Billy Dick."

Trudi was scrunched down in the seat, but at the mention of her name, she flinched and said, "You little worm, I didn't want to do anything. You and your creepy friend came up with this scheme all by yourselves. I just went along for the hell of it."

"Scheme?" I repeated.

She shoved her hair out of her eyes and glowered at them. "Yeah, they were gonna steal some jars of moonshine and sell 'em to the kids at the Dee-Lishus. That's what they said, anyway. Then it turns out they don't even know where the still is, and he gets this bright idea we ought to go to some old shack and burn it down, just for kicks."

"Which one of them had the bright idea?" I asked. "Billy Dick MacNamara?"

Billy Dick's eyes began their now familiar retreat. "Not me. I might steal some hooch, but I don't start fires."

I shook my head. "Then why did you lie to me and make threats?"

"I d-dunno." His voice thickened as he struggled with the words. "For once, s-somebody thought I was important. Somebody noticed me, didn't dare laugh at me. So maybe I lied, acted g-guilty, said things to keep you curious." He gulped noisily. "I don't start fires."

Willard giggled again. "Sure you do, Billy Dick. Remember in the tunnel below Balthazar, when the dragon belched and I was burned to a crisp?"

"I was the one who was burned," Billy Dick said, frowning. "You were the d-dungeonmaster. You ordered the dragon to attack."

"I couldn't help it, Billy Dick. The dragon can't be stopped, you know; he can only be controlled by a wizard. I'm not a wizard. I can't be Willard the Wizard until somebody's been sacrificed. I thought about you, but the dragon demanded a female sacrifice."

"Sacrifice?" Trudi gasped. The blemishes on her face were bright red against her sudden pallor. "Is that why you wanted me to go inside that shack? Damn it, Willard, you're a sight spookier than I ever dreamed. I thought that lacy red slip in your closet was Billy Dick's, but now I'm not so sure it doesn't belong to Willard the Wizard!" She raised her hand as if to slap him, then lowered it and looked at me. "It won't do much good, will it? I reckon you'd better get hold of my parents. They're at my great-aunt's hospital room. I'll give you the telephone number."

"Thanks," I said. "You'll all have to wait at the barracks until we can notify them, and Billy Dick's mother."

The only sound in the barroom was a wheezy sigh

from the sow as a trooper escorted the three away to locate their parents.

Once the door closed, I forced myself to move along to the next pair of miscreants, Ruby Bee and Estelle. "And you two? Why were you on Cotter's Ridge?"

Ruby Bee looked almost as defiant as Billy Dick had. "We did it to save you the bother, so there's no need to squawk at us like we were interfering in your official investigation. We went up there to save Fuzzy's backside."

Fuzzy smiled benignly at her. "Always nice to have your backside saved, isn't it?"

Estelle snorted. "Ruby Bee happened to notice he was stewed to the gills when he came back from Raz's on the morning they were making the movie there. We discussed it, and realized he'd most likely been drinking moonshine and might have gone up on the ridge to look for more. Raz got mighty perturbed when we delicately inquired about it."

I looked at Raz. "How very curious that the kids, and now Fuzzy, would anticipate finding something as illegal as a moonshine still on Cotter's Ridge. Why would they all entertain such a possibility?"

"How would I know?" Raz said. He started to spit, heard Ruby Bee's hiss, and thought better of it. "I jest took Marjorie up there on account of her fondness for snufflin' for acorns. Ol' Fuzzy came lunging out of the bushes and liked to scare the britches clean off me, and Marjorie nearly run up a tree. I may have took a shot at him, and then got all worried he might be a-bleedin' and tracked him down to the shack." He went ahead and spat on the floor. "Marjorie still ain't up to snuff. She was too upset to ride in the back of the truck with a dead man, and she's always had a hankerin' to ride in a station wagon."

"Are you claiming there's not a still somewhere up the mountain past Robin's shack?" I persisted.

"No, there ain't, and iff'n there was, I wouldn't have told that feller anything except mebbe the general area, and I wouldn't have dun that iff'n he hadn't come by one evening and started admiring the quality."

"Took me hours to find it," the feller contributed with a hiccup. "It's dynamite hooch. Blow your head off—kaboom!"

Raz and Marjorie were sent away. I was going to get rid of Fuzzy, but he fell across the seat and began to snore. I moved along to Kevin and Dahlia.

"And you two?"

Dahlia's tongue was on the trigger, so to speak. "It's all Kevin's fault. He kidnapped me and almost got me killed, and I want you to arrest him and lock him up in a filthy jail cell for the rest of his born days."

"My beloved . . ."

"Well, it was your fault, and you know it." She proceeded to relate a farfetched tale of a wild ride up the mountainside, a wire thrown in the bushes, a body in the shack, and a miserable night in the car. "He didn't even bring anything to eat or drink," she concluded in condemnation. "I could have died of starvation up there."

"Kin you ever find it in your heart to forgive me?" Kevin said, clasping his hands together.

"Not unless I get to be in the movie."

Carlotta winced. "I think we'll close down production of *Wild Cherry Wine*. It's not feasible now that we've lost three of our five principles and the director."

Dahlia was berating Kevin as they left. The room seemed larger and much more manageable. Ruby Bee offered to make fresh coffee, and although I wanted to throttle her, I gestured curtly at her to get on with it.

"I can't believe Buddy's dead, too," Carlotta was saying to Anderson and Frederick. The three were huddled in one booth. Anderson had his arm around her, but she was shivering and nervously ruffling her hair.

"Gwenneth's still missing," Frederick reminded her. "No one can do anything for Kitty, Buddy, or Hal, but we've got to find Gwenneth before something happens to her."

I listened to them from the middle of the dance floor, gnawing on my lip as I tried to see through the professional facades. Based on what I was observing, Carlotta was frightened, Frederick was genuinely distraught about the missing girl, and Anderson was depressed and defeated by what he'd seen in the mirror.

I caught myself wondering if my emotions were reflected so precisely. Plover didn't seem to think so, but he was hardly the person to offer a critique.

Ruby Bee put a cup of coffee in my hand. Estelle carried a tray with more cups to the others. Harve wandered over, and in an attempt at optimism, slapped me on the back and said, "We're only missing the blond actress, so I'd say we're making progress."

"Buddy Meredith wouldn't agree with that," I said, slurping coffee and sighing. "How in the hell did he end up at Robin's cabin, Harve? We don't have a local chamber of commerce that passes out maps detailing points of interest. Except for Fuzzy, the others couldn't have known about the road and the shack. How could any one of them have taken Meredith's body there?"

"It's not exactly something that comes up in your basic conversations," Harve said. He went to the bar and put down his coffee cup to dig a cigar butt out of his shirt pocket. I stared blankly at his back as I recalled a remark from an earlier conversation.

"Are you okay?" Plover asked, nudging me.

"I need to make a telephone call, but not from here.

Hold down the fort while I go to the PD.'' My frown deepened. ''And I need to hunt up something in my notebook, too. I knew there was a reason for all my copious scribbling.''

When I arrived at the PD, I made the call, then took out my notebook and found the page of notes from the interrogation of Hal Desmond. What I'd thought would be there wasn't, and I made myself sit still until I remembered the gist of my first conversation with him, when he and Carlotta had dropped by the PD to discuss the schedule.

Even though I knew Plover and Harve were waiting impatiently for my return, I leaned back in the chair and mulled over my theory until it made sense. The motive was obvious, and after staring at my notes a while longer, the means became obvious, too. All I lacked was proof.

I walked back to Ruby Bee's, my fists in my pockets, and entered the barroom. Fuzzy was snoring peaceably. The remaining three members of Glittertown Productions, Inc., were in the same booth. Ruby Bee moved behind the bar, refilling coffee cups for Harve and Estelle. Plover was pretending to ponder the selections on the jukebox, but his shoulders were rigid and he snorted periodically.

I went to the booth. ''I want to know precisely where each of you was the night of Kitty's murder,'' I began coolly. ''This time let's skip the evasions. Carlotta?''

''Gwenneth was in the room, so I went to the launderette and used the pay telephone to call my friend at Cinerotica,'' she said. ''Kitty and Buddy were shrewd enough to figure it out. I needed to make sure he'd shredded any paper trail.''

''And then?''

''I went to Anderson's room.''

''Why?''

"I took him a check to reimburse him for something he picked up before he left California. I like to keep the books up to date so I can tell if we're on budget."

"Cocaine is one of your standard production costs?" I said.

She shrugged. "Preproduction, actually. Hal insisted it was necessary to boost his creative flow."

I looked at Anderson. "Will you confirm this?"

His eyes lowered, he nodded. "After she gave me the check, we just relaxed for a while, talking about the town and the script."

"Sure you did," Frederick said, smirking.

"Don't be so quick to cast the first stone," I said to him. "Darla Jean told me the truth about your evening in a motel in Farberville. Sergeant Plover suggested we book you on contributing to the delinquency of a minor, but I lean toward handing you over to Darla Jean's father. Who knows? He might use a shotgun to make you marry her. I wonder how she'd do as a Hollywood hostess. I'm confident that she knows how to make cornbread, but I wouldn't count on her for anything fancier than that."

"Don't be ridiculous. You're not gonna encourage her to tell the world that she got blind drunk and screwed the night away with someone she barely knew."

"She did get blind drunk, didn't she?" I glanced over my shoulder at Harve and Plover, who were only a few feet away and clearly interested. Ruby Bee was glued to the nearer end of the bar, and Estelle was leaning at such an angle she was apt to topple off the barstool. I explained for their benefit. "I called Darla Jean from the PD to make sure I'd heard her story correctly. After she drove him to a drugstore, Frederick bought a bottle of whiskey and insisted they take a motel room. He started pouring booze down her, and even though she protested that she wasn't like slutty Robin Buchanon, he forced her to have sex with him.''

"I didn't force her. She wanted it," Frederick said. "Now she may claim she didn't, but at the time she was a hot little number."

I shifted my attention to Carlotta and Anderson. "Robin Buchanon was a rather unique individual who lived in the shack where Meredith's body was found earlier this afternoon. You may not care about a decrepit, abandoned shack, but Frederick was interested enough to ask Darla Jean for details. He then poured more whiskey down her until she passed out. When she awoke later, a second bottle mysteriously had appeared in the room. She can't remember anything about the trip home except for a brief episode of vomiting. She's just grateful she made it home at midnight and the car was parked in the driveway the next morning."

Frederick grinned. "So what if I drove home? She was cross-eyed, and I was doing her and the car a favor."

Carlotta looked as if she wished she had her clipboard on which to make notes. "Are you saying Frederick got the girl drunk intentionally? It's sleazy, but it's a long way from—"

"Murder?" I suggested. She nodded, watching Frederick as if he were a cobra poised to strike. "I'm afraid so. He left Darla Jean unconscious in the motel, came back here to kill Kitty and Meredith, and put Meredith's body in the trunk. He bought another bottle of whiskey, and after he'd finished with the girl, took her home and waited until she was inside the house. He then had the use of her car for several hours."

Cigar smoke drifted over my shoulder. "Why not leave both bodies in the motel room?" Harve asked. "Seems a sight easier."

"Easier, but not as ironic," I said. "Buddy Meredith

had escaped his rural roots and gone off to the big city. Frederick must have felt it was only justice to allow the body to decompose in a piss-poor excuse for a shack. Lots of maggots and big green bottle flies. A godawful stench. Rats and other vermin to gnaw on it. A charmingly ironic location for Buddy Meredith's final scene, don't you think?''

"And why would I do that?'' demanded Frederick.

"Because he abandoned your mother," I said more gently than I'd intended to. "Did she point him out at the movies? Did she tell you how he'd run off the night before they were supposed to be married?''

"You're full of it, Chief Hanks. I told you I lived in San Diego, not St. Louis.'' He was inching toward the outside edge of the seat, but Plover stepped forward and impassively blocked the egress.

"Who said anything about St. Louis?'' I said.

"You must have said something," he said. He assessed his chances of getting past Plover, then slumped into the seat.

I continued. "We will track this down, eventually, over the phone or in person, if we have to. Your grandfather denied your existence in order to appease his guilt, but we'll find your birth certificate. You can change your name, but not your little baby footprints on the birth certificate. You let Hal send you to an orthodontist to get rid of the gap between your front teeth, and send you to a speech coach to correct your 'hayseed' accent. Correct, but not erase entirely, I might add. No one from San Diego does anything as quickly as 'a snake goin' through a hollow log.' That's a colloquialism indigenous to the Ozarks region. You must have learned it from your mother.''

"Nice Mr. Meredith refound his accent," Ruby Bee said from behind the bar. "And you know, I was thinking Frederick looked familiar, but I've never seen him on television. It must have been a passing family resemblance, like—"

"Like all the Buchanons have," Estelle interrupted. "This wasn't near as ugly, but there was something about the shape of the head and ears. I saw it, too."

"Didn't hear you mention it," Ruby Bee said with a sniff.

"You neither, Miss Automatic Recognition," Estelle countered.

"You can dig through records until your toes turn up," Frederick said, resuming his smirk. "Hey, you ought to team up with Carlotta and write screenplays. Then you could watch your fabrications in living color."

Carlotta slid out of the booth and looked down at Frederick. She no longer resembled the confident, efficient assistant who could put a film into production by sheer force of personality. Her face was damp, her eyes red and swollen, her voice ragged. "Did you kill Hal, too? And Gwenneth? Is there some twisted reason to kill all of us because your father didn't marry your mother?"

"Ask her," he said, cocking his thumb as he aimed his forefinger at me. "We may end up with a regular miniseries."

"I don't think he killed Gwenneth," I said. "I'll admit I don't know where she is at the moment, but Frederick seemed to have a real obsession with the kid sister characterization."

"Somebody has to watch out for her," he said. "She's such a stupid thing, letting Hal use her whenever he was in the mood. She's going to look fifty before she's thirty, and be waiting tables forever after. Can we get this over with? I'd like to find her, even if she's screwing somebody else."

I looked at Anderson, but I was struggling to connect

something he'd said with an elusive idea. It finally came
to me, seconds short of a migraine. "Becky Hopperly
died when her son was ten years old or so. We'll know
for sure when we get the death certificate and a copy
of the coroner's report, but her father went into a guilt-
stricken decline when he heard about it. He told a
neighbor it was fitting for her to die for her sins—and
we know which sin he felt most strongly about. Maybe
she died during an abortion. Not the kind done in a
sterile clinic, but the kind done in a kitchen for a few
dollars."

"Done by a butcher!" Frederick exploded. His boyish features almost distorted out of recognition, he began to pound on the tabletop. "She couldn't afford a
clean, decent place, because her father refused to send
a few goddamn dollars. While my mother was bleeding
to death on a table, the butcher patted me on the head
and said I would have had a baby sister. Would have! I
would have had a mother if her old man hadn't written
her off! She died because everyone abandoned her—
Meredith, her father, and even the fat pig who bought
his way into her bed with groceries and a little something to help with the rent. He always gave me a quar-
ter when he left."

"Did he look like Hal?" I asked.

"He looked like a fat pig, lady," Frederick said with
a snarl. He ducked his face for a moment, and when he
lifted it, he was once again the innocent, boyish heart-
throb who had kept the local girls in a tizzy with his
freckles and pectorals. "It was a long time ago. I
wouldn't recognize the guy if he walked through the
door in a pastel polyester suit. I hope you've got some
evidence tucked away somewhere to back up these
slanderous accusations. My reputation's important in
the industry, you know. Once you're tagged as a homicidal maniac, it's impossible to work."

"I've already shown motive and opportunity," I said, as always unnerved by the sudden transformations at which these people—better yet, chameleons—were so adept.

"What about Hal?" Carlotta said.

"Yes, what about Hal?" Frederick said, mocking her. "I can assure you he didn't knock up my mother in St. Louis twelve years ago. He was much too busy making porn movies and snorting coke to bother with a sad country girl trying to survive in a cold-water tenement on the wrong side of the river."

"Maybe I'll think of something while you're sitting in a cell," I snapped.

Plover went through the door and returned with a trooper, who took Frederick out of the murkiness of the barroom and into the relentless glare awaiting him outside. Carlotta was slumped against Anderson's shoulder, crying, while he numbly stroked her hair.

"And then there were two," I murmured, watching them from across the darkened expanse of the dance floor.

"We're back up to three," Plover said. "I just got the word that Gwenneth D'Amourre was spotted at the supermarket. She was very perturbed that they didn't carry a particular brand of hairspray. The checker reported as much to the manager, who hustled her off."

"Then she's okay," I said as we went over to the bar. "I wouldn't go so far as to say she's in good hands, but I'm not going to worry about her. We need to concentrate on nailing our homicidal friend. Impound the car Darla Jean drove that night and test the exterior of the trunk for Marland's fingerprints"—I waited for a twinge of nausea to pass—"and the interior for blood. Once it's matched with Meredith's, we'll have a decent case. Still a gawdawful mess, but at least it's a beginning."

"So it was all linked to Pineyville," he said. "I suppose I was being foolish to harp on the other murder, although the similarity was hard to miss."

I put an elbow on the bar and propped my chin in my hand. "I'd better call Detective Cannelli before too long."

"To schedule your weekend of passion in Las Vegas?"

"I don't think so," I said morosely. "That place is as unreal as these people. No, I need to tell him who murdered the St. James woman."

Plover stiffened, and if he'd been a hedgehog, he would have bristled. "Did St. James confess to you?"

"No, but the night of the murder he was sharing a room with Frederick, and started talking about his wife's unilateral decision to have an abortion. It may have ignited something. Anderson's afraid he doesn't remember driving to L.A., but I think it's more likely Frederick decided to save him the trouble of a divorce."

"A real wacko."

"The parallel between his mother's story and the plot of *Wild Cherry Wine* must have hit him where it really hurt. That, along with the confusion of Gwenneth, his self-proclaimed sister, playing the role of Loretta, who symbolized his mother, and Buddy, his father, being her father . . . and poor Kitty, who made the mistake of making Buddy happy. Jesus, what a mess." I was about to sigh when it hit me. I must have had a peculiar look on my face, because Plover narrowed his eyes and leaned away from me.

"What?" he said.

"What about Hal, to be precise," I corrected him. "In Fredericks' grossly disturbed scenario, everybody was somebody else. The only person who was adamant about his position in the hierarchy was Hal Desmond."

"Producer? Director? Dope king?"

"The company was just a big, happy family, and Hal seized numerous opportunities to cast himself in the role of its head. A regular Daddy dearest, demanding an incestuous and abusive relationship with his daughter, also known as Frederick's sister. He not only demanded it, he flaunted it in their faces. I think Hal might have lived longer if he'd chosen another role for himself."

"Other than Father Phallic, that is," Plover murmured. He mulled over my theory for a moment, then said, "We'll have to prove it, but at least we know whose prints to look for first. Frederick Marland really was out of control with all this swirling around him. Fathers, daughters, sons, and lovers. A saner man than he might have snapped, too, just from trying to keep it straight in his mind."

"I'm sure his lawyer will be eager to mention as much. On the other hand, Frederick didn't join Glittertown by accident, and he was careful to provide himself with alibis. He knew what he was doing—and why. The why is sick, but it makes sense." I put my hand on my face and rubbed my temples. "The what isn't all that charming, either."

Plover leaned over the bar and got me a glass of water. "Here, you look like last year's laundry."

"Oddly enough, that's what I feel like," I said. "Dirty and wrinkled and beginning to mildew."

Ruby Bee approached cautiously. "By the way, you had a call while you were gone earlier. Les said to tell you he'd finally talked to the folks what live on the Hasty road. The wife let Billy Dick in to call the fire department, but at about the same time, the husband was driving up the road on his way home from Hasty, and he passed a skinny kid on a bicycle, going the opposite way and pedaling so hard his rear wheel was smoking. Thinks he can identify him if he sees him."

"Bingo," I said, although without enthusiasm. "One red taillight going over a hill. That's a case against Willard Yarrow. Billy Dick's not willing to take the blame; he must have suspected Willard was behind the fires." I took a mouthful of water and let it dribble down my throat as I considered an unpleasant idea. "I'm surprised I wasn't invited along on the so-called picnic. Willard was stalking me, and making sure I knew it by leaving little messages. It's comforting to know I wasn't paranoid."

"Nobody accused you of that," Plover said. "Well, except for the bomb squad. Your breathless demand that they examine the two cars with microscopes cost them several hours. All they found in yours was a loose battery cable. Oh, and tell Ruby Bee to have her oil changed and stop leaving apple cores under the front seat."

"So I'm a little bit paranoid," I said gracelessly. "Blame it on the lack of a father figure in my formative years, and congratulate me on becoming such a charming, intelligent, law-abiding person—compared to all these other products of dysfunctional families." I finished off the water and banged down the glass so hard that everyone turned to stare at me. "I wish somebody'd tell me one thing: What the hell happened to Ward Cleaver?"

"Bring me a fresh compress when you have a moment," Mrs. Jim Bob called from the living room to Perkins's eldest, who was scouring pans at the kitchen sink. "I don't remember when I've had such an excruciatingly painful headache—and it's entirely the fault of those lascivious Hollywood people and their corrupting influence. To think they could pull the wool over Brother Verber's eyes like that!"

Perkins's eldest put the last pan on the counter, removed the plug, and listened to the gurgly water swirl down the drain.

"He never would have allowed nakedness in the house of the Lord," Mrs. Jim Bob continued as she adjusted a throw pillow under her head. "He may have slipped on occasion, but he was truly repentant when I pointed out his sinfulness. He was grateful, too, although it was nothing more than my Christian duty. Are you bringing that compress?"

Perkins's eldest went out to the breakfast room and looked at the couple in the backyard. Gwenneth D'Amourre looked real sweet as she lay draped in the hammock, and Jim Bob looked pleased as he sat close enough to rock the hammock and twirl golden curls around his finger. It occurred to Perkins's eldest that the two might like some lemonade, so she slipped back into the kitchen and carefully opened the cabinet.

"You don't suppose anyone in the Missionary Society's going to look askance at me because my house was supposed to be in that filthy movie?" Mrs. Jim Bob said, sitting up so quickly that the folded washcloth fell off her forehead. She waited for a moment. "Well, of course you don't know how anyone in the Missionary Society might react; I was merely airing my concern aloud. Membership is restricted to those women of the congregation who've shown unfailing piety and a willingness to aid the unfortunate."

Perkins's eldest fixed a tray and took it out to the backyard. She came extremely close to smiling when the actress cooed at the dainty linen napkins and the porcelain plate with artfully arranged lemon cookies, but she didn't.

"I imagine you're wondering how we display our

Christian zeal," Mrs. Jim Bob said. She held the compress to her forehead and, despite the flickers of pain, patiently explained to Perkins's eldest how the society prayed for heathens and sinners everywhere for fifteen minutes straight before they broke for coffee and dessert.

Darla Jean reluctantly answered the telephone, not in the mood to talk to anyone and especially not in the mood to talk to Heather.

"Want to go shopping?" Heather began, even though she knew what the response would be.

"I'm grounded for the summer."

Heather gave Traci a mischievous smile but turned on the sympathy as she said, "Oh, Darla Jean, that's terrible. How come?"

"Because I had to go to the state police office to tell them about something, and my parents kept nagging until I told them what I said. That's how come I'm grounded—as if you didn't already know. Arly came by and talked to them a couple of times, so I may be allowed out of the house for the first football game next fall."

"Is there any chance you're . . . pregnant?"

"No." Darla Jean hung up and lay back on the bed, thinking that famous Hollywood movie stars weren't all they were cracked up to be. The more she thought about it (and she had plenty of time), the better Dwayne looked, and before too long she called him to tell him as much. Sad to say, access to her second-story bedroom window was discussed.

Kevin Buchanon held three large sacks emblazoned with the logo "Jim Bob's SuperSaver Buy 4 Less." When the door opened, he took a deep breath and said, "My beloved honeybee, I've brought you vanilla sandwich cookies, chocolate-covered raisins, a dozen doughnuts, a six-pack of orange soda pop, and all the cream-filled sponge cakes they had at the store. Please accept them and—"

He broke off as the sacks were yanked out of his arms, and he was still gaping as the door slammed in his face, missing his nose by no more than a scant inch. "Women!" he muttered as he trudged back down the road. "I just don't understand 'em."

"Did you come out of desperation?" Plover asked amiably.

"Yeah," I said, settling my feet on the dashboard, "I did. Now that Glittertown Productions, Inc., is long gone and the fire department's watching the ninth inning, there's nothing else to do."

"Nothing at all?"

"Oh, I tried to find Raz's still yesterday, but he was crafty enough to move it. Ruby Bee said she heard it's in a shallow cave toward the south end of Cotter's Ridge. Estelle, on the other hand, heard it was near Boone Creek. Once my poison ivy eases up, maybe I'll take another stab at it. Or let it go."

"I wasn't sure you'd come tonight," he said.

He looked as if he had something more to say, but I didn't want to hear any awkwardly phrased sentiments. I didn't want to hear any elegantly phrased ones, either. I held up my hand and said, "Don't forget I was reared on the timeless adage 'Save the last dance for the feller

what brung you.' If you'll turn up the speaker, I'll share
my popcorn.''

The opening credits of *Tanya Makes the Team* began
to flash on the vast screen.

FADE-OUT